IF YOU WERE HERE

Also by Abigail Johnson

Every Time You Go Away

Every Other Weekend

Even If I Fall

The First to Know

If I Fix You

If You Were Here

ABIGAIL JOHNSON

STORYTIDE
An Imprint of HarperCollins*Publishers*

HarperCollins Children's Books,
a division of HarperCollins Publishers,
195 Broadway, New York, NY 10007

HarperCollins Publishers,
Macken House, 39/40 Mayor Street Upper,
Dublin 1, D01 C9W8, Ireland

Storytide is an imprint of HarperCollins Publishers.

If You Were Here

harpercollins.com
Library of Congress Control Number: 2025947092
ISBN 978-1-335-01410-8
Typography by Chris Kwon

26 27 28 29 30 LBC 5 4 3 2 1

First Edition

For Gideon.
Creativity crackles off you, kid.
I can't wait to watch more of your brilliant life.

And for Smike, my little sir.
Eighteen years wasn't nearly long enough.

ONE
Lili

The briny air takes on a suddenly sweet note as I step off the ferry. Not that my stomach pays any attention, choosing instead to clench as that final swell of sea lurches the gangway beneath my feet. Sweat slicks down my neck as I battle with what's left of my breakfast, urging it to stay put. It's touch and go as descending tourists jostle my shoulders on the left and right. I push my damp, blonde curtain bangs to the sides, and lift my face to a sun so bright it looks white against the watercolor-blue sky. I don't care if it costs me a few extra freckles, I just need to see anything that is not the Atlantic Ocean.

I don't get seasick in a cute, movie-montage way. There's no dramatic moment of leaning over the railing, wind in my hair, staring mournfully at the horizon. The past two hours have been a nauseous, sweaty, miserable ordeal, punctuated with more than one bout of public vomiting.

Throwing up in public: 0/10, do not recommend.

I clutch at the railing as we disembark, *we* being me, the vomit queen—an actual name given to me by an evil little boy with curly brown hair on the ferry with us—along with my ten-year-old sister, Goldie, who chased said evil little boy off by threatening to have me aim at him the next time I threw up, and our mom, whose olive complexion hadn't been as green tinged as mine, but who felt seasick enough that all she'd said in response was "Lili, don't get sick on any kids, okay?"

I think she was kidding. I'd been too nauseated to really tell.

More people pour past me, so many, and even more crowd around the pier. I forgot what it's like on Nantucket during this time of year.

Off-season the island has a population of around twelve thousand people, but that number swells to over fifty thousand during the summer. For an island only fourteen miles long and less than a third of that wide, it's a lot of people.

And after seven years away, I get to be one of them again.

That thought is a sliver of sunshine piercing through my cloud of nausea.

Seagulls cry overhead and a wooden dock far older than my seventeen years creaks underfoot. In the distance, the familiar clang of the harbor bell sounds, and my fingers stretch automatically, searching for the hand that used to hold mine all those years ago.

A hand does find mine, not the one my memory longed for, but a familiar, comforting one all the same. Mom gives it a squeeze and me a knowing glance before letting go.

"Feels the same, doesn't it?"

It really does, and though we both sigh, we couldn't sound more different. Despite the unpleasant journey here, when I inhale, a mix of sweet honeysuckle, fresh bread, and salty kiss of ocean in the air makes me smile. Mom's expression turns resigned as she focuses on the burnt French fry scent of diesel coming from the ferry and the fishy seaweed wrapping around the wooden pilings of the dock.

I reach for *her* hand now and squeeze. "It's just us this time. And whatever we want this summer to be."

She gives me a resolute nod, patting our joined hands with her free one before striding forward to catch up with Goldie.

That nagging sense of guilt pricks at me before I can shove it away. I had promised Mom over and over again that we would make brand-new memories here to chase away the old ones that clung to her. So as much as I'd like to linger by the harbor, hopping along the cobblestones with my sister and doing more than window-shop in all the picture book–esque stores with names like Faraway Chocolate, the Petticoat Café, and the Sunken Ship, I become the one marching Goldie straight past the wooden placards hanging above colorful awnings as we walk the couple blocks to our car rental.

"Later." I gently steer her by the shoulders. "Don't you want to see the house?"

Mom brightens at this. "Oh, I hope it has roses climbing all over it."

The picture we'd seen had indeed shown beautiful pink and white roses all but swallowing the tiny gray shingled house, but I bite my lip, remembering the words of caution from the property manager that the house had been somewhat neglected since that rather idyllic photo was taken.

"We can plant more if it doesn't. It's ours now so we can do whatever we want."

Mom usually renovates and stages houses to appeal to current market trends rather than any personal preferences we might have, but unlike the houses she flips, we won't be selling this one. It's ours, or at least Goldie's and mine, and I don't ever intend to let it go.

My still-hesitant stomach is thankful for the smooth drive outside Nantucket Town to the house, no starts and stops since there aren't any traffic lights on the island. I find myself gripping the seatbelt as the tires crunch over the pea-graveled driveway, curving around huge silver maple trees that nearly block out the sky in places, until the branches thin and the sunlight pours down over a single house up ahead.

When Mom puts the car in park, we all stare at the house that I'd begged, pleaded, and implored them both to spend our summer at.

No one gets out of the car.

Goldie scrunches her nose. "All in favor of going back to Arizona right now, raise your hand."

She's being dramatic; the house is just old. There are about eight hundred pre–Civil War homes on the island, and while this one isn't reaching the level of the 1687 Jethro Coffin House in terms of hauntability, it's going to need more than a few new rose bushes to make it look inviting to the living.

"Is this why Dad died? He found out he was gonna have to live here?"

I suck in a breath at my sister's careless words. She'd been only four when Mom and Dad divorced and he moved back permanently to his childhood home of Nantucket. He never did get the hang of consistent calls or visits, so while I pored over the postcards he sent, being so young, Goldie always cared more about the pictures on the front than the words on the back. She never went through the kind of grief that I did when he died six months ago.

"That's not funny, Goldie," Mom says with a weary reprimand in her voice. "This house has been in the Gardner family for generations, and Dad couldn't say no when the opportunity came to buy it back."

"Well, Lili and I are the only Gardners left, so can we say no?"

I get out of the car, hugging my bare elbows against a sudden breeze and the sound of Goldie continuing to argue with Mom.

One of his last postcards to me was the day he got the keys.

> *A Gardner house, Lili! A family house. And one day, it'll be yours and Goldie's house, your legacy to continue. Let me fix it up first and then you can both come visit next summer.*

It's summer now, and I'm here, but he isn't.

It probably looked much the same back then. I'm sure he had plans for it, but Dad's plans had a way of never quite making it out into the real world. But I know he would have seen this house and instantly understood its worth, and with a not-unpleasant ache in my chest, I see it too.

An older woman with short, spiky gray hair and tan skin kissed by years of salt and sun walks out of the front door. "Hello, Gardner family!" she calls out in a warm voice as she carefully navigates the porch steps while holding a huge furry cat in her arms.

Mom and Goldie step onto the patchy grass with me, the late-afternoon sun catching Goldie's pale hair and turning it nearly white. The woman doesn't hesitate—she walks right up to Mom and gives her a one-armed hug, deftly avoiding squashing the enormous Maine coon cat in her other arm.

"You must be Mia," she says, pulling back. Her smile sweeps over the rest of us, wide and bright enough to make me feel immediately at ease. "And these are your girls, of course. All that blonde hair!"

"Mrs. Mayhew?"

The woman laughs. "That's me. And this"—she lifts the cat slightly—"is Ollie. Or maybe Stan? I never can tell the difference. Anyway, come on in, and let me show you the house."

She waves us toward the small saltbox home without waiting for an answer, her energy more inviting than demanding. The cat stays perfectly docile in her arms, its thick fur rippling in the breeze as we follow her inside.

The house is dim, the light filtering through wavy glass windows that distort the view of the garden. It smells faintly of lemon polish and something older, deeper—like wood warmed by the sun for decades. Mrs. Mayhew leads us through the narrow rooms, her voice lively as she talks about the house's history.

"No renovations or improvements since your late husband bought it last year," she says cheerfully, her heels clicking on the wood floor.

I glance at Mom, waiting for the inevitable flared nostrils or the tightening of her mouth. But there's nothing—her expression is perfectly neutral, her lips pressed into a polite line. I can't tell if she's doing it for my sake or Mrs. Mayhew's.

"Too busy chasing the past to worry about the present, hmm?" Mrs. Mayhew shakes her head and adjusts the cat in her arms. "My Henry was the same way. Kept a whole attic full of his collectibles—refused to show a single soul. A friend offered to assess it after he passed, but I'm quite sure it only had value to Henry. So there it sits."

"Maybe you could sell some of it online," Mom suggests, her hand landing lightly on Goldie's shoulder. "Goldie is great with eBay, aren't you, sweetie? How many items did you sell last year? Two hundred?"

"Two hundred sixty-one." Goldie shrugs, but there's pride in her expression. As part of her homeschool math curriculum, Mom had her start a business for a mini-entrepreneurship unit. So far, she's already made enough money flipping thrift store finds to buy her own gaming laptop.

Mrs. Mayhew brightens. "Come by anytime if you want to make a little money this summer."

She doesn't wait for a reply, plunging right back into the history of the house. It was lovingly restored in the 1920s, she explains, then less lovingly updated in the '80s. Now it's dated but clean, the walls a mix of faded wallpaper and peeling paint.

When she mentions previous plumbing leaks, Mom's expression wavers—just for a second—but I catch it. Her pallor hasn't improved much since the ferry, and talk of water damage isn't helping.

Mrs. Mayhew pulls an envelope from her bag. "The plumbing issues have been repaired and were isolated to the second story, so nothing down here was damaged."

Mom nods as Mrs. Mayhew hands her a stack of papers and a full keyring. "Those will open any room in the house. The iron one is for the shed, which has two bikes with freshly aired-up tires in it." She winks as Goldie perks up at that announcement. "And the brass one is for the study." She indicates a closed door just off the kitchen that I'd assumed was a closet. "I'm sorry to say I never could find one for the old locked desk in there, but maybe you'll have better luck."

It's my turn to look excited. "Desk?" Dad's death blindsided us all, but the one silver lining had been learning he'd left us this house. I'd wanted to come right away, as if setting foot on the island could somehow right a world that had just been turned upside down. But Mom had looked at me with those green eyes of hers, wild and panicked like a cornered cat.

So, I backpedaled. Compromised. We made plans to come in the summer after I graduated and Goldie finished homeschool for the year, and instead held a memorial service in Arizona while some of his smaller, personal effects were boxed up and sent to us. I thought we already had everything important of his—the watch from his grandfather, his first edition of *Moby Dick*, the framed Gardner family tree he'd researched all the way back to the 1700s—but what if he left something else behind?

Mrs. Mayhew nods. "Looks like something that would have come over on the *Mayflower*. I hate to say it, but I'm glad my husband never saw it. He'd have no doubt tried to buy it for some exorbitant amount of money, and I just don't know where we would have put it." She laughs, oblivious to the way my eyes are now focused on the closed study door.

"I think old desks are gonna have to wait," Mom says. "We need to unpack and do a million other things first."

Mrs. Mayhew smiles. "Of course. Well, Ollie and I will leave you to get settled then. I wasn't sure what you'd have on hand to eat, so I left you a basket out on the porch including some of my homemade blackberry jam. The wild shrubs grow all along the harbor from Monomoy to Quaise, and lucky for us, they bloomed early this year." She gives us a warm smile. "If you need anything else—or want more jam—I'm just a mile down the road."

As soon as Mrs. Mayhew steps out the door, Mom exhales like she's been holding her breath for hours. She sends Goldie to pull the sheeting off the furniture, then drops onto the couch with a thud. The cushions puff out a faintly musty smell, but she doesn't seem to notice.

"I'm fine," she says, though her voice is thin, as if she's trying to convince herself as much as me. "How about you? That ferry ride was rough, huh?"

"Not super fun, no." I eye the keyring in her hand. "But Dad always told me an upset stomach is a small price to pay for paradise."

She nods, remembering. "Never quite felt that way to me, but"—she carefully removes the brass key to Dad's study and offers it to me—"I know it did to the two of you."

I hesitate before taking it. "What about unpacking and the million other things first?"

She smiles before pushing to her feet. "Tell you what. I'll let you disappear into that study for the night if you promise to meet me outside early tomorrow to tear down that death trap of a porch railing."

I take the key from her fingers and grin. "Deal."

Mom and Goldie head upstairs, and though their footsteps creak overhead, I feel a strange sense of quiet as I turn the brass key in the study door and push it open.

Books line the wall-to-wall shelves, and I trail my fingers along their linen spines as I breathe in air that I foolishly expect to still smell like him—black licorice and coffee. The breath I take awakens an ache because of course it doesn't. It smells stale and dusty and empty. I quickly pull off the sheets covering the rest of the furniture and let my eyes skim over things that haven't been touched since he was here. A worn leather chair, a brass floor lamp, his old rug, some framed paintings of ships on the walls. And heavy, forest-green curtains that I throw open to let light in.

All through the air, tiny dust motes glitter and cascade down to rest on a huge honey-colored desk in the middle of the room. I don't know much about antique furniture, but it looks maybe eighteenth century, and beautifully preserved. Only a few tiny edge pieces are chipped away from the rosewood inlay. I can't help but touch it, tracing the swirling carved branches on the sides and drawer fronts, stopping at the keyhole centered on the top-right drawer.

I give it an experimental tug, but it doesn't move.

Slowly, turning around the room, I try to imagine Dad in this position. He knew he was dying in the end. He didn't have a lot of time, but he had enough. He left us this house, and that means that he left us whatever's in his desk too. So I start looking.

I open all the unlocked drawers first but don't find anything significant. I move on to the bookshelves, flipping through each title and checking all the notebooks that he kept about our various ancestors that he researched. I check floorboards and behind picture frames, and even carefully stand on the desk to peek inside the light fixture in the ceiling.

No key.

"Come on, Dad. Would you really make it this hard for me?" Stepping down, I realize that no, he wouldn't. From the moment I showed the first spark of interest in history, specifically our family's history, he'd been overjoyed and had set about teaching me everything there was to know about the Gardners and our legacy here on Nantucket. Nothing was more important to him than imparting that knowledge to me. Which means I'm looking too hard. He would make sure that of all people, I could find it.

I sit back at the desk, looking around now, not for hiding places, but for things that connect to me.

And that's when I see it.

The brass floor lamp in the corner. It looks like an antique except for the cheap plastic whale charm hanging from the pull chain.

It 100 percent doesn't belong in this room, but it's there because I gave it to him when I was eight, maybe nine? It had initially been filled up with little candies, but as I give it a shake and hear a rattle inside, I already know it holds something far sweeter now. Cracking it open along the seam, an ornate, basket-handle carved key spills into my hand.

I rub the cool metal between my thumb and forefinger, smiling before returning to the desk and unlocking the drawer.

TWO
Lili

The scent of coffee is what wakes me the next morning, and I'm smiling before I open my eyes.

"Morning, sleepyhead."

I sit up at the sound of Mom's voice, and immediately wince as I realize the rock-hard pillow I'd been sleeping on is actually a desk.

"Want to tell me what kept you in here all night?" She's perched on the corner of the desk and offers me one of the steaming mugs she's holding. As soon as I wrap my hands around the warm ceramic, she plucks a sticky note from my cheek and squints at the words I vaguely remember scribbling down last night. "Or who Mr. Fanning is and why you need to talk to him first?" She taps at the word I'd underlined twice.

I scald my mouth on the too-hot coffee, but I need my brain to fully wake up, and fast. I spot the plastic whale and sit up straighter, eyes instantly scanning for the worn, leather-bound notebook I'd found in Dad's locked drawer. I slide it to me and set my coffee mug far on the other side of the desk.

“Because of this,” I say in a croaky, morning voice that makes her smile.

“One of his notebooks? That’s good. I know he would’ve wanted you girls to have those. After all, his history is your history.”

I shake my head, ignoring the sore muscles from sleeping bent over on a desk. “No, this one wasn’t just for his own genealogical research.” All my life, he’d traced family members that came before him, trying to track down every name and every significant contribution, unearth the forgotten details about the people who shared his bloodline. He had a shelf of notebooks in this very room that each covered hundreds of people, but this one that I hold right now is all about one woman. “It’s about Kezia Gardner.”

“Oh?” Mom’s expression goes carefully neutral. I know she’s heard the name. Dad was talking about her even before the divorce.

“Mom, I think this is what he was working on when he died.” I start to open the notebook, but her hand moves to rest on mine, stopping me.

“Lili, he was always working on theories about her.” Her voice swells with old-fashioned-newscaster delivery: “One of history’s most notorious female smugglers, who swindled both the colonies and the Brits during the war.” She drops the act with a slight sigh. “And yet he’d go on for hours about how he thought she was just misunderstood.”

I run a finger over the smooth leather cover, trying to prod her own curiosity. “He might have been right.”

She takes a long sip of her coffee before answering me, but when she does, her voice is almost sorrowful. “You look just like him right now.”

A smile lifts one side of my face. "Yeah?"

She nods, even though we both know she's not exactly telling the truth. I look like her, the same round cheeks and button nose. Her hair is an ashier shade of blonde than mine, but it's the clothes that differentiate us the most right now. I'd fallen asleep wearing the same vintage white eyelet sundress from yesterday, whereas she's got her favorite oversized Hansen T-shirt on.

I like hearing it though, and she knows it.

She picks up the sticky note again. "And this guy? Is he a Kezia believer too?"

"Not exactly, but he might be able to help me figure out some of Dad's research." I puff out my cheeks as I exhale. "Dad's notes are kind of all over the place, but I thought I might go into town today and see what he thinks."

She raises her eyebrows. "Is that your way of asking if you can bail on helping me tear that porch railing down this morning?"

"No." I hastily gulp more coffee, feeling more awake with each swallow. "But maybe after?"

She presses the sticky note to my forehead before heading for the door. "Fine, but that means we'll all be up late removing wallpaper tonight. And you're going to get stuck holding the steamer."

It's funny how places can feel different without ever changing at all. After so many years away, Nantucket is not the same summer vacation destination I remember from my childhood; it's bursting with sights and sounds I must have experienced countless times before that I'd either forgotten or never appreciated until now.

This morning, as I bike into town, I'm reveling in every cobblestone bumping under my tires as I coast down narrow lanes, thrilling as I pass all the historic homes adorned with bursts of blooming hydrangeas in brilliant shades of blue, pink, and purple, savoring every breath of sea air filling my lungs.

Before I even glimpse Main Street, I'm smiling at the faint sound of people laughing and bustling in search of coffee, souvenirs, and the ineffable magic of this tiny coastal island.

I'd almost forgotten it.

I come to a stop outside a café I can't specifically recall but that has the familiar weathered charm of a building that has stood for countless decades, and inhale the scent of freshly baked cinnamon rolls so sweet I can almost taste the sugar crystals as they crunch beneath my teeth. I'm tempted to join the line already forming outside. Dad would. He'd have instantly abandoned whatever plans we had and already be betting me which of us could eat more.

I loved his spontaneity and the ease with which he could change the course of his life—and ours—whenever the impulse struck him. As a child, our summers always went the same way. As soon as we got off the ferry, he'd scoop me onto his shoulders and head straight to Dionis Beach. I'd shriek as I teased the gentle surf, build sandcastles until they were taller than me, and later lay on a towel with the sun warming my skin and the comforting rhythm of the waves lulling me to sleep.

And then there were the history days, when we'd go on long hikes to barely discernible landmarks, take dull museum tours that often as not ended with Dad arguing with guides over details he insisted they got wrong, or go nowhere at all while he'd read aloud from some old book that I barely understood.

It wasn't until after he left that I realized how much I missed those days and him. He wasn't there when I started having my own history days, reading the books I knew he'd want me to read, watching the documentaries he'd love—or love to dispute—and learning as much about our history as I could so that when those rare phone calls came, I'd be able to say something that made them last that little bit longer.

Leaving the bakery and the rest of Main Street behind, I keep moving toward a destination I know better than almost any other place on the island: the Whaling Museum, whose collections chronicle four centuries of Nantucket history, including the only known copy of one of Kezia Gardner's diaries. The one the Whaling Museum has ends right before the Revolutionary War, leaving the rest of her story to be told by others, but it's a good place to start.

Parking my bike outside the redbrick building, I shade my eyes as I glance all the way up to the patinated whale-topped weathervane that almost seems to wink at me in the morning light. "I'm going to take that as a good sign," I whisper to the whale, then walk through the thick white columns flanking the entrance, purchase a ticket, and pass under the always-impressive forty-seven-foot sperm whale skeleton suspended high overhead.

The museum is quite large, but I remember the layout well enough to find my way around. Urgent as my task feels, I can't help from seeking out Kezia's diary. Standing over the glass case, I indulge in a quick fantasy where I manage to silently break the lock, slip the diary into my bag, and disappear among the tourists until I can dash outside before anyone even notices it's gone. But I know I'm not as daring as my ancestor was.

I wouldn't have minded lingering, and I probably would have if Dad hadn't made me memorize the two displayed pages years ago.

I know all about Kezia's take on the Great Nantucket Bank Robbery and her emphatic doubt regarding the guilt of the eventually convicted men. The museum does occasionally showcase a handful of other select pages, but I know those too. It's everything else I needed to find out now, everything else that will remain hidden away until I help bring it to light.

Finally, I stride off in search of Mr. Fanning. I have vague memories of the collections manager at the museum, mostly of how red his pale face would turn when my dad loudly and vehemently questioned his mental fitness to tie his shoes, let alone to accurately display an exhibit. He looks perfectly normal colored when I catch up to the man and hear him say he's leaving to grab his second cup of coffee of the morning.

Short and slightly rounded, he wears his thinning light-brown hair neatly parted and, despite the warm weather, a navy sweater vest with an azure-blue tie patterned with gray whale silhouettes. He looks like a kindly teacher type and gives me an inquisitive smile when I call his name.

"Hello there, young lady, and what can I do for you on this fine morning?"

"I have a request regarding access to some of the restricted materials in the museum's possession."

"Oh? Are you a history student?"

Not yet, I think, since I know he means college and the ink on my high school diploma has barely dried at this point.

"Aren't we all?" I say, thankfully earning a chuckle from him.

"Why don't you tell me which materials you are hoping to access and a little about your project."

"The Kezia Gardner diary, for a start. I'm working on a theory that the reports of her alleged smuggling activities were misleading or inaccurate."

It takes only that one sentence for the gentle expression on Mr. Fanning's face to shift into stiff aloofness. He hasn't seen me for years, but as his eyes narrow, I feel certain in that moment that he realizes exactly who I am.

"As your father was told before being banned from this museum, along with several others, if I'm not mistaken, we don't make a habit of exposing sensitive materials to agenda-driven hobbyists, and especially not to those who have berated and harassed our staff for years."

Banned? Dad hadn't mentioned that to me, though I guess it's not a complete surprise. "I have no interest in berating or harassing anyone," I say, moving to keep pace beside him when he continues down the street. "I just want to look more fully into her life, and her diary would be a huge help. And," I add when he starts to interrupt me, "I'll abide by any guidelines you set forth."

"Your father—"

"Is dead," I finish for him, doing my best to hide how devastating it is for me to say the words. "Earlier this year."

He pauses. "My condolences. But unfortunately we do not allow public access to vulnerable materials at this time. You're welcome to view any items currently on display, but—"

"That's not good enough." I can feel color flushing hot in my cheeks. "I need to see more than two pages through a display case. And I really need someone to help me sort through all the accounts. Don't you care that history, our history"—I gesture around us to the buildings that have lined Broad Street for centuries—"may have gotten it wrong?"

"As someone who has studied all the available materials, I can tell you the same thing I told your father." He leans closer to me. "We didn't. And I promise that you won't get a different answer from any of the other museums on the island."

I resist the urge to call or chase after him as he walks off, but if I'm being honest with myself, that went about as well as I expected. Dad burned a lot of bridges around here, and it's going to take more than a cute dress and friendly smile to rebuild them. I don't know exactly what it's going to take, but I'll find out. Maybe tomorrow I'll show up with coffee for Mr. Fanning. He'll have to talk with me then, right? And if not, I'll try something else the day after, and the day after that, and . . .

I stop with a sigh. I know that with enough time I can change his mind. After all, Nantucket was the last place Mom wanted to set foot on a few months ago, and I'd made that happen. But I don't have endless weeks to gradually persuade him that my idea is the right one. My time here is limited.

Gnawing at my bottom lip, I take a deep breath and try not to feel too discouraged. It helps that the cherry tree–lined streets are literally snowing pink petals in the late morning breeze. And then I spot a familiar face winding toward me with a cheerful hand lifted in hello.

"Lili? I thought that was you."

"Hello, Mrs.—Mrs.—"

"Mayhew," she offers, seemingly not the least bit offended that I forgot. "Now why do you look like a hungry cat staring at an empty food dish? Is there something wrong with the house?"

I shake my head and retrieve my bike. "The house is fine. I just"—my eyes land on Mr. Fanning's retreating figure—"didn't get the answer I wanted to a really important question."

Mrs. Mayhew follows my line of sight. "Something about the museum then?"

I turn to her, surprised.

"You live here as long as I have and you tend to get to know everyone, even little men like Mr. Fanning whose ego trips are legendary."

I choke back a laugh. "Little or not, I really need his help finishing a family research project, and I was just told in no uncertain terms that not only will I not get it from the Whaling Museum, but I shouldn't bother with any of the other museums on the island either." Of course, I plan to bother anyone and everyone I have to until somebody helps me, but I keep that detail to myself.

Mrs. Mayhew gives me a tight, one-armed hug. "That just shows that his mind is as little as the rest of him. I happen to know of a museum right around the corner that I'd wager would be happy to do the exact opposite of anything Mr. Fanning approved of." Keeping her arm around me, she starts guiding me down the street. "And an exceptionally smart friend who works there and knows more about the history of this island than just about anyone, my late husband and your dad excepting."

Her last few words push everything else she just said out of my mind. "How well did you know my dad?"

"Oh, not well. He and my Henry didn't get on, some kind of historical disagreement."

I catch one more glimpse of Mr. Fanning before he disappears around the corner. "Sounds like my dad had historical disagreements with a lot of people."

"But he was always kind to me. In fact, after I lost Henry, he came by every year to help me get my Christmas decorations down from the attic."

I smile, liking the image of him helping her even as it collides with one of Mom and me struggling every year with ours. "You said you know someone who might be able to help me?"

"I sure do, and I think with a bit of inventive persuasion on your part, you might find the exact help you're looking for."

"Really?" I try to rack my brain for the museum she could be referring to. There are quite a few on Nantucket, all with different focuses, everything from the Shipwreck and Lifesaving Museum to the tiny Lightship Basket Museum. But the only museum on this particular street is . . .

I come to a halt outside the building that would have never been on my list in a million years. "Mrs. Mayhew, this isn't—I mean, I appreciate the kind thought, but this *museum*"—I have to force myself to even use the word—"isn't going to be of any help to me."

Mrs. Mayhew only smiles. "Have you ever been inside?"

"No." Dad had refused the one and only time I'd asked. He'd said there was nothing in there but fairytales masquerading as fact, and with an island as rich in history as Nantucket, it was better left for the tourists, which we were not. Despite the fact that our family only visited during the summers, Nantucket was in our blood.

"Well, then you don't really know, do you?" She lets her arm fall from my shoulder and gives me a gentle nudge. "What could it hurt?"

THREE
Wren

Bethany is late. Again.

Which means instead of leading tours—where at least I can slip some actual history into the fiction on display around here—I'm stuck behind the gift shop counter, ringing up plastic snow globes filled with iridescent glitter, seashell-shaped bags of mermaid poop slime, and overpriced T-shirts that say *I Met the Real Little Mermaid at McCleave's Mermaid Museum*.

The register, as always, is fighting me. Two out of every three attempts, it refuses to cooperate, blinking back at me like it knows I can't do a damn thing about it.

At least the shop is empty now, except for one girl.

She's about my age, maybe a little younger, but I'd have noticed her even in a crowd. Not because she's loud or trying to draw attention—she's not—but because she doesn't look like the usual flip-flop-wearing, sunburned tourists who roll in off Main Street. She's wearing a sundress with a ribbon in her hair, like she walked straight out of a black-and-white movie.

She doesn't even glance at the shelves, heading straight for the arched entrance to the exhibits.

Then she hesitates. Doubles back. Drifts toward the round table in the center of the shop, fingers skimming over the T-shirts before picking one up.

"Which one of you will Goldie like enough to forgive me for ditching her today?" she murmurs to the fabric.

A minute later, a shirt lands on the counter.

"Hi," she says, her voice light and neutral, the kind of greeting you give to strangers without thinking about it.

I nod and start ringing her up—or I try to, because naturally, the register picks now to rebel.

"I had one of those," she says, watching as I jab at the buttons. "I worked in this vintage clothing store in Arizona, and I swear the register had a personal vendetta against me."

Tourist. Called it.

I don't bother responding beyond a quiet "Hmm," still trying to get the stupid machine to cooperate. It finally does, spitting out a receipt like it expects a thank-you.

I bag her shirt and slide it across the counter. "Anything else?"

She smiles again, not forced, just easy. "Actually, I had a question—" She glances at my name tag. "Wren." Then at the words beneath it. "Oh, you're a guide. Perfect. When does the next tour start?"

It doesn't.

I check my phone again—nothing from Bethany—before answering. "We're short-staffed today, so you'll have to settle for the placards by each exhibit." Then I shrug. "But you can make up whatever you want. It's all fiction."

The words land like I just popped her beach ball.

"Is there maybe a curator or collections manager I could speak with?" she asks, still hopeful.

I almost laugh. "Nope. But there is a full-sized mermaid skeleton waiting for you just through there." I nod toward the museum's main hall. "Captain Lawrence McCleave 'discovered' Nerissa during a whaling expedition in 1893. Before that, this place was a cabinet of curiosities—his wife's way of sharing all the interesting finds her husband brought home, and turning a profit at the same time."

She turns toward the exhibit. I can't see her face, but I can imagine the expression well enough.

Most people expect drawings. Models. Cute little Disney-esque displays for kids to laugh at.

They do not expect *her*.

There is nothing laughable about the six-foot skeleton standing eerily upright, its form suspended by a thin metal wire that runs from the skull down through a narrow ribcage, past flared fin bones at the hips, and along an extended vertebral column that tapers into a sweeping, curved tail. Delicate, spindly bones fan from the tail's edges, resembling skeletal fingers stretching a couple dozen inches on either side.

"They come for the fantastical, Wren, so that's what we gotta give them," Dad says every time he sets up a new display. "We need them to be so wowed that they have to tell everyone they know how much they love McCleave's."

Personally, I find the whole thing to be rather grotesque. Not just the skeleton's wide eye sockets and sharp teeth, but the way we've accessorized her over the years. A crudely carved whale bone knife, a shark tooth cuff, and a seashell necklace, all conveniently available for purchase in the gift shop.

Tourists eat it up.

Usually.

But this tourist girl doesn't walk straight toward the display like most people do. Instead, she turns back to me.

"What else can you tell me about how the museum started and the kind of early exhibits it had?" Before I can do more than blink at a question literally no one else has ever asked me, she glances past me. "Oh, is that him, Captain McCleave?"

I follow her gaze, and my stomach tightens.

She's looking at the McCleave's History display wall.

I keep my expression neutral, but I really don't want to be here while she studies it.

She scans the display, skipping over the daguerreotype photo of Captain Lawrence McCleave himself on his schooner, the *Greasy Luck*, in favor of an early copy of the 1889 Ewer Map of Nantucket Island (now sporting a few colorful mermaid additions not included in the reverend's meticulously detailed original). She barely glances at the artist's rendition of a living Nerissa—just long enough to read the caption declaring her a member of the *Hydronymphus pesci* species, a supposed Asian lineage of merfolk.

And then—just as I expect—her attention turns back to the photograph of Captain McCleave.

Then to me.

Then back to him.

Her lips twitch. "Your name is Wren? As in Lawrence? Are you related to Captain McCleave?"

I brace.

Then, right on cue, a grin spreads across her face. "You are." She gestures between me and the photo. "The dark wavy hair, the eyes, and that jawline—" A splash of pink colors her cheeks as she realizes what she just said.

I grip the edge of the counter, fighting not to react.

Fortunately, a little girl of around six is pawing through a bin of stuffed starfish at that moment and has angled herself just far enough around to see that I'm not sitting on a regular chair behind the counter.

"Hey, you're in a wheelchair."

Observant kid. And by far the observation I prefer over anyone telling me I look like the good captain there. I avoid looking at Tourist Girl as I unlock my wheels and turn to face the kid. "I am."

"Did you get hurt?"

Gotta love the bluntness of children. I'm used to it though. "I broke my back four years ago. Don't try jumping off Sunset Cliffs, okay?"

She bobs her pigtailed head, moving to study me. "You look like you can walk, but you can't?"

"Nope, no walking for me. My chair gets me everywhere I need to go though." I pop into a quick wheelie to demonstrate while I cast a glance around for the mom in case this turns into full-on interrogation. She's hunched over a stroller trying to keep a toddler from grabbing at a row of blown-glass siren figurines.

"You should get a bright blue chair or maybe a yellow one," the kid says, unimpressed with my solid black frame when I set the casters back down. "Or lights!" She kicks up her sneakered foot then brings it down hard on the ground to show me the way it lights up. “See how mine do?”

I can’t not smile at that. “I’ll look into it.”

“Is that why you work here? Because they don’t have any stairs?”

My smile turns tightlipped. “Uh-huh.”

The kid runs off, sneaker lights flashing when her mom calls her over, and I’m left with just Tourist Girl again. She’s moved right up to the museum’s history wall to read the rest of it, while casting increasingly frequent glances my way.

I’ve always hated the way guests study me once they make the connection, picking apart every feature like I’m some kind of relic of the past. I hated it even before I broke my back and gave them another reason to stare. Me and my wheelchair have been a fact of life for a while now, and we mostly don’t fight anymore—but I have no interest in being a tourist attraction.

Not now. Not ever.

“You’re really his descendant, aren’t you? So this place has been in your family for nearly a century and a half. I bet it’s changed a lot, more than just Nerissa out there?” Her eyes focus intently on me and she swallows before opening her mouth. “I was curious though—”

I cut off her question since I doubt it’s the innocent-kid kind. “I am related to him,” I say flatly. “But no, I’ve never seen a real mermaid. I don’t believe they exist. I don’t believe in sea monsters or krakens or anything else like that. But if you do, then by all means.” I flick a hand toward the lobby then move back behind the counter. “The Siren’s Hall is to the left, where we pretend mermaids played a pivotal role in maritime history. Inside, you’ll find old sea charts marked with dubious sketches of fish-women, dramatic paintings of sailors documenting their encounters, and an entire wall dedicated to mermaid sightings. The timeline stretches from ancient Babylonian mythology all the way to 2017—when police discovered a so-called mermaid wandering Fresno, proudly displaying webbed toes on both feet."

I don't check if that ruins the magic for her before I keep going. "If you're in the mood for more, there's the Sunken Kingdom Exhibit to the right—McCleave's attempt at creating an immersive merfolk city. It's got artifacts like *The Little Mermaid*'s actual 'dinglehopper' and a water tank where guests can fish for mermaid eggs, crack them open, and if you find an elusive golden mermaid figure inside, redeem it for anything on that shelf." I point to the one above my head then lean my forearms on the counter. "And even more exhibits beyond those. Either way, I think I'm done answering questions for the day."

"Oh, no, I wasn't . . ." She trails off as the little girl returns, this time accompanied by her mom, and plops a full set of Nerissa accessories on the counter, excitedly talking about wearing it all to the beach later.

My original customer starts to back away as I take up arms against the register once again. From the corner of my eye, I catch her biting her lip as she glances between the entrance that leads into the exhibits and the exit as if trying to make up her mind which way to go. I could offer her a suggestion, but a moment later she sighs and starts to head farther into the museum.

"Hey. Tourist Girl."

She turns back to find me holding up her bag.

"Don't forget your T-shirt."

FOUR

Wren

I watch as Tourist Girl walks past Nerissa, finish helping the little girl and her mom, then turn back to the stoic Captain McCleave and throw a stuffed starfish at his picture. It bounces harmlessly off the glass but I still wheel forward to retrieve it, ready to take aim again when hands clamp down on my shoulders from behind, hard enough to force a grunt out of me, as Tate's laughter rings in my ear. "Hey, man. I've been looking all over for you."

I side-eye my best friend and his *Rhode Island Sucks* T-shirt. "Where?"

"I don't know." He rakes a hand over his dense, coiled hair that is barely a shade darker than his deep brown skin. "Out front? Here?"

I huff out a laugh. "I'm stuck in the gift shop until Bethany shows up."

Tate points a thumb over his shoulder. "I just saw her coming in."

A moment later a middle-aged red-haired woman blusters in with the usual excuses about hectic mornings and faulty alarm clocks.

"If you could call next time," I say, *or, I don't know, answer a text*, "that would help."

"You got it, boss." But we both know she won't, just like we know I'm not the boss. Yeah, sure, I could complain and maybe my dad would fire her, but then I'd be stuck in here all the time instead of just when I'm covering for her. It's not like we've got a lot of people begging to work at McCleave's.

"We're running low on Nerissa necklaces. I need to go grab some from the back room."

Tate falls into step beside me, his long, lanky strides easily keeping up as I push my wheelchair without any real force.

"Are you working today?"

He shakes his head. "Little dudes are driving me nuts." Tate has eight-year-old twin brothers. "Figured I'd keep you company. Unless you've got a tour group waiting."

There's no one gathering around the Tours Start Here sign, so I guess not. "Why, you want to try your hand?"

"Hey, I'm here to mop floors and occasionally work the gift shop," Tate says. "Not to give in-depth lessons about stuff that your family made up a hundred years ago."

He's not wrong about his role—or the exhibits. For some reason, I scan for Tourist Girl among the guests and catch a glimpse of her ponytail disappearing around the corner toward the Grotto, a dimly lit room meant to mimic an underwater cave with a bunch of fiberglass rocks, fake plywood shipwrecks, and a fog machine that gives you a headache if you stay too long. I quicken my pace. I'd really rather she not come back out here until I'm gone. "Please tell me the FeeJee mermaid is still being repaired."

Tate bares his teeth in a grimace. "It's fine. The lighting over there is bad, so instead of an actual monkey-piranha nightmare come to life, it's more like a *shadowy* monkey-piranha nightmare. Bonus: no photo of your great-great-whatever-grandfather claiming he found it."

"Just the cage he supposedly trapped it in," I mutter.

"Right. Forgot about that." But Tate is grinning now. "Speaking of mermaids, Eryn got her new tail. She show it to you yet?"

"She mentioned something." I wheel toward the door marked *Private: Employees Only.*

Shaking his head, Tate strides ahead to push it open. "Another fundamental difference between us. If my girlfriend was an actual mermaid, I'd be front and center for that fashion show."

"She's not an actual—"

"Hey, hey, be careful what you say to the now official captain of McCleave's Famous Mermaid-Sighting Tour," he says, backing into the room with a smirk. "On Tuesdays and Saturdays from 9 to 11 a.m., she's as real as Nerissa out there."

"That real, huh?"

Then I stop, immediately hit with the smell of dust, stale coffee, and the faintest trace of old wax that never quite faded from the building's past life as a candle factory as the door swings shut behind me, sealing out most of the light. The space feels cooler, the kind of dim that makes you instinctively blink to adjust. "Wait—does that mean you passed your certification class?"

Tate grins and switches on the overhead lights. The fixtures buzz to life, throwing a dim yellow glow over the expansive room, once the production floor. It still holds some of that history—the exposed beams stretching high above, the scuffed wooden planks that creak underfoot—but now it serves as the museum's multipurpose space.

"Feel free to start saluting me anytime now."

I don't salute him, but I do pull him in for a hug, clapping an arm around his back. "And this is how you're celebrating? Why aren't you over at your uncle's shoving that paper in his face and telling him it's time to make good on his promise and finally sell the *Siren's Call* to you?"

Tate flops onto the sagging green velvet couch that, along with two mismatched beige side chairs and a scuffed oak coffee table, forms what passes for an employee lounge. "He's off-island for the next couple of months, but I'll be there waiting the second he gets back." He stretches his arms behind his head, staring up at the ceiling like he can already see his future mapped out there. "This was my last hoop, so as long as he doesn't raise the price again, by the end of summer, I'll be the owner of the sweetest twenty-six-foot Classic Crosby Launch to ever grace the seas."

He dives into his plans for a private charter company—his dream since high school—while I wade deeper into my own reality: sifting through storage shelves for trinkets to pawn off on tourists. I push the bitterness down, eyes skimming over crates of old display artifacts—historical pieces that no one else cares about. Instead, I focus on the task at hand, spotting a box of Nerissa necklaces and hauling it onto my lap, gritting my teeth against a wave of self-loathing as I do.

"Hey, you think I should start signing my name Captain Tatum Raleigh?" From out of nowhere, he produces a bag of sour cream–and-onion potato chips and starts munching. He's never not eating.

The guy should weigh a million pounds; instead he looks like a strong breeze would blow him over.

"As long as you don't start wearing the hat Eryn gave you everywhere." I pass when he offers me the bag on my way back out, only to stop just before I reach the door when my legs start to spasm.

Tate's seen my legs bounce often enough that he doesn't comment. My spasms don't hurt—but they're annoying as hell. My quads jump and twitch like I'm riding an invisible bull. Hanging on to the box, I press my free hand against my thigh, trying to force the muscles still.

A minute passes. I have anti-spasm meds, but I never take them. They only sort of work and I don't like pills.

So I deal with this crap.

Another minute goes by.

Tate watches me for a beat, then gestures at the box. "Want me to run those over to the gift shop?"

I hesitate, jaw tight, before handing it over.

He salutes me with a chip on his way out.

He's nearly out the door before I'm able to will my frustration away and say the word *thanks*.

"Never have to say it, man." He knows I appreciate the help just like he knows how much I hate needing it.

My legs eventually settle, leaving the constant pins-and-needles feeling sharper than usual as I push out into the lobby—only to spot my dad in full Poseidon mode.

A groan builds in my throat, but I swallow it down.

He's standing near the exit, surrounded by a half circle of eager tourists, his white shell crown gleaming under the lights. A fake beard, trident, and even a ridiculous padded-muscle chest complete the costume. He looks like a cross between a superhero and Santa Claus as he waxes on about all the mermaids he's seen along our coastline. And the worst part? It works. Even Tourist Girl is listening from a few feet away.

"You can see them too," he proclaims with practiced enthusiasm. "Just sign up for McCleave's Famous Mermaid-Sighting Tour. Not only will you learn all sorts of history about Nantucket—pirates, smugglers, shipwrecks—but we guarantee that you'll see a real live mermaid."

I will my legs to spasm again, just for an excuse to leave.

They don't.

"Our guide is a direct descendant of none other than Captain McCleave himself. He alone knows the secret location where Nerissa's kin still swim."

I feel it coming a second before it happens.

His gaze lifts and settles on mine.

I barely have a second to brace myself before he sweeps an arm toward me with a flourish.

"There he is now!" he announces, his grin unwavering. "Wren, come tell these people about the tour."

Every head in the room turns.

I clench my jaw so hard it aches.

It doesn't seem to matter how many times I've told him I don't want to be an act the way he inexplicably does. When I was a kid, I tolerated it. Barely. I preferred reading, combing through the museum's original collections—the ones with actual historical value. But as I got older and my resemblance to my many-times-great-grandfather increased, Dad stopped letting me stay in the background.

I finally agreed to take over the boat tours, not because I wanted to play into any of this, but because they get me out of the museum. On the water, nobody complains too much about the actual history I choose to share as long as it all ends with a mermaid sighting, which, thanks to Eryn, it always does. At least I got him to stop insisting I dress up the way he does.

Dad calls my name again, his voice thick with expectation.

I don't say a word. Instead, I jerk my chin toward the gift shop, where Tate and Bethany are already handling customers, before pushing my chair in the opposite direction, ignoring the way Dad's grin falls as several people, including Tourist Girl, take flyers.

FIVE

Lili

The morning fog still clings to the edges of the island, blurring the world as Goldie and I pedal down Madaket Road toward the Walter S. Barrett Public Pier on Saturday. The air is thick with salt and sweetly damp from last night's rain, and yet, even with the fresh sea breeze in my face, my stomach turns at what I'm about to do.

I am voluntarily getting on a boat. Again.

I'd gone back and forth about this at least a dozen times since my somewhat disappointing visit to McCleave's a few days ago. But somewhere between prying off old baseboards and measuring for the new ones, I made the mistake of leaving the flyer for the mermaid-sighting tour in view of Goldie.

That was the end of the debate.

"Do you think she'll look really real?" Goldie asks, pedaling faster as we pass the Stop and Shop and fire station, her oversized Nerissa T-shirt flapping against her arms like a sail, "or like somebody's sad Halloween costume?"

"The skeleton looked pretty real." Unsettlingly so. Sadly, not much else in the place did.

But I keep coming back to what I read in the gift shop—how McCleave's was once a historical museum before they went all-in on the fantasy. Since it's still run by the family, there's a chance they still have some of those original pieces in their collection.

It's a long shot, I know. But the guy dressed as Poseidon did specifically say they'd be talking about more than just mermaids on this tour. I'll just keep my eyes on the horizon and my ears trained for anything about smugglers. And if the guide doesn't know anything that can help me? At least Goldie will get to see more of the island she barely remembers.

"There it is!" Goldie practically skids to a stop, pointing ahead.

The *Siren's Call* bobs at the dock, its navy hull trimmed in white, the name painted in gold across the stern. A sign on the dock announces: *McCleave's Famous Mermaid-Sighting Tour*.

I grip my handlebars tighter as we coast down toward the bike rack, passing a bright white-and-turquoise ice cream truck parked nearby, its side labeled Hang Loose Helado. The striped awning shades a growing crowd of customers, the sweet scents of vanilla and melted waffle cones clashing pleasantly with the sharp bite of salty air.

I fully expect Goldie to beg to grab something, but she just looks.

"You don't want any?"

She side-eyes me. "I don't want you eating ice cream before I have to sit next to you on a boat for an hour."

I elbow her. "Wow. The concern."

She grins and runs ahead, flashing our ticket confirmation before boarding.

I hesitate, watching the boat rock gently in the harbor. Even with zero dairy in my system, I already feel my stomach preparing to stage a rebellion. I stare across the deck, and for a second, ice cream or not, I don't know if I can actually do this. But then I think of Mr. Fanning and his pinched, patronizing face.

I take a breath, square my shoulders, and step on board.

Goldie beelines for the front, weaving through the narrow rows of benches until she claims a spot right next to the guide.

Wren.

I follow, forcing myself to sit down calmly beside his wheelchair, determined to make a better impression this time. And who knows—maybe I imagined his irritation the other day. I know *I* was occasionally short with customers for no reason back when I worked retail. I flash a warm smile. "Hey. Remember me?"

His expression says he does, and not fondly.

I push forward anyway. "I didn't get to introduce myself the other day. I'm Lili, and that's my sister, Goldie." I nod toward her, though she's too busy kneeling on the bench, practically vibrating with excitement as she stares at the water.

"Um, listen," I continue, shifting slightly. "I wanted to apologize for any misunderstanding in the gift shop. I have a—"

A crackle of static cuts through the air as Wren's headset comes to life.

"Eryn's in place. Just saw we had two last-minute cancellations, so we're setting out with eighteen."

"All accounted for," Wren responds, pressing a button on his mic.

A Black guy in a captain's hat hops on board, squeezing down the narrow aisle until reaching the front. "Well, all right then." He straightens his hat, then steps forward, addressing the passengers with a broad, practiced grin.

“Good morning, lads and ladies! Mermaid lovers from near and far! My name is Captain Tatum Raleigh, Tate to my friends, and I have the great honor of being your captain for today’s adventure! And yes,” he adds, winking at an older woman seated near the front, “I am a real captain.”

She giggles.

I’m pretty sure Wren rolls his eyes.

Captain Tate launches into a very well-rehearsed introduction, pacing the deck with a theatrical flourish. “I will keep you safe, secure, and smiling as we travel all around this faraway island of ours. So! Get your cameras out, your eyes trained on the water, and let me hear how many of you are ready to see a real mermaid!”

The chorus of excited cheers is loud—louder than I expected. Goldie practically screams in my ear.

“Oh, so it sounds like some of you don’t really care about mermaids,” Tate continues, letting his shoulders sag dramatically. The passengers play along, responding with an exaggerated *Boo!*

“I mean, we could cancel the tour,” he says, turning as if to head back to the wheel. “Maybe try and find some other folks who would appreciate seeing the family of our fair Nerissa swimming in these very waters . . .”

“No! No!”

A few of the younger kids look genuinely panicked at the thought.

Tate sighs, shaking his head. “Maybe I should ask one more time, just in case anyone wants to change their mind.” He sucks in an exaggerated breath, then booms—“How many of you are READY to see a MERMAID?”

The deafening roar that follows physically startles me.

Tate beams. "That's more like it!" He claps his hands. "Then let me introduce you to the man who's going to guide you back in time through treacherous tales of pirates, smugglers, shipwrecks, and, yes, mermaids. Not only does he know more about this island's tumultuous history than just about anyone, but he is, in fact, the many-times-great-grandson of Captain Lawrence McCleave—the very man who discovered the world-famous Nerissa skeleton nearly one hundred and fifty years ago!" He points two fingers in Wren's direction. "Wren, take it away."

Eighteen eager faces swing toward the guy sitting beside me, primed and pumped for the show.

Wren clicks on his mic, leans forward slightly, and—in the flattest, most uninterested voice I've ever heard—says, "Yeah, thanks. This is your reminder to remain seated when the boat is moving and not to crowd your fellow passengers when our mermaid appears at the end of the tour."

I blink. Even airline pilots giving tired safety speeches have more enthusiasm. The contrast between him and Tate is so jarring, I almost laugh. But then the boat starts moving and my stomach lurches with it.

"Nantucket, which means 'faraway land' in Algonquin, the language of the native Wampanoag people, wasn't inhabited by Europeans until the middle of the seventeenth century. At that time, it's estimated that there were around three thousand Wampanoags on the island. Due to European disease, and specifically an epidemic known as the "Indian Sickness" in 1763, they were all gone in less than a century. Abram Quary, the last Wampanoag in Nantucket, whose portrait you can find in the Atheneum, died in 1854."

Momentarily distracted from cold sweat starting to prick along my neck, I quietly tell my sister, "That's wrong. Dorcas Honorable outlived him by six weeks."

Goldie slow blinks at me. "What?"

"Just tell him." I nudge her arm.

With a sigh, she raises her hand. Wren stops mid-sentence, frowning.

"Um, what about that dork lady?"

"She meant Dorcus Honorable," I say, somehow not throwing up on the spot.

Wren pulls his brows together. "She's not officially listed in any of the census data."

I know I'm right, but I don't push it. Maybe I'll bring it up after everyone disembarks. That thought helps keep my nausea at bay—until he does it again.

"Among the more than seven hundred shipwrecks surrounding our island, the sinking of the *Titanic*-like *Andrea Doria* in 1956 is perhaps the most well-known, as it was the first televised tragedy of its kind. Due to intense fog and a radar misinterpretation, the *Doria* collided with the MS *Stockholm* and sank along with fifty of its passengers."

This time, I don't prompt Goldie. "Actually, their lack of communication is often cited as the primary reason for the collision, not the fog."

He sweeps an irritated glance in my direction. "Thanks for sharing."

"I'm just saying, they would've avoided each other if they'd just used their radios."

There's a flicker of something on his face—irritation or

amusement, I can't quite tell—but he turns back to the group and keeps talking.

I don't notice until a full minute later that I've kept my eyes open the entire time. My stomach is far from happy, but arguing with Wren is proving to be an incredibly effective distraction. I scoot to the edge of my seat, eagerly waiting for another questionable fact.

Unfortunately, he doesn't give me much to argue with. Tate wasn't lying in his introduction—Wren knows a lot, and not just regurgitated facts either. Within the first twenty minutes of the tour I'm 95 percent sure that he's the "friend" Mrs. Mayhew mentioned, and I decide to press just a little more to be sure when he brings up Captain William Kidd's rumored buried treasure.

"Some people say that he was a privateer rather than a pirate, arguing that Captain Kidd was commissioned by the Earl of Bellomont to *hunt down* pirates."

Wren looks at me, and this time I swear he almost smiles. "He sailed under French colors in order to flat out steal the *Quedagh Merchant*, and it was Bellomont himself who had him hung for piracy."

I shake my head, thrilled I can move without turning into a human sprinkler. "The 1698 Act of Grace would've pardoned him from any highly disputed acts of piracy, if not for his political affiliations."

Wren laughs, loud enough that Tate looks over. Then he mutes his mic and leans closer. "Whether he was a Whig or not is irrelevant. He was guilty of piracy."

"Not according to Margaret Ellison and her book, *Pirates and the Crown*." It was a poorly researched book that I read last year, but it did indeed try to defend Captain Kidd. "Clearly, you haven't read it, or maybe any books that go against more popular accounts."

His expression sharpens, like he's enjoying this too much. "Oh, Tourist Girl, I guarantee I'm reading all the right books. Both Geoffrey L. Finchley and Eleanor Beecham ripped Ellison's book apart for its absolutely embarrassing research practices."

His stare grabs hold of mine, and for a moment, it's like I'm not seasick at all. Because he's right, they did.

But then a spray of cool water mists over us, and his expression chills with it.

"Look, I don't have the time or the crayons to explain this to you if that's the kind of nonsense you're reading."

My face heats, but before I can defend myself, Goldie interrupts. "Um, we own a house here, and our family comes from Nantucket, so you should maybe call her Local Girl."

"Or Lili," I say, turning my attention briefly to her and then back to Wren. "Can I ask you another question?"

His laugh is entirely humorless. "Can I stop you?"

Not about this. "What do you know about Kezia Gardner?"

His brows lift slightly, but he doesn't hesitate to switch the mic back on. "I was just asked about Kezia Gardner. Show of hands, who knows who she was?"

Only one woman in the back raises a tentative hand. Goldie turns to me with a grin and shoots her hand high into the air, her bracelets jingling with the motion.

"Only two of you, huh?" Wren says, before meeting my gaze and adding, "Three." He gestures toward the sandy dunes slipping past us. "Kezia Gardner was the most notorious smuggler in Nantucket history, operating right along this shoreline.

"Married to a whaling captain, Kezia took control when the Revolutionary War crippled trade with Britain. She had a nimble mind and flexible morals, and refused to let her fortune disappear. Instead of bowing to new trade restrictions, she worked both sides of the Atlantic, protecting her ships and smuggling contraband goods. No one ever cracked her method of communication, but some claim she had a smuggler's hole hidden among the blackberry bushes right along the harbor."

These are not commonly known details. I grip the edge of my seat as Wren continues.

"She dodged prosecution, but the people of Nantucket have their own form of justice. Many involved in legitimate trade lost their businesses and even their homes due to economic instability while she grew richer at their expense. One night while Kezia and her husband slept, a group set fire to their home in Quaise."

A lump tightens in my throat. I already know how this ends.

"They survived but fled soon after, claiming the damp sea air was ruining her health." His tone is skeptical, like he finds the excuse laughable. "She died five years later, never returning to the island that made her infamous."

His eyes lock on mine. "Does that answer your question?"

I nod, heart pounding. It really does.

Before I can say more, someone calls from the back of the boat.

"Now eventually you do plan to have mermaids on your mermaid tour, right?"

A few passengers laugh.

Wren's mouth tightens but he gives a nod to the captain, and the boat makes a sharp left. My stomach flips in protest and I squeeze my eyes shut.

"If you'll all turn to your left as we round this cove—" Wren's voice fades as a girl around Goldie's age gasps.

"Look! It's the mermaid!"

Goldie grips my arm so hard I lose circulation. "She's so pretty!"

I risk opening my eyes—and okay, yeah, the mermaid is breathtaking.

Perched on the sun-warmed rocks, she's framed by the glittering Atlantic, a cherry blossom woven into her long, glossy black hair. Her golden-tipped aquamarine tail catches the light with every movement, shimmering like something straight out of a Japanese legend.

Phones click, kids squeal, a boy near the back bounces in his dad's lap. "She's waving at me!"

Despite my nausea, I smile.

The captain slows the boat, letting everyone get the perfect photo. Wren recites a few practiced lines, but no one is listening, not even me.

My stomach clenches as the boat drifts, so I clamp my eyes shut, breathing through my mouth until Goldie announces that the mermaid is leaving. I force my eyes open just in time to see her dive into the water, her tail flashing once before disappearing beneath the waves.

The moment the boat turns back toward the harbor, Wren says, "Thank you for taking the tour. Watch your step as you disembark, and please remember to take all trash and belongings with you." He switches off the microphone with a click, and just like that, he's done.

"I'm going to go get in line for ice cream." Goldie bumps into me on her way off as soon as we dock. "I'll meet you at the bikes!"

I nod vaguely. Talking feels dangerous. Walking even more so. I focus on standing.

"Hey, ride's over, Tourist Girl." Wren's voice drifts over my shoulder when I realize I'm the last guest on board. "Time to get off my boat before you turn any greener."

"Uh, my boat," the captain interjects, flashing me a grin. "And I do private tours."

The idea of another boat ride nearly finishes me off. I shake my head slowly.

"No?" Tate props one foot on the seat and gazes dramatically out over the water. "The sea, she is a fickle mistress, but she owns my heart. And if I have to choose between the two of you, pretty-girl-I-just-met, I'm sorry to say it's the sea for me."

Wren shoves him aside. "Would you just go help Eryn? I'll meet you both back at the truck after cleaning up."

Tate goes, and Wren's eyes turn to me. "You gonna make it, or do you need a bag? I'd rather you not puke on my boat."

I exhale slowly, leveling him with a look. "I thought it was the captain's boat."

"You're still arguing?" He tilts his head toward the gangplank. "Maybe try getting on solid ground first." I manage to step onto the dock without humiliating myself, but Wren watches me like he expects me to drop.

"You took the ferry, right?" he asks, tying off a bag of trash in his lap. "Which means you knew you'd get sick today. You barely glanced at the mermaid. So why take the tour?"

I hold up a finger, bending slightly to rest a hand on my knee. He rolls down the ramp as I mutter to myself under my breath. "See? You didn't throw up. You did not throw up on the boat, and you are not going to throw up now."

“Let me get you a water.” Wren says.

I shake my head, take a slow breath, then straighten. “I’m good.”

“Are you?” He sounds skeptical.

“I will be good,” I amend. “And I’m sorry for arguing with you on your tour.”

He studies me. “You were technically right about Dorcas. And the *Andrea Doria*.”

I grin. “You were right about Kidd.”

“Oh, I know.” He doesn’t grin, but I kind of get the feeling he wants to.

“And you’re right that I’m not interested in mermaids. What I want is a lot more important.”

“Oh yeah?” He tosses the trash bag into a nearby can. “And what’s that? A coupon for another Nerissa T-shirt?”

“Is that my prize for fact-checking your tour speech?”

He laughs.

The sound is rough around the edges but surprisingly nice. I tuck that away before I can think too much about it. “I need a research partner for the summer. Someone who knows Nantucket history, specifically the Revolutionary War era.” I draw a deep breath. “Kezia Gardner is my as-many-times-great-grandmother as Lawrence McCleave is your grandfather.” I rock my hand from side to side. “Or near about.”

His mouth flattens. “And? Everybody around here is related to someone noteworthy.”

“My dad spent years trying to prove we got her story wrong and died before he could. The museums wouldn’t help him, and they won’t help me. I think you can.”

Wren sighs, rubbing the back of his neck. "Look, I'm sorry about your dad, but McCleave's is a mermaid museum. We don't do real history."

I study his face. "Then tell me how you know about blackberries hiding the entrance to her supposed smuggling hole?"

His jaw ticks. "I read it somewhere."

"Where?"

He hesitates.

I step closer, watching his expression flicker, a subtle shift that catches me off guard. "You do have records at McCleave's, don't you? Books and maybe even artifacts from before 1893? Things that not even the Whaling Museum seems to know about?"

His gaze lowers, and in that split second, I know.

My heart thuds in my chest, a warm rush of triumph and possibility spreading through me. "I don't think you care about mermaids any more than I do, but McCleave's is literally your family's museum, so why not help me and rediscover some of the actual history I'm willing to bet you still have?"

He's about to brush me off, his lips already parting to say something dismissive. But then he stops, his posture shifting, his eyes narrowing in a way that suggests he's weighing something deeper. He lifts his head, meeting my gaze with a deliberation that makes my breath catch.

"I'm not saying we have anything," he says slowly, like he's testing the words on his tongue, "but if you want access, to McCleave's and to me for the summer, I'd have to get something out of it."

His words hang in the air, a subtle unexpected challenge that makes my pulse speed up. I probably should ask more questions, but the only word I say is "Anything."

SIX
Wren

"She offered to do what?"

Tate is sprawled in the open bed of my truck, twirling his captain hat around one finger while Eryn changes in the cab.

"Work at McCleave's. For free," I repeat, still not believing Tourist Girl had agreed. She hadn't been thrilled by the terms I'd offered her; in fact, she'd looked distinctly uncomfortable, but she'd said yes.

Eryn slides out of the cab, fully dressed in cutoffs and a tank top, then hops up beside Tate. She folds her legs beneath her with effortless grace and tucks a loose strand of still-damp hair behind her ear as she turns to face us. "Doing what?"

"Running the gift shop, for one, whenever Bethany can't."

Tate raises an eyebrow, his mouth tilting into the beginnings of a grin. "That could be good. Anything else?"

"I haven't thought it all the way through yet, but I guess anything."

Tate's grin widens. "So does that potentially mean any sort of job? Like, 'Oops, someone flushed a hot dog again—better call the new girl'?"

Eryn frowns at him. "I'm sure he doesn't mean that." Then she looks at me, tilting her head. "You don't, right?"

"She did say she'll do anything that doesn't involve getting on a boat."

Tate's smile is now so comically wide I could count his molars.

"But neither of us agreed to anything yet. She said she had to figure some things out on her end, and I'm not thrilled with the idea of spending a good part of my summer on some pointless research project."

His grin crashes like a toppled sandcastle. "What—why?"

"Did you miss the part where she has this delusional theory about Kezia Gardner, of all people, that I'm supposed to help her prove?"

"And did *you* miss the part about her doing all the stuff that makes you a miserable bastard to be around? What is the matter with you?" Tate swipes at my head, but I duck just in time.

"Um, you're the one who cleans the bathrooms," Eryn points out.

"Um, we can all be miserable bastards, Eryn," Tate says. "Wren doesn't get a monopoly on that."

She loops her arms around my neck, her wet hair brushing against my cheek, and I shift infinitesimally away from the cold contact. "He's not miserable."

Tate steps back with mock outrage, hands raised in defense. "Whoa, whoa. Are you just going to sit there and let her get away with calling you a bastard?"

Eryn immediately releases me and straightens. "I never said that."

"No? Cause I called him"—Tate makes air quotes—"a miserable bastard. Then you said"—he moves to drape his arms around my neck but I shove him away with one arm, so he pretends to hold an invisible me while doing a not-terrible Eryn impression—"'he's not miserable.' The only implication is that you think he *is* a bastard."

Eryn rolls her eyes.

They keep going, bickering the way they always do, the rhythm of it familiar, comfortable. I watch the way Eryn shakes her head at Tate's dramatics, the way he jabs at her just enough to keep her entertained. They've been this way since third grade. There was a time, back in junior high, when I thought they might end up together, but neither of them showed any interest in being more than what they were.

If someone had asked me back then if I thought I'd ever end up with Eryn, I'd have said never. But here we are, going on four years.

"It doesn't matter since I doubt she'll even come back. She didn't expect me to ask for anything in return and there's no way she actually wants to work at McCleave's. She's got that tourist energy."

"Tourist energy?" Tate hangs his head. "Man, you've got to let that go. Not everybody is the same as—"

"Okay, okay," Eryn interrupts. "This conversation isn't going anywhere helpful."

"I'm just saying . . ." Tate leans back on both hands. "This could be a good deal. Just don't be an idiot and run off free help. See how I avoided calling you a bastard? That was for you."

A laugh slips out before I can catch it, but Eryn doesn't join in. Instead, she says, "I think it's a good idea too." Her voice is calm, but it feels like a jab.

I shift more fully toward her. "Really? Because I'd have to spend time helping her, time we already don't get a lot of."

Her gaze meets mine, steady and unwavering, her unnaturally blue contact lenses from her mermaid costume still catching the midday sun. "I'm working at the café more this summer anyway, so really it's only Tate who'll have to share you."

Defeat rolls over me, inevitable as the tide, and when I turn to Tate, his triumphant grin tells me he knows it too.

"You're not an idiot," Eryn says, her tone softer now. She shoots a pointed look at Tate, who throws his hands up in mock surrender. "No matter what you decide. But what's so bad about offering someone a little help? And a research project for the museum might even be fun."

Fun. Right. Now I feel like I'm seasick.

I can't help this girl. That much was obvious on the boat. She argued with me the whole time, like she thought she could wear me down if she just kept at it. Like I was enjoying it as much as she was.

Okay fine, maybe I didn't completely hate that part, but that still doesn't mean I want to spend my summer with a tourist.

Tate shoves my knee with his foot, dragging me out of my head. "Dude, relax. You look like someone just poured sand in your soda."

I force a scoff, shoving his foot off me. "I'm fine."

Eryn doesn't say anything. Just watches me for a beat longer before hopping off the truck bed. "I should go." She stretches her arms over her head. "I told Teresa I'd take an afternoon shift today."

I nod, trying to shake the strange unease creeping into my ribs, the feeling that something is shifting and I don't quite have control of it.

"Promise me you'll give it a try?"

I glance away, staring at the edge of the truck bed where the paint is chipped, exposing the dull metal underneath. It's easier than looking at her. I haven't liked anything about McCleave's since I was a kid. And maybe not even then. The things I care about—the real things—are crammed onto shelves in the backroom, forgotten because nobody else gives a damn. And honestly, I'm no better. I'm just a guy a year out of high school with no qualifications beyond, hopefully, keeping those artifacts from falling apart. The kind of degree I'd need to make anything of them doesn't exist here on Nantucket. Not that it matters; I couldn't leave if I wanted to, which thankfully I don't. I love this island.

I'm just stuck.

My gaze travels to Eryn again and I think about how utterly incapable I am of saying no to her. I never really could, even before the accident. And after?

How many girls would stay with their brand-new fifteen-year-old boyfriend after he broke his back and spent months in the hospital? How many would step up to take care of that boyfriend's dad, cooking him dinner every night, keeping the house from falling apart, so his dad could fight with insurance companies to get him a wheelchair? How many would still be there four years later, dressing up in a mermaid tail every week for his family museum?

How many would talk about a future and a family with a guy who couldn't even get down on one knee for them?

The thought twists in my chest, sharp and unwelcome, like a splinter I can't get rid of. I lower my head. "I'd have to talk with my dad," I say finally, my voice low, resigned.

"That shouldn't be too hard." Eryn's hand brushes against mine, her touch light, but it only makes the unspoken expectations between us feel heavier.

"Sure," I agree, forcing myself to meet her gaze. "But I can't help her find something that isn't there."

"You can help her find closure," she says, her tone quiet but insistent.

I seriously doubt that. Some people don't know when to give up. My gaze drifts over Eryn's face, and I realize just how true that is.

SEVEN

Lili

The day after the mermaid tour sees us up bright and early, and for once, I'm not the only one in a dress.

"Stop," Mom tells Goldie when my sister makes yet another face at her reflection in the bathroom mirror, squirming as though ants are crawling all over her. "I checked all the seams and cut out the tag. You'll survive one morning."

Goldie stills as Mom finishes braiding her hair, her small frame rigid, but her mouth still turned down in a pout. "I got to wear shorts back in Arizona."

"And you can still wear them under your dress if you want to."

Goldie looks up at Mom to make sure she's serious, then, with a grin, races back to our room.

"You look really pretty," I tell Mom, watching her smooth the blue silk scarf she'd tied loosely around her neck for the third time. It's a delicate thing, with tiny golden anchors dotting the fabric, like a map to the sea. "Very nautical chic," I add with a teasing smile.

Mom catches my eye in the mirror, a crinkle of warmth spreading across her face. "Thanks."

I watch her for another moment, trying to decide if this is the right time to bring up the offer Wren made me yesterday. Before I can work up the nerve, Mom is ushering us both down the stairs.

"Move your butt. I've been wanting to step inside that steepled white church since before Goldie was born, and we are not going to be late for our first service." She gives me a gentle swat, and I can't help but laugh.

The church is located in the heart of downtown, only a few minutes away. When we arrive, there are still plenty of people walking up the stepped brick pathway, greeting each other with smiles and laughter, the quiet hum of their conversations mixing with the sound of a bell tolling overhead. It's all very welcoming, but my hands curl into my skirt. Now that I've decided to talk to Mom, I can't stop rehearsing how I'll say it.

We slip through the old wooden doors to find that, like the exterior, the inside is bright and white. Every surface glows from the sunlight streaming through the tall arched windows that line the walls.

As we settle into one of the white, boxed pews, I notice the baskets of purple hydrangeas hanging from the arched rods that stretch across the sanctuary. The smell is light, like summer rain, just the right balance of floral and fresh. I release my skirt. Even Goldie, who usually can't sit still for five minutes, seems to take a deep breath, her fidgeting finally slowing, as her eyes touch on each one, counting.

The service is simple and familiar, the kind of steady rhythm that makes you forget the passing of time. When it ends, the hush lingers before conversations begin again, spilling warmth into the space.

Several locals introduce themselves, all friendly, but a couple of men with smiles just a bit too polished hover near Mom. Gazing at her bare ring finger, they suddenly seem very eager to give her personal tours of the island.

I brace myself, but before Mom even has a chance to respond, a familiar face elbows her way through, looping her arm through Mom's like they've been best friends for years.

"You'd think they'd never seen a pretty woman before," Mrs. Mayhew declares, steering her away. "Most of the people here are lovely, but God didn't give those two enough sense to tie their shoes."

Goldie bursts into laughter.

"But it's wonderful to see all the Gardner girls here this morning. How are you getting settled?"

"Just fine," Mom says, the tension in her shoulders easing. "I really enjoyed the sermon, and the church is even more beautiful than I imagined. I'd love to hear more about its architecture—I mean, the trompe l'oeil design on the ceiling alone is stunning." She looks up. "I took an art class years ago and fell in love with the way artists can use paint to create that kind of illusion. It's all flat, but it looks like you could reach up and touch carved stone."

Mrs. Mayhew beams. "It is a beautiful church, that's for sure. I don't know all the details about the building myself, but I'd be happy to introduce you to someone who does."

Mom's face lights up. "I'd love that."

Mrs. Mayhew nods. "If you don't mind, I'd like to take Goldie over to meet some of the other kids first. We've got a handful her age, and they usually gather out back to play tag and red rover and such."

Mom looks down at Goldie, who practically vibrates at the idea. "That sound good to you?"

Goldie nods so vigorously her braid nearly comes undone, and a second later, she and Mrs. Mayhew are off, leaving Mom and me to wander through the sanctuary as she continues studying the space.

"What do you think about adding chunky trim like that to the windows at the house?" she muses, pointing. "It'd be more historically accurate than the simple kind we have up now."

I nod, grateful that she's giving me an opportunity to bring up the topic. "Sure. Actually, can I talk to you about the house?"

"Just look at the crown molding," she says, still lost in thought. "It'll take a little longer, but I've got my miter box. I could do it."

I step in front of her. "I need to talk to you about something, and it kind of affects the house."

That gets her attention. "Oh no, please don't tell me you found a leak in the ceiling."

"No, nothing like that," I assure her. "It's more of a request."

Her brows knit together.

"You know how I found Dad's notebook and have been trying to figure out all his research?"

She nods slowly. "You tried to get a couple of museums in town to help, but it didn't work out."

"Right." I exhale. "Only, it turns out one of them might be willing to help me after all—"

Her expression shifts, the tension lifting. "They are? Lili, that's great."

"—in exchange for me volunteering there for the summer."

She stops walking.

I take a couple more steps before turning back to her.

She isn't frowning, but she isn't smiling either. She opens her mouth, then closes it again.

I don't say anything.

She catches up to me. "What about renovating the house? We've barely started."

"I still want to work on the house. I wouldn't be volunteering full-time."

"When are you going to research Kezia Gardner? Not while you're volunteering, right?"

"I don't know how that's supposed to work yet. I wanted to talk to you first, but I'll figure it out."

She studies me, her green eyes searching mine. "And Goldie? All the things you promised to do with her? Is one boat ride all she gets?"

I shake my head. "I'd be doing this for her too. She doesn't remember Dad the way I do. To her, he's more like a character in a story than a real person."

Mom inhales deeply and looks away. "That's because he spent too many years chasing after history—years he took from you and your sister."

I know she feels that way. But I can't. And I have a whole stack of postcards reminding me why.

"That's why I need to do this," I say quietly. "I finally have a chance to show her that he did something important with his life."

Her voice wavers when she says, "You two were the most important thing he did with his life."

I shift, uncomfortable, my gaze slipping from hers.

"Lili."

I glance back at her, startled by the softened tone of her voice.

"I understand this is important to you," she says, carefully, like she's weighing every word. "I know you wouldn't be asking if it wasn't." She hesitates, then exhales, thoughtful. "I also know how badly you wanted to come here to feel closer to him, and if this is how you think you need to do that . . . then okay. I won't stop you."

A slow, uncertain smile tugs at my lips. "Really?"

She hesitates again, then nods. "But promise me you won't disappear the way he did."

"I won't." My answer is immediate. Certain. "I promise."

She presses her lips together, searching my face. "I'm going to hold you to that."

EIGHT
Wren

Bright and early Monday morning, Tate strides into the museum's back room with Tourist Girl trailing behind him.

"—probably going to involve some janitorial work," he's saying, his voice full of fake encouragement. "But nothing a plunger and a can-do attitude can't handle."

She hesitates just inside the doorway, looking thoroughly distraught at the idea. I bite back a laugh, but my attention catches on her outfit—high-waisted sailor-style shorts in a soft red, matching flats, and a sleeveless white top tied at the waist. It's the kind of thing you'd expect to see in an old summer postcard, like she should be leaning against a vintage convertible with an ice cream cone in hand. Instead, she's standing in the dusty back room of a museum, framed by bookcases full of Nantucket history books and an old dehumidifier rattling in the corner.

It's not that she looks bad. If anything, she looks too put together, especially in a place where the unofficial uniform is wrinkled T-shirts and an air of mild discontent. Case in point: Tate, whose shirt is both wrinkled and vaguely insulting. Today's selection simply says: *Newport: Because Some People Fear Happiness.*

"You're not going to be cleaning bathrooms," I say, dragging my focus back to my laptop.

Tate turns to me with an exaggerated *What gives?* expression. "What?" he says, all innocence. "She's asked what kind of work she'd be doing. I'm just giving her some possible options."

She lets out a small breath, visibly relieved, though she still clutches the strap of her red bag like she's already regretting showing up today.

"Bye, Tate," I say flatly.

He sighs dramatically but heads out, muttering something about wasted opportunities under his breath as he goes.

"So, he works here too?" she asks after a moment, her voice light but probing.

I nod, keeping my eyes on my screen. Then I remember that he's about to own his own boat. He won't be here much longer. "For now." I'm happy for him, but I'll hate it when he's gone. "Give me a minute and we'll talk about what you'll actually be doing around here." When a beat passes without so much as a sound from her, I look up, half expecting her to have left too.

She's staring at the rows of shelves filling half the room. Gone is the uneasy expression she'd worn with Tate and in its place is open-mouthed awe I don't expect from anyone, let alone a tourist. She might as well be seeing the ocean for the first time.

Her bag slips from her fingertips, landing with a soft thud. She moves toward the nearest shelf, craning her neck to take it all in before crouching down, then shooting back up. I watch her for a while, distracted despite myself, noticing how she reaches out a hand only to draw it back as though afraid to touch anything,

When she stops in front of a long, rectangular crate, one of the oldest in the McCleave's collection, she reads the label and her eyes widen. "Tell me that's a joke."

"We keep the jokes outside this room," I say, unlocking my brakes and moving closer even though I know the exact contents of the crate she's looking at. "A salvage crew working near Henderson Island found it along with other remnants of the wreck that matched the account of the surviving first mate, Owen Chase, exactly. McCleave's paid $248 for it in 1903," I add absently. "The old ledgers are in the filing cabinet behind you if you want more details."

She whirls on me, her blonde hair swinging around so fast she nearly hits herself in the face. "You're claiming to have a harpoon from the wreck of the *Essex* back here," she breathes, her voice trembling with awe. "That's like . . . having the weapon that took on Moby Dick hidden in your storage closet."

"Melville only took inspiration from the sinking of the *Essex*, you know. Or did you miss that book while you were reading Margaret Ellison's pseudohistory?" I say, my tone light, though part of me wants her to argue with me, to go toe-to-toe the way she did on the tour. But she just shakes her head, clearly stunned, and shifts her attention to another shelf.

"Edward Coffin, Andrew B. H. Wilson, Joseph Starbuck . . ." She says the names like they're celebrities instead of some of the most important whaling captains of the nineteenth century, and for a second, it's hard to watch. It's the kind of reverence I never see around here.

When she spots the item currently set out on the table for routine cleaning and inspection, her voice drops to a whisper. "Does that bell say *Rising Sun* on it?"

She can see the embossed metal as clearly as I can. "Want to know how much we paid for it? It was a bargain."

"No." Her hands slide over the sides of her head and she spins away like she's too overwhelmed to look at any more of it. "Why do you have all this back here and not out there?" She gestures vaguely toward the lobby.

"And where exactly would you suggest it go?" I head back toward my desk. "Next to the authentic mermaid anatomy chart or beside the golden comb of the infamous Rhine River siren?"

She trails behind me, voice cracking. "It just feels wrong for all of this to be hidden away back here."

I bristle at the truth in her words, and the fact that there's not a thing that I can do about it. "Yeah, well, tell that to the other tourists."

"I guess I should be grateful that I'm seeing something few people ever will." She stops walking and I can feel her stare. "Thank you for letting me back here. And for taking such obvious care of so much history."

I tense at the praise. "And how would you know about that? Run a lot of conservation labs when you're not out sightseeing?"

She doesn't take the bait. "No, but I have been in a lot of museums. Someone is maintaining these items. I'm guessing it's the same someone who knows the contents of the crates without looking."

I don't respond. I'm not a curator, and I'm well aware of how far short I fall.

She stares back at the shelves, her red lips caught in a thoughtful bite before she slowly releases them in a smile. "You know, you shouldn't have shown me this place, because now I'm never gonna want to leave."

Except the tourists always leave, even the ones who swear they won't.

"You'd rather I met with you in the taxidermy lab?"

Her nose scrunches up. "Ew. No. You have one of those?"

"Mermaids don't make themselves."

Her expression shifts from disgust to intrigue, back and forth, all in the span of a few seconds. "Something must be wrong with me because I kind of want to see it. Just once," she adds quickly. "For the life of me I cannot tell how Nerissa . . . *is* Nerissa. I can't stop thinking about it." Then she shakes her head. "But that's not why I'm here. We have a deal, right? I'll work here for free, doing whatever you need, and you'll help me research my ancestor's history." She reaches for her bag. "My dad already has a lot of information but—"

"Whoa," I say, drawing her attention to me. "That's not how any of this is going to work. Seeing all this back here, you're convinced I can help you, right?"

Her nod is slow, like she already knows there's a follow-up to that question.

"Well." I lean my forearms on my desk. "Now it's your turn to prove that *you* can help *me*."

NINE
Wren

Ten minutes after she leaves, I'm still processing our meeting. We've agreed to a loose schedule, but nothing's final until Dad signs off on her.

I check my watch. It's just before one. He'll be in the lab.

As a kid, I thought the taxidermy lab was some unholy mix of Dr. Frankenstein's black-and-white movie lab and an unaired episode of *Hoarders*, the kind deemed unfit for television. The space used to be an old rendering room where whale blubber was boiled down in massive cauldrons, and even though it's been more than 150 years since it was operational, it still feels like the walls, the doors—hell, even the air—are slick with grease. The acrid stench of formaldehyde slaps you the moment you step inside, clawing at your throat and stinging your eyes and nose. There are no windows. Not even a skylight. Dad says he's fine with it, swearing his dozens of lamps do the trick, but to me, the room feels like a tomb. Glass-eyed animals stare blankly from every surface, their stiff bodies trapped midsnarl or frozen in eerie calm. Jars filled with murky, amber-tinted liquid line the shelves, their floating contents just indistinct enough to trigger a visceral unease.

Dad's hunched over something with his rotary tool when I come in, the whir of the motor drowning out the sound of my movement until I'm halfway across the room. He makes a half-hearted show of brushing what looks like white powder off his chest and arms, raking it from his dark hair and the beard he hasn't shaved in over a week. He doesn't come close to getting it all and it doesn't matter anyway because I can now see exactly what he's working on. The stone table in the center of the room—the one with the deep scars and grooves from years of use—holds the remains of what I'm guessing are a grouper, a pelican, and—*shit*—an eel. My entire body clenches at the sight of that long, spindly eel skeleton, perfect for shaping into mermaid tails.

"Making a sister for Nerissa?" I ask flatly. Already I can feel the chemicals starting to sting my eyes and nose.

"This one's going to be male, so he'll be her mate," he says, offering me his safety goggles. I shake my head. "It'll be quite a few more weeks before Nereus here is ready for any kind of introduction, but . . ." Dad leans back so I can see the size he's going for—easily eight feet—and I'm already envisioning the schlock accessories we'll end up selling because of Nereus. Seashell slingshots? A seaweed lasso? "Once he's part of the display," Dad continues, "we'll need to revisit Nerissa's story to incorporate him into it."

My voice is deeply suspicious. "What does that mean?"

"New T-shirt designs, for one, a second mermaid for the tours, and a new tour script focusing more on the story of the two of them."

"The current script is fine."

"We'll give you some time to think about it."

"Dad, no. I barely have enough time as it is to cover a fraction of the island's history before we get to Eryn on her rock." I pause to eye him. "And why do you keep saying 'we'?"

Dad sighs, the sound deep and resigned. "I mentioned the idea to Eryn and she offered to come up with a backstory for how they were star-crossed lovers, Romeo and Juliet style, got separated, but are now reunited forever. I'm not asking you to recite all that," he adds, no doubt seeing the look of disbelief on my face. "I thought Eryn and whoever plays Nereus could act out a scene. She's on board."

"Yeah, Eryn would 'be on board' for anything you asked because she's a sweet person who likes helping people." I try not to let myself get worked up here, but it's an effort.

I know the pattern. After my accident, Dad and Eryn got used to figuring things out for me, and while some of that may have been necessary back then, it hasn't been for a long time. I'm sure Dad knows that. He also knows that I'd have a harder time pushing back against something he'd already gotten her to agree to.

Dad's safety goggles are back in place as he continues shaping the skeletal structure with his rotary tool. "Did it ever occur to you that we're all just trying to help you invest more in this place?"

I side-eye him. "How does cutting part of my script help me do that?" He glances my way, and I know instantly that isn't the only change he wants to make. "What are you saying?"

He lowers the rotary tool and looks at me. His face is tired, like this conversation has been brewing for too long. "I figured you'd be grateful to let the tour go. You've never liked it. I know you're trying to find your place here and I'm trying to help you, but the tour needs something different, and you . . . you could use a break."

I inhale through my nose and fight to keep my voice even. "You wanted me to lead the tours, I did. I finally found a way not to hate them and that's when you decide to pull the plug?"

He doesn't rise to this at all, and why should he? We have some version of this same fight every few months. I get angry; he finishes a new specimen. That's it.

Finally—and clearly with great reluctance—he says, "We're starting to get more complaints. About you."

"Like what?" I don't exactly yell, but with the acoustics in the rendering room, it's close enough.

"Low energy. Off-topic discussions. Arguing with guests."

"I argued with one guest on one tour," I correct. "And the situation's been resolved."

"Well, it was mentioned in one of the reviews. And overall, our bookings are down compared to last season, not much, but some."

"So your immediate answer is to cut my tour?" The tendons in my neck start to tighten and clench up along my jaw, and my teeth grind together.

"Not cut. People love seeing Eryn. And they love something else too."

I scoff. "Let me guess, the discount you offer when they wear our T-shirts?"

"No, Captain Tate. Several have suggested he lead the whole thing."

My stomach drops before I even understand why. It's not that I don't know Tate's good at what he does. He's a crowd-pleaser, gets laughs, keeps the tourists engaged. He's made for this. But hearing that people want him to take over . . .

I try to breathe evenly, but something in my ribs feels wrong. "Have you talked to Tate?"

"We haven't decided anything yet, but he's open to the idea if you are."

My voice is quieter now. "Why didn't you tell me any of this?"

"I'm telling you now."

Yeah, after he, Eryn, and even Tate already discussed it without me. Forget this. "Fine, then I'll talk too. I want to bring somebody else on here. Unpaid," I add when I see him start to shake his head. "Somebody who's interested in learning about museums and is willing to volunteer over the summer."

His jaw shifts to the side as he considers. "I don't have time to search and interview anyone. You're going to be busy too. The tourists aren't even all here yet and we're going to need all hands on deck to make sure McCleave's is where they want to be."

"I already talked with her and she'll pick everything up quickly." I'm not even lying when I say that.

Dad's stool squeaks as he leans back. "Not sure that's a great idea."

I'm not sure either, but he will agree to this. I'm not leaving until he does. "She'll literally be volunteering. If it doesn't work out, I'll let her go."

We look at each other, neither one all that happy with the other.

"You want me to be more invested, that's what I'm doing."

"Fine," he says. "But I want you working on a new script for Tate or I'll write one myself."

TEN
Lili

"Oh no," I whisper, skidding my bike to a stop beside Barrett Pier, my stomach dropping faster than my kickstand. So this is how my first official day volunteering is going to start.

I'd foolishly thought Wren wanted me to meet him here so I could pass out flyers or sell T-shirts or something. I forgot that McCleave's does their boat tours on Saturdays *and* Tuesdays. He can't possibly think I'm getting back on that boat again, can he?

"And the Tourist Girl finally arrives."

Wren's voice—dry as driftwood—draws my attention to him wheeling around the back of a gray pickup truck.

"I'm not late," I say, locking my bike and joining him. "So you can't say 'finally' like that."

"What is it with you and arguing with everything I say?"

"I'll stop arguing when you start being right."

I catch the briefest tug at the corner of his mouth.

"Want to tell me why I'm here, since we both know you're not mean enough to put me back on that boat?"

"No boat rides for you today," he agrees, and I deeply dislike the way he says *today*.

"Then I'm here to . . . ?"

"Help." He starts down the pier.

"Right, but how exactly? And when are we going to talk about Kezia Gardner?"

His arms flex as he grips his wheels to stop them. "Do you always ask this many questions?"

"All you said was to meet you here. I think I'm owed a few answers."

"Okay," he says, bending to pick up a crumpled mermaid tour flyer. "Then you can start by picking up the stuff you guys leave everywhere."

I scoff. "I have never left trash behind in my life."

He glances up, like he's weighing the truth of that statement. "What, do you want a cookie?"

"I wouldn't say no to one."

"I'll see what I can do."

His tone is easy, almost teasing, and something about it makes my pulse tick up a notch.

By the time we reach the boat, I've nearly convinced myself this day might not be so bad. Then he tosses me a bottle of SPF and a pair of ancient-looking motion sickness wristbands.

"Um, in no world is this better than a cookie," I say.

"They're for after the tour," he says. "Cleaning out the boat. Thought you might need them. Even docked."

Oh.

I look down at the wristbands again, my grip loosening slightly. They're fraying at the edges, the once-black fabric now faded to charcoal, but they suddenly feel less like a joke and more like . . . a gesture. Kindness, maybe, if you squint hard enough. It would've been *kinder* not to make me get on the boat at all, of course, but it's better than being on plunger duty.

Before I can react, his phone buzzes and whatever he sees on the screen hardens his expression.

"Can you head back to the truck and wait for Tate?" He hands me a set of keys. "The sign for the tour is in the back. Just unlock it for him and he'll set it up."

"Pick up trash and wait by a truck." I sigh somewhat dramatically. "How did you ever live without my immeasurable help?"

He huffs out a reluctant laugh. "Oh, don't worry. You'll be doing a lot more than that today."

Good, I think, as I stroll back to the parking lot, though I think he was trying to rattle me. That might have worked before he gave these worn wrist bands to me, but after? Not so much.

The truck's tailgate groans as I lower it and decide I don't need to wait to lift out a single sign. I mean, how heavy can it be?

The answer is very. The steel pole weighs a ton, but I manage. The large, solid-wood sign is another story. I'm about to psych myself up for a third try when a pair of slim, tanned hands grips the opposite corner.

"Here, let me help," the girl I instantly recognize as the mermaid from McCleave's tour says, crouching down beside me. "On three?"

We both groan under the weight, but together, we wrestle the sign into place, securing it onto the pole's rolling base.

"Thanks," I say, shielding my eyes from the sun. "Kind of my first day, and I may have overestimated my own strength."

“It’s not you,” she says, shaking out her hands to force the feeling back the same way I am. “Leon from Salt & Timber Signworks made it last year to withstand a hurricane. I’ve never been able to lift it by myself.”

“Oh, good. I don’t feel so bad now.”

She keeps smiling. “It’s Lili, right?”

I nod. “And you’re the mermaid. I’m sorry, I don’t know your name.”

“Eryn,” she says.

“Eryn! Pop the trunk!”

Tate’s voice cuts through the lot, and without looking, Eryn hits a button on her key fob. A little red compact car beeps in response.

“I’m so glad Wren brought you today.” Her smile turns shy as she shifts her feet, the sunlight catching the pearlescent shimmer dusted over her skin. “I thought for sure he’d keep you cooped up in the back room hunched over a desk all day. I mean, who would choose that over this?” She stares out over the choppy water.

She clearly doesn’t share my reservations about boats bobbing like corks on the waves. She spots Wren on the boat and raises a hand in greeting.

He hesitates before lifting his own in response.

Behind her, Tate straightens from the trunk. “Okay, we’ve got your tail, your towel, your neoprene socks, your conditioner. And . . . yep, all set.” He notices me for the first time, grinning around a Twizzler that’s hanging from his mouth. “Oh hey, Tourist Girl.”

“What did you call her?” Eryn frowns, brushing back a wisp of her black hair that’s escaped from the messy bun on her head.

"It's a Wren thing," I say quickly. "Apparently, it's easier than using people's names." The nickname itself doesn't bother me, not really. It's the way he sometimes says it, like I don't belong here, that feels unfair.

Tate shrugs. "Yeah, well, it's what you are, isn't it?"

"Tate," Eryn says, her voice weary but laced with quiet authority.

"What?" His grin is unrepentant. "She wanted to know."

"I really didn't," I mutter, shaking my head.

Eryn moves to do her own scan of the trunk, her fingers brushing over the intricate shell crown I spot nestled beside the mermaid tail. "Ignore him."

"Oh, I plan to."

She laughs. "Good. Because I'm tired of being outnumbered."

"Well, I know when I'm not wanted," Tate quips, his voice rising over the sound of the waves lapping at the dock. "Text me if you need anything or when you're back on dry land."

As he heads down the dock, Wren watches him, but when Tate hops aboard, Wren says something that makes Tate's entire body stiffen. He replies with a sharp gesture, Twizzlers still clutched in one hand. Then, after a beat, he tosses the candy onto a bench and shakes his head, clearly exasperated.

The conversation ends abruptly. Wren exhales, shoulders rising then dropping, as if shaking something off before wheeling toward the other end of the boat.

Tate watches him, his jaw set. A few seconds pass before he moves—slowly, almost reluctantly—into the captain's chair.

They don't speak after that.

I glance at Eryn, expecting some reaction, but she's still rummaging through her trunk, oblivious to whatever just went down.

She straightens a second later, holding a phone in her hand that has a screen so cracked I'd be shocked if it still works.

"One sec," she tells me, reaching back into her car and pulling out another phone, this one light blue with a golden croissant sticker on the back. She taps the screen and lifts it to her ear.

On the boat, Wren answers his own phone at the same time.

"Hey, babe, can you let Tate know he dropped his phone in my trunk?"

Babe?

I glance between them, an odd realization hitting me. She's his girlfriend. I don't know why I hadn't considered the possibility before. Maybe because he's kind of on the grumpy side, though I guess not with her. So much for the banter between him and me that I thought I'd picked up on earlier. It's not like it had been much, just a hint. And a wildly impractical one at that. This is better, I tell myself. I don't even have to let my mind ever start going there.

"Okayyy," she says, drawing out the word. "I'll tell her." A pause. "Are you sure you don't just want me to—? Right, yeah. Sure, later." She flicks her eyes to me and kind of shifts away, voice lowering. "Actually I can't tonight. I have to be at the café super early, but whatever it is, we can just talk later." There's a stretch of silence. "I will, 'kay, bye."

She tosses the phone into her bag before turning back to me. "Sorry about that."

I shrug off her apology. "Did you say café?"

Eryn's expression shifts, a spark of excitement lighting up her eyes. "It's my other job, my main job. I'm an assistant baker over at the Petticoat Café. I waitress some too."

"I passed by that place my first day here. There was something that smelled so good I was halfway across the street before I even noticed. Maybe a cinnamon roll?"

"That's my recipe! They're called morning buns." She points back at her car. "Want to try one? I always bring a couple for the guys, but Tate can miss out today."

The second she opens the door, I catch the scent—warm, buttery vanilla with a hint of cinnamon. It's better than I remembered.

She grabs a box from the backseat, then spins to reveal pastries that look like the love child of a croissant and a cinnamon roll—golden, sugar-crusted spirals dripping with ooey-gooey vanilla icing. My eyes widen on instinct.

I tear off a piece of one and pop it into my mouth. The crisp, caramelized edges give way to soft, flaky layers, and the sugar practically melts on my tongue. I set a hand on the car door to steady myself.

Eryn laughs. "First time, huh? Yeah, they tend to have that effect on people."

I tear off another piece, then another, barely chewing before going in for more. "These are amazing."

"Thanks." She beams. "Oh, I almost forgot. Would you mind running Tate's phone down to the boat? I need to start getting ready."

"Sure." I take the cracked phone from her. "Need help with anything else?"

"Thanks, but I've got it down." She nods toward the boat, where the guys are still barely interacting. "You know, I could talk to Wren about dropping the 'Tourist Girl' nickname if it really bothers you."

I shake my head quickly. "No, I'm good. He'll come around once he gets to know me."

She seems to like that answer. "I'm sure that's true. I'm really glad he accepted your offer. I think it'll be good for him to have somebody around who's into all the history stuff he loves. I've tried, but I just don't have it in me. And Tate, well, I don't think he's actually tried."

We both laugh.

"Well," she says, hesitating for half a second before leaning in for a quick hug. "I'm sure we'll be seeing more of each other. Maybe we can even hang out sometime?"

I exhale slightly, relieved that I hadn't misread the friendship signs. "I'd like that."

She drives off as I head down to the boat. Tate is still in his captain's chair, watching Wren but not saying anything.

Something is definitely going on there, but as curious as I am, I don't know either of them well enough to ask. Instead, I lift up Tate's cell as I approach.

"I can now officially add phone delivery to my list of duties for the day." I pass it up to Wren, who tosses it to Tate without a word.

"Thanks," he says, then considers me as though a thought just occurred to him. "You got a camera on your phone?"

"Of course. I like my clothes to be from another time, not my phone. Why?"

"Then that's what you're doing today," he says matter-of-factly. "Taking pictures of the tour guests interacting with the mermaid for the website." His tone tightens slightly, jaw flexing before he adds, "We're making some changes."

Behind him, Tate stiffens.

I eye them both, curiosity flaring. "I can do that."

"Make sure Tate's in plenty of the shots," Wren says, his voice deceptively even. "And get some before we reach Eryn."

"Before? Where exactly do you want me to get them?" I scan the shoreline, mentally retracing the route Goldie and I took on our tour. My head starts to spin. We covered so much ground. Does he actually expect me to—what—chase the boat? "How many pictures are we talking here?" I ask, attempting to mask my anxiety at the sight of the waist-high, spindly beach grass that promises to shred my bare legs.

"Every few minutes is fine." His voice carries just enough challenge that I can't ignore it, even as I feel Tate watching me.

I take a step closer, lowering my voice so it's just between us. "Why do I feel like I'm being punished for something I didn't even do?"

Wren flinches—his eyes shift with a hint of realization, as if the thought hadn't crossed his mind until now. He tightens his grip on the railing, then exhales slowly, the tension in his shoulders still there but easing now. "I just need the photos. Can you do it or not?"

Deciding that now isn't the time to push back, I nod. "Not a problem. I take listing photos for my mom's house flips. I'm good. In fact, if you'd told me that you wanted pictures today, not only would I have not worn this romper, but I'd have brought my DSLR camera and offered to edit the photos too."

There's another slight crack in his armor, and I can see it for just a second—maybe a flicker of approval or maybe just a shift in how he sees me. “Good, huh?” he says, a bit more dry than usual.

“Really good. So good that you won’t have a shred of doubt left about my capabilities.”

He stares at me, his expression giving nothing away. “All right then. Let’s see what you’ve got.”

ELEVEN
Wren

I pull off my glasses and half close my laptop with what I hope passes for nonchalance just as Lili strolls into the back room the next morning, all breezy confidence, like she owns the place.

"Morning."

Her outfit catches me off guard, and I hate that I notice it at all. She's put-together, like always—some kind of green shorts and a top with tiny cherry clusters all over it. Even her hair, loose and wavy, looks like it took effort.

Everything fits like it was made for her.

"Yeah, hey. Can you give me a minute? I need to finish something." Before I can reopen my laptop, she spots the nametag I set out for her on the table and grins at it like it's made of gold instead of plastic.

"I guess this makes me official, huh?" But as she goes to pin it on, she hesitates. "Is there maybe a lanyard? I'd rather not put a hole in my top."

"No, but we do have polos," I say, managing to keep a straight face even though the mental image of her trading that outfit for one of the McCleave's uniforms is almost too much. "There should be extras in that storage closet."

I lean back slightly and watch as she heads toward the door. Honestly, the polos are enough to make anyone reconsider their life choices, but she's the one who wanted another option.

I let out a breath as she digs through the box, listening to the rustle of fabric and the soft, distressed sounds she makes.

It takes her forever to settle on one, and even then, she doesn't put it on. She holds it up—shapeless navy blue and way too big for her—and looks at me.

"Rethinking putting a tiny hole in your own shirt?"

She looks genuinely conflicted. "Hey, how come you're not wearing one?"

"I'm management." Sort of.

"What about Tate?"

"Janitorial." Then I add, "Bethany wears one, but if you'd rather help Tate clean bathrooms—"

"Nope, I'm good. I just want to wash this before I wear it," she says, setting it aside on the couch. "Tomorrow, okay?"

We both know she's not going to wear it, but maybe she'll opt for something a little less distracting. If that's even possible. "That's fine. I need you back here today anyway."

Her eyes brighten. "Because we're researching Kezia?"

The hope in her voice is enough to make me wince. For a second, I feel bad about disappointing her.

"No." I shake my head. "Inventory. I need you to go through all the gift shop merchandise on wooden shelves, mark down what's running low and what we need to push. There's a clipboard hanging by the door. Forms are self-explanatory."

She sighs, but it's more resigned than dramatic, like she saw it coming. Without arguing, she spins on her heel to grab the clipboard.

I wait until she's fully distracted before reopening my laptop. The cursor on the blank document blinks at me, slow and accusatory.

Blink, blink, blink.

Shit, shit, shit.

The words won't come.

In the background, Lili hums. It starts low, a soft undercurrent, but soon it grows into a murmur of lyrics. Then actual words.

It's from a song I recognize, "Seaside" by the Kooks, and it pulls at the edges of my focus, dragging me back from the screen until I'm aware of nothing but the hum of her voice and the too-quiet room around us.

I put my glasses back on and force my attention back to the laptop, fingers hovering over the keyboard. The nonsense script for Tate's new "more engaging" tour isn't going to write itself.

Finally, the rhythm of the keys drowns her out, and I manage a few paragraphs. It's all crap, but at least it's something.

"So, did you look through the photos I took yesterday?" she asks, breaking my fragile concentration. "I emailed them to you last night," she persists, her voice closer now. "I'm particularly happy with the last one."

Curiosity gets the better of me. Anything to avoid this awful script. I click over to my inbox and open her email.

The photos are . . . good. There are the requested shots of Tate, Eryn, and plenty of smiling tourists. But then I get to the last one, and I can't help but laugh.

It's a perfectly focused shot of her grass-scraped arm, hand, and one flipped-off finger.

She appears beside me, leaning in to scroll through the images herself. "What are you working on so intently anyway?"

Without thinking, I nudge her hand aside and close the email. The new tour script pops back up, filling the screen.

Her eyes dart to it and before I can shut the laptop, her curiosity shifts to confusion. "You're rewriting the tour? Why?"

I'd have to physically shove her aside to keep her from scanning the rest of it, and at this point, I don't care that much.

"This is for Tate," she says, frowning, and then with an almost accusatory note in her voice adds, "and you took out almost *all* of the historical facts."

She looks at me again, her sea-glass eyes sharp and searching, close enough that I catch the darker green ring circling the outside. "That was the best part of the tour."

I hold her gaze longer than I should. "Yeah, well, you might be the only tourist who thinks that way."

She breaks the connection effortlessly, turning back to the screen and scrolling farther down. "I'm sure that's not true."

I could argue. Tell her she doesn't know what she's talking about. But at this point, it's easier to just show her.

Without a word, I reclaim the trackpad, open the latest reviews, and move back to let her read them for herself:

Pretty mermaid but the guide talked too much about boring history stuff. I'd rather listen to a Wikipedia article read out loud. Captain was funny.

I came for mermaids, not a dissertation on 18th-century shipping regulations. My kid asked if we were being punished. Honestly, it felt like it.

They shouldn't call it a mermaid tour. All you do is listen to some guy talk about history for an hour and catch a glimpse of a mermaid at the end. Rip-off.

We thought this would be the highlight of our trip, but it was a mess. The live mermaid was the only good part, she looked amazing and stayed in character the whole time. The guide, though? Yikes. I think I fell asleep. I don't know why they don't have the captain do the whole thing. He was great.

I'm torn. The mermaid was incredible, and the kids were mesmerized. But the guide gave a full-on history lesson. He even had a bit of a spat with a girl on our tour, which was uncomfortable. Would I do it again? Probably not.

She draws back when she's done, quiet. "I guess this is what you guys were fighting about yesterday?"

I cut a glance toward her.

"I could see you from the parking lot," she explains. "Seemed like things were a little tense."

I hesitate. I didn't plan on talking about this with anyone, especially not her. I'm still pissed at Tate for not telling me the second my dad came to him. He said he didn't take my dad's idea seriously and wasn't sure I'd care either way. Right now, that doesn't feel like a good enough excuse.

"It's fine. We worked it out." Maybe not entirely, but I know we will, because that's what we always do. Plus, I don't get to stay mad at him when I didn't even bring it up with Eryn, even though she essentially did the same thing.

Besides, it's not really either of them I'm truly mad at.

"The reviews are clear about what they want," I say.

When I don't say more than that, her gaze lingers on me, softening like she's piecing something together. "It wasn't your choice, was it? Poseidon? He's your dad, right?"

I haven't explained that I'm not the one making decisions around here, but it sounds like she doesn't need me to.

"You look a little like him," she adds. "Just in the eyes."

That's not something I want to hear.

"Is there anyone else from your family that helps run the museum?"

I don't want to go down this conversation trail. "Just us. Look, I really need to finish this, so can you just—" I gesture toward the shelves she's supposed to be inventorying.

She doesn't move. "I'm sorry for arguing with you on my tour. I wasn't thinking about it impacting someone else's experience so much that they'd leave a review about it. I was just trying to distract my stomach at first, then sort of test you, you know?"

"Glad I passed." My tone is flat, but the corner of her mouth tugs up.

"Oh, you definitely did," she says. "I didn't expect to like any of my time on that boat, but arguing with you was kind of fun." She leans her head from side to side. "All things considering."

I'm not going to say it to her, but I can admit to myself now that I didn't hate having someone onboard who knew about the 1698 Act of Grace either. Even if she tried to misapply it.

"But I'm still sorry," she says again, glancing at the laptop.

"One review isn't the problem. Most people taking a boat ride to see a mermaid don't care about Abram Quary or Dorcas Honorable."

She makes a face. "They should, but fine, okay, I take your point." Then, more carefully, she adds, "But you know the answer doesn't have to be him instead of you, right?" She turns fully, leaning back on the desk, facing me directly now. "It doesn't even have to be all fluff over facts. Why not work on something that brings in more mermaid lore but weaves in entertaining historical stories too?"

"It's a little late for that," I say.

"Because of what your dad wants? What if we give him a revised version first and then maybe work on amping up your delivery? Let him see you try out some new material before he makes you hand the tour over to Tate?"

I don't miss the way she says *we*. "Amping up my delivery?"

She ignores the question. "I'm just saying, maybe we could get him to give you another shot before changing everything."

My laugh is bitter, sharp. "*We* aren't going to do anything."

She half rolls her eyes. "Fine, but have you tried? I mean, really tried? Because I think you care about this more than you're letting on."

My irritation flares. "My dad and I don't work like that."

"It sounds like *you* don't work like that." She pushes off the desk, crossing her arms. "How do you know he won't change his mind? Just because it's hard doesn't mean you don't try."

I slam the laptop shut with more force than I mean to. "And what would you know about hard, Tourist Girl? What have you ever done that wasn't easy?"

"Easy?" Her voice cuts through mine, sharp and incredulous. "Are you kidding me? It took my dad dying to get my mom to let me come back here."

I freeze.

Her breath is uneven, her cheeks flushed. "She swore that she would never set foot on this island again after the divorce because, in her mind, he chose his past here over our present there. I spent months trying to convince her to let me have one more summer in a place that she hates almost more than I love. You have no idea how hard it was, but I did it because there wasn't another option for me. I wasn't going to stop."

Her voice catches on the last word, emotion pressing against it. I suddenly have a hard time not staring.

"Okay, I shouldn't have said that," I say, quieter now. "But this is my whole life here. Don't you think I would've taken the chance to change things around here by now if I could?"

Her answer is immediate. "That's the difference, Wren. You're waiting for opportunities. I'm telling you to create them."

Before I can argue, she flips open the laptop, starts a fresh document, and looks at me expectantly, her fingers hovering over the keyboard.

"Not enough mermaid details—easy fix. Dry historical facts—just about the delivery." She lifts her chin. "Between the two of us, we can fix this. So stop being a baby and help me write the best damn mermaid *and* history tour possible."

Her determination is a physical force, pressing into the space between us. My irritation spikes, but somehow, I can't look away from the blank document.

It's not that I believe this will change anything.

But something about her confidence makes it impossible to say no.

TWELVE
Lili

Over the next week, Wren and I settle into a rhythm. Each morning, I either check inventory or run the register in the gift shop. It's not glamorous, but I don't mind. The familiarity of retail work is grounding, even if the mornings drag. Wren leads the occasional tour of the museum, but mostly he's holed up in the back room. Without him around, time crawls.

By noon, though, the energy shifts. Eryn arrives like clockwork, balancing paper bags filled with lunches from the café that make my stomach growl before she's even through the door. Her presence inevitably summons Tate from whatever corner of the museum he's been lurking in, like some kind of caloric bat signal has been activated.

He and Wren seem good, but then, I didn't see them interact much before.

The three of them have an easy shorthand together that took me a few days to adjust to. Inside jokes, stories, and more than a decade of shared experiences. It should have felt isolating, but Eryn made sure it didn't. She never let the conversations veer too far off into past territory and always wanted to hear about how house renovations were going (good, but if I ever have to use a drum sander again, it'll be too soon—it took me three long nights just to refinish the downstairs floors) or about my plans for after the summer (college, history degree, and hopefully a job in a museum somewhere).

Wren never asks questions, but he's always listening to my answers.

I learn more about Eryn too, like how she's hoping to get more of her recipes on the café's menu and eventually wants to become a full pastry chef there. She's definitely talented enough as far as I'm concerned. I still think about her morning buns an unhealthy amount.

When she leaves, though, there's always an awkward moment. I feign interest in a napkin or a stray ketchup packet while she gives Wren a quick goodbye kiss. It's nothing over the top, but it's enough to make me overly conscious of my own hands, suddenly unsure what to do with them.

After lunch, Wren and I dive into his tour speech. The afternoons fly by in a blur of revisions, debates, and full-blown arguments. Mostly arguments. His stubbornness is maddening, but if I'm being honest, it's also kind of thrilling. There's an unspoken rhythm to our back-and-forth, like sparring partners who secretly enjoy the fight.

On Thursday evening, a full week since we started working on his speech, Wren insists it's too dark for me to bike home.

As we cruise down the narrow dirt roads of Nantucket, he puts on "The Weight" by the Band, and the sound fills the car, warm and nostalgic. The windows are rolled down, and I let the breeze whip through my hair as I surf my hand against the air currents outside. The mix of sweet grass and salty sea scents the car, and for a moment, everything feels right.

"You know, I think the tour script is done," I say, glancing at him. His profile is lit by the glow of the dashboard, his strong jaw and broad shoulders solid and steady. "I mean, we can tweak it more tomorrow if you want, but honestly? It's good."

He doesn't answer immediately, his hands relaxed on the wheel. The quiet between us isn't uncomfortable—it's satisfying, like the calm after a storm.

"I might even call it great," I add, leaning back against my seat with a small smile.

That earns a snort of disbelief. It's barely a sound, but I recognize it for what it is: almost a laugh. I've heard it a few times this week, and every time it feels like a win.

"It's not terrible," he finally says.

At a stop sign, he stretches his arms overhead, groaning softly as his shoulders crack. The movement tugs his shirt up, and for the briefest second, I catch a glimpse of the skin above his waistband. My cheeks heat immediately, and I turn to face the window, hoping he doesn't notice.

"So, what's next?" he asks, dropping his arms with a sigh. "We work on delivery?" He says it like it's some great inconvenience, even though he's the one who brought it up.

Before I can answer, my phone buzzes with a text.

Mom: Home soon? Goldie wants a movie night, she said we can even watch *Roman Holiday*.

I make a groaning sound.

"Something wrong?" Wren asks.

"No, I mean, yes. My sister picked one of my favorite movies for us to watch tonight, but I've seen it so many times." I side-eye him. "Don't suppose you want to start rehearsing your speech tonight?"

"*Now?* I mean, I guess. You want to go back to the museum?"

The road ahead dips into shadow, framed by weathered white picket fences tangled with wild roses. My gaze catches on a towering elm tree set back from the road, its branches reaching over a patch of the greenest grass I've ever seen. Without fully thinking it through, I point.

"There," I say. "Pull over by that tree."

He raises an eyebrow but doesn't argue. The tires crunch against gravel as he shifts the car into park. While he waits, I text Mom a sad-face emoji and let her know I'll be late and to start the movie without me.

Turning to Wren, I grin. "We'll have you reciting this speech so perfectly your dad won't be able to do anything but clap."

His lips twitch, but he doesn't reply. Instead, he reaches for his laptop.

And for the first time, I can tell he's starting to believe me.

"You want me to ad-lib jokes?" Wren's tone is incredulous, as if I'd suggested he hurl children overboard during his tours. His brow furrows, and that muscle in his jaw—the one I've noticed flexes whenever he's annoyed—tightens noticeably.

"Not *jokes*-jokes," I say quickly. "Just, you know, funny historical stories. Haven't you ever taken one of those tours at Universal Studios or something? They're funny. People laugh. They tell their friends." I lean forward, stressing my point. "They leave good reviews."

"Anything else?" His voice is cool, but I know him well enough by now to catch the warning undertone. He's not really asking for suggestions—he's daring me to add more.

Well, challenge accepted. I was saving the best for last anyway. "You've got to smile more."

He responds by baring his teeth at me in a grin so exaggerated it's borderline feral.

"Or not," I say, trying not to laugh only to have it turn into a yawn.

He exhales sharply and sets the laptop on the dashboard. "It's late. You're tired."

I am tired. My fifth—or maybe sixth—yawn in as many minutes proves it. But I'm not letting him shut this down. "Just read through it one more time," I urge. "Try the jokes. See how it feels."

He studies me for a long moment, taking in my slumped posture and the way my head rests against the passenger-side window. His gaze softens just enough to make me think he's about to agree, but then he shakes his head. "You look like you're ready to pass out. And I'm not about to sit you in my lap and carry you into your house."

His engine rumbles to life before I can respond, the low purr vibrating through the truck.

"It is late," I murmur, suddenly wide awake as my mind conjures an unhelpful image of me sitting in his lap, his arms around me. Heat floods my face. I press my palm against the cool glass of the window, hoping it will shock my brain back to order as Wren drives me home. My hand is on the handle, ready to hop out the second he parks.

But just as I'm ready to open my door, he stops me.

"The other day, you told me how hard it was getting back here, but you said there was no other option for you." His voice is measured, unreadable. "Tell me why."

I remember the conversation, and while I don't understand why he's choosing now to bring it up, I instantly know my answer.

"This place is important to me," I say, my voice steadier than I expect. "My family built its legacy on this island; it may not be a historically celebrated legacy, but it's still mine. And once I was old enough to understand what that meant, the generations that came before me, I wanted to know more." I flip my arm over and trail my fingers over the faint blue lines of my veins, following the patterns I used to trace as a kid when I pretended I could feel my history running through them. "Nothing was more important to my dad than this place, and I wanted to be a part of that with him. So I read everything I could. It's the only way I've ever felt connected to my dad." I let my arm drop. "He wanted to show the world who our family really was, and I want that too. Isn't this"—I gaze around us, taking in more than the cab of his truck—"the same for you?"

Something flashes across Wren's face, but it's gone before I can name it. His posture doesn't shift, but there's a stillness in the silence between us, like my words landed somewhere deeper than he's willing to admit.

Then, his expression cools, his voice flat when he finally speaks. "Mermaids are my family legacy, and I'd just as soon the world forget about that. But if you want to dig into yours, be my guest, Tourist Girl. Just don't blame me when you find out they're exactly who the history books say they were."

I should probably be put off by his warning, but I just smile. "'Tourist Girl'? Still? I do have a name."

"I know."

For some reason that makes me smile wider.

"Still want to do it?"

"Research my family?" My expression becomes serious. "More than anything."

His eyes trail over the blue veins that I showed him. "Then bring your dad's stuff tomorrow. His notes or whatever he has on Kezia Gardner."

I blink. "Wait, really? We're actually going to start?" A burst of happiness swells inside me so fast it almost knocks me off my seat. I have the ridiculous, overwhelming urge to throw my arms around him and hug him. I grip the door handle instead, my fingers tight around the cool metal.

"Yeah," he says, and it's almost like my excitement infects him. His expression doesn't shift much, but there's something lighter in his eyes as he looks at me. The moment is gone almost as soon as it appears. He clears his throat.

"Does that mean I'm officially off probation?" I ask, barely containing my grin.

"It wasn't probation."

I shake my head, but I don't argue. I don't want to do anything that might break whatever this is—this quiet, unexpected moment when it feels like we might be on the same side.

THIRTEEN
Lili

While Wren turns pages in my dad's notebook the next day, I allow myself to do a little poking around on the Shelves, as I've started calling them in my head. I'm having a pretty good time looking through the collection of books there too, until Wren barks at me to stop touching everything.

"I'm hardly touching *everything*." I glance over at the neat stack of books I had started, and not even really old books, just interesting ones. I wasn't going to so much as breathe on anything that looked old or fragile.

"Just stop moving around." He frowns in my general direction. "You're distracting me."

I'm distracting *him*? He's the one who keeps snorting and making derisive sounds every time he reads something he doesn't like, which is apparently often. I'm literally standing in front of a single shelf. He's just looking for a reason to be grumpy. But fine, I can look with my eyes until he's not paying attention.

"What are you doing?" he asks, suddenly sitting up straighter when I make the mistake of resting my hand on the shelf's edge, not even near anything. "Okay, here is the first rule: Only I touch the old books, and only if necessary." He stares at the other shelves, the ones full of boxes and crates. "Actually, maybe just check with me before you touch anything you're not sure about. Which should be everything."

I nod very seriously. "So then I probably shouldn't have opened that glass display case in the back and scribbled my name on the parchment inside with crayons?"

He gives me a patronizing smile.

"Oh, and what if I need to sneeze but can't find a tissue? It's okay to keep blowing my nose on that ship log from the *Perseverance's Cry*, isn't it?"

Wren shifts his back to me and continues turning pages, but I swear he uses more force each time.

I want to ask how it's going a few minutes later, but he seems grumpy enough for the both of us right now. And the more time I spend back here, the more I think I understand why. Glancing back at the Shelves, I think I'd be less than cheerful too if I had to stare at all this history, day in and day out, and yet know I'll never get the chance to display any of it. Until I figured out what I was going to do about it. Wren, on the other hand, seems to have just accepted his fate without a fight.

I'll never understand that.

I turn back to the pile of books I started. I'd thought I was bringing quite a bit to the table when it came to this place and its past. But being back here has shown me just how much I still need to learn.

I know my Nantucket history. I'd clean up if it were a *Jeopardy!* category. But we're just working on a theory about Kezia Gardner at this point, and a vague one at that. I don't have any proof that she wasn't a smuggler.

And unfortunately, I'm not the only one.

For years, I thought my dad was the foremost expert when it came to Melville's "elbow of sand." He could recall obscure facts and quotes in an instant, spinning stories so vivid and persuasive that no one ever questioned him. Least of all me. But since finding his notebook I've realized his research practices left a lot to be desired.

The pages are a mess—snippets of quotes with no sources, shorthand that might as well be a secret code, and exclamation points scrawled in the margins like Dad was mid-conversation with himself. He also drew maps covered in rough sketches of coastlines that are unlabeled and so vague they might as well be doodles, and lots of ropes tied with sailor knots that I can't make any sense of.

I'm not even going to think about how bad his handwriting is on top of all that.

I know he'd never just *give* me the answers. He'd expect me to work for them. But I thought he'd at least have left me more of a head start than this. I've been reading it for two weeks and it still feels like trying to decipher the thoughts of someone who never expected—or wanted—anyone else to follow them.

I glance at Wren, hunched over the notebook at the far end of the table. If anyone could help make sense of my dad's notes, I thought it might be him. But the frown carved into his face tells me otherwise.

Finally, Wren snaps the notebook shut with enough force to make me jump.

"Well?" I ask, already bracing for the answer.

He exhales sharply, pulling his glasses off and dragging a hand through his hair before fixing me with a look that's equal parts frustration and disbelief. "This isn't research," he says flatly. "This is . . . rambling. It's like he had ideas faster than he could write them down and didn't bother organizing anything."

I stiffen, feeling defensive even though he's not wrong. "There's got to be something helpful in there. Somewhere."

"Unless you've got some kind of secret decoder ring, this"—he holds up my dad's notebook—"is practically useless."

It's crushing to hear my own thoughts echoed back at me. Wren is supposed to understand all this far better than I do, but he's already calling it a lost cause after a few hours. "You're telling me you can't make sense of anything?"

"He keeps referencing the same number." He squints, trying to read my dad's awful handwriting. "Forty-three, over and over again. What does it mean?" He adds with dripping sarcasm, "You don't know because, you guessed it, he never cites any of his sources."

"We don't know what it is *yet*."

He spreads his arms wide as if inviting me to enlighten him.

I spread my arms too. "Well, I didn't want to work with you for your sparkling personality."

"Working out for you, is it?"

Yeah, great. Can't wait for the part where I end up chasing another boat. "Look, if it were easy rewriting history, everyone would be doing it."

"Or . . ." he prompts in an overexaggerated voice.

I swallow down a note of frustration. "There is information out there about Kezia, pieces of her story that nobody's heard yet. My dad knew it and I know it too." I grab my dad's notebook and flip to the end, where I tucked one of the last postcards he sent me next to my favorite photo of the two of us.

> *It's all right here in this Faraway Land, the truth that no one else is compelled to search for. But we are, aren't we, Lili?*

"He wouldn't let me search for something that wasn't there, he wouldn't." I shift it to the side so he can see the photo of me and Dad. I'm probably only seven, crouched barefoot in the damp sand at the beach, turning a rusted iron nail over in my hands. Dad kneels beside me, his cap on backward, pointing toward the empty stretch of water where the *Bonito* wrecked over a century ago. There's nothing left of it now, but I'm watching him like if I listen hard enough, if I look long enough, history might still be hiding somewhere beneath our feet.

I've never forgotten that feeling and I can't now.

Beside me, Wren stares at the photo, his gaze lingering a little longer than I expected. There's a shift in his expression, a subtle tightening of his jaw, as if the image has triggered something he's not ready to talk about. For a moment, I wonder if he's seeing the same kind of connection between me and my dad, maybe even feeling a bit of regret about his own relationship with his father. But then he looks up, his face unreadable.

"Where is that, Great Point?"

I nod. "It was always one of our favorite beaches. We went there every summer, until we stopped coming to visit. But I know my dad spent a lot of time there over the last few years."

Something about that answer makes him uncomfortable. I can't tell if it's pity or understanding on his features, and honestly I'm fine with either if it means he's willing to try a little longer.

"The notebook," he says after a moment. "Is that all your dad has or—"

"No," I answer too quickly. "He had an entire home study full of research material on Kezia and our family. I thought the notebook was the most important, but maybe there's something else."

"Yeah, maybe," he says, rereading over the words on the postcard. Then he groans, a sound so deep and almost primal that it makes me shiver. "All right, let me grab something real quick and I'll meet you outside."

FOURTEEN

Lili

Twenty minutes later, we both go quiet as we pull up in front of my very historical, very not accessible home.

Before, when Wren dropped me off at night, it had just been a shadowed outline, a place I disappeared into while he drove away. I don't think either of us considered the logistics before, but looking at it in the afternoon light, the problem is glaring. Short of army crawling up the front steps and through the door, I don't see how he's supposed to get inside.

I'm sure he's done worse living on Nantucket, but I'd rather he not have to struggle just to get inside my house. But since feeling bad doesn't actually solve the problem, I start thinking. "How many inches of clearance do you need on each side to fit through the door?" I ask. "And are you okay with me pushing from behind if it's tight? Taking the door off the hinges is probably the easiest first option, otherwise—hmmm," I mutter, chewing on my bottom lip.

When I glance at Wren, his eyes quickly dart away, like I've caught him staring.

“We’re not taking the door off,” he says, his voice uncertain, as if he’s trying to convince himself as much as me. “Back door?”

I brighten. “That could work.”

There’s only a slight step up over the threshold in the back, which Wren pops up and over without too much difficulty.

I follow behind him, the now smooth-as-butter floorboards creaking as I move through the living room. There’s a mug on the table, probably mine, still half-full from hours ago. Before I can make it to the study, Mom’s voice calls down.

“Lili? Is that you back already?”

I hurry to the base of the stairs, tilting my head up to answer. “Yes, and I’m not alone!”

A beat of silence. Then, clomping footsteps.

Goldie appears first, leaning over the railing at the top of the stairs. “Hey, Tour Guy.”

“Yeah, hey,” Wren says, but he’s looking at me as if I told her to call him that.

I didn’t, but I’m happy to take credit for it.

A second later, Mom emerges. I’ve told her about Wren, of course, but I still introduce him.

“Wren, this is my mom, Mia. Mom, this is Wren, my sort of . . . boss?” I turn to him for maybe a better word, but he seems fine with that one.

Mom smiles warmly. “It’s great to finally meet you, Wren. Lili’s told me about your family’s museum. It sounds incredible. I hope I’ll get to see it before we leave.”

I watch Wren closely, half expecting him to tense at the mention of the museum, but he just shakes her hand. “Great to meet you too. And you’re welcome anytime.”

Mom eyes me, a silent *Why are you home unannounced with company?* written all over her face, but before I can explain, Wren does it for me.

"Lili thought I might like to see some of her dad's research materials. Help us figure out what's already been done and what we still need to cover."

Hearing him say my name makes something flutter in my chest. I know he's only doing it to be polite in front of my mom, but still—I like it more than I should.

"If you don't mind, that is," he adds.

Mom waves a hand. "Oh, I don't mind at all." She starts toward the heavy door off the stairs, then hesitates. "You know what? I really need to finish getting the upstairs windows open. I'll never understand why people keep painting them shut, but these have at least five or six layers on them."

"I'll try not to keep her long," Wren says, nodding toward me. "Hopefully she'll be upstairs to help you in no time."

I shoot him a glare that he pretends not to see.

"That would be great," Mom says. "But please don't rush on my account or I'll never hear the end of it. Goldie and I can manage today, right?"

Goldie scowls. "She makes us wear masks."

Mom places a hand on her shoulder, steering her toward the stairs. "That's because we tested, and there's lead paint. And what don't we do with lead paint?"

"Mess around," Goldie drones.

"Right."

As they pass behind Wren, Mom turns to me and mouths, *He's really cute*, then gives me an exaggerated thumbs-up.

I shoot her a pointed look, my eyes growing wide. I can't believe she just did that right behind him. To be fair, I never mentioned that he has a girlfriend, but I definitely don't need her telling me things I already know.

"Your mom seems nice," Wren says, all innocence, once they've gone upstairs to start the windows.

I look at him deadpan. "Uh-huh. Don't think I don't know what you just did. If I end up upstairs chipping away at lead paint, I'm dragging you up there with me."

He muffles a laugh while I unlock the study. The door creaks open and he squeezes through the narrow doorway after me, his knuckles scraping against the frame. I wince.

"Oh, I'm so sorry. Did you get cut?"

He doesn't even hear the question as he stares at the piece of furniture in the center of the room. "Is that a Lombard desk?"

Of course that's what he notices before checking if his hands are bleeding. "I'm not sure. Goldie's looking into it. All we know so far is that the carved leaves all over it are called acanthus and there are exactly one hundred thirty-seven of them."

"That's an oddly specific thing to know."

I just shrug. "My sister likes to count things."

His fingers trail over the polished wood. "If it's real, it probably cost more than my truck. You could sell it."

My reaction is immediate and vehement. "I would never."

"I wouldn't either." He looks away from the desk, his gaze catching mine. "But most people would."

His eyes hold mine, and for a second, I almost forget to breathe. My fingers twitch at my sides, and I have to force myself to look away.

"Anyway, this is it." I step back so he can see the room. "All the books on those two bookcases are Nantucket related. The ones on the far left focus on our family history, including his notebooks on the bottom shelf. The one I brought you is about Kezia, but we should check the others just in case."

I crouch down, reaching for the first notebook. But before I can pull it out, Wren's voice breaks through the quiet. "What about boxes or maybe the drawers in the desk? Did you find anything in there?"

I twist on my heel, frowning at the unexpected question. "Yeah, I found his Kezia notebook."

He shakes his head, his frustration rising. It's clear he's looking for something more. "Nothing else? Maybe some pictures? Or did he have a computer?"

"Now who's being oddly specific?" I raise an eyebrow, irritated that he's already got something on his mind that he's keeping from me. "No, no computer. He was strictly analog. Why don't you just tell me what you're looking for?"

He hesitates for a second, like he's debating whether or not to speak. Then he says, "I don't know."

"Well, that's a lie. You're obviously thinking of something." I walk toward him, my voice sharpening with the frustration of not knowing something he clearly does.

His jaw clenches as he meets my gaze. For the first time since I've known him, I catch a hint of discomfort, a flash of something almost guilty.

"Years ago, a guy came into the museum. He didn't care about any of the mermaid stuff, and it was off-season, so it wasn't like we had a lot of people around. He and my dad got to talking, and the next thing I knew Dad was letting him in the back room to look around."

Something about his tone makes the hairs on my arms stand up.

"I was just barely in high school at that point," he continues, "still trying to teach myself how to take care of all the items McCleave's had collected over the years, but I knew enough not to just let some guy wander around unsupervised. So I stayed back there, watched him like a hawk. He walked around, taking in everything, but he only asked to look at one thing."

My heart skips. "What?"

Wren pulls something from his bag, and my stomach flips when I realize it's a dark blue archival box. He places it carefully on the desk and lifts the lid.

The scent of leather, dust, and something faintly musty wafts toward me as I catch sight of a book inside. It's old, with a cracked leather cover that's charred almost black in places. My heart rate quickens as I step back. "What is that?"

"I don't know. I've never been able to read a single page of it. I didn't think anyone could." His voice is thick with frustration, his fingers gripping the edge of the box. "It was clearly in some kind of fire, and there's water damage, too. The pages are stained, smudged . . . I couldn't even tell how old it was. When I found it, wrapped in burlap, there was no info on it. No provenance. Nothing in the ledger. Best guess is my great-great-grandfather got it at an auction in the twenties."

"But this guy . . . he knew?"

"I don't know how he could." He meets my gaze again, his eyes clouded. "He didn't say anything. Dad and Tate came and went, but he just sat there at the table, not touching anything. Just staring at it for hours."

My breath feels too shallow, like it's trapped somewhere in my chest. "And then?"

"I had to leave for a few minutes, and when I came back, he was gone. I never saw him again." His eyes lock onto mine, and I feel a knot twist in my stomach. "Until today, when you showed me that photo of you with your dad."

The world shifts beneath me. Everything clicks together—too many pieces falling into place at once. "He must've thought . . . now you think . . ." I can't wrap my mind around it fast enough. I lift my eyes to Wren, searching, but he just shakes his head.

I take a step back, trying to steady my breathing. "Okay, wait—let's go back to the book. Is it a diary? Could it be another Kezia diary?"

He blows out a breath. "If that's what he's referencing in his notebook, I guess he could have taken pictures or something in those few minutes I was gone." His tone turns skeptical. "But he would have had to spend every moment of the last four or five years trying to read it, and even then I'm not sure it's possible."

We both lean in toward the desk, our attention fixed on the cracked leather-bound book that looks more like a relic than a record, but my thoughts drift elsewhere. I think about those last few years, the space between me and my dad, the conversations we never got to have because of the possibility Wren is voicing. He shut himself off from so much, even ignoring the warning signs of the illness that ultimately took his life. A tightness creeps into my chest. It's not something I can put into words yet, but it's there. A small, unsettled feeling that follows me as I stare at the book.

"Where's your dad's notebook? Can we look at it?" Wren asks, pulling me back to the present.

I hand it to him, my fingers brushing his as I do, and I try to focus on that warmth even though I don't follow him to the other side of the desk.

"Hey," Wren says, his voice quiet. "You okay?"

I don't respond at first, the question hanging in the air. Wren sets the notebook down and moves closer to me, his gaze steady. "Lili?"

It's the first time he's said my name just for me. The sound of it fizzes through me, quick and bright, like the first sip of something sweet and sparkling. It's ridiculous how much I want to hear it again.

I press my lips together, pushing the feeling aside before it can turn into something I have to deal with. Instead, I focus on the book, on the thrill that's been there all along. "Let's see what's possible."

I open Dad's notebook, while Wren slips on a pair of white gloves he also brought and carefully opens the other one. I turn page after page of atrocious handwriting that looks like a doctor was trying to write behind his own back. While running. I have to smile thinking about how some of Dad's postcards had taken me literal hours to decipher, and those usually only contained a few lines. Looking at a full page makes my eyes want to cross. Occasionally, something stands out, if it's repeated enough. The number forty-three, for one, and as I stare, something else.

I stop turning pages, the oddest sensation trickling through me as I glance between the two books, like I've got my emotions crossed again and I'm not feeling the way I'm supposed to.

I know Wren sees it too because he lets out a laugh.

Most of the ink on the aged, faded page of the mystery book has bled beyond recognition, smearing and staining until the entry is all but lost. But in the corner, untouched by the damage, is a drawing of an intricately knotted rope.

My fingers tighten around the edge of my dad's notebook as I stare down at the page I'd already been studying. Carefully sketched in the margin is the exact same knot.

It hits like a current—recognition, certainty, *yes*.

I sit up straighter. Everything in me is buzzing. All that time, all the guessing, and now something solid. Finally.

I look at Wren and grin so wide my cheeks hurt. He's already smiling back.

Before I can overthink it, I launch over and hug him. Quick, tight, completely on impulse. My whole body needs *somewhere* to put that feeling. But when his arms come up around me after a moment, I let myself hold him just a second longer.

FIFTEEN

Wren

Late nights are a semi-regular thing for me. Usually I stay in my room, but I linger in the kitchen tonight. The house is quiet except for the hum of the fridge and the faint whistle of the wind squeezing through the old windows.

Our house, like everything else in our lives, is functional and no frills. A two-story Cape Cod with low counters and wide doorways Dad modified after my accident. The living room doubles as a workspace for McCleave's, with old maps and binders spilling across the worn coffee table. The kitchen is the best part of the house—bright, a little cramped, with scratched cabinets and a scuffed-up butcher block island that still smells faintly of lemon oil from when Eryn last tried to clean it.

I'm just about to pour myself another coffee when Dad walks in, his pajama pants hanging loosely around his waist, the faded T-shirt he's been wearing for years barely holding on to its shape. He was clearly already in bed, his hair mussed from sleep. He doesn't seem surprised to find me still up. He never does. Instead, he heads straight for the fridge, yanking it open and pulling out eggs, cheese, and vegetables that look like they've been in the crisper too long. He drops everything on the counter by the stove and grabs his skillet, the one he treats like a museum piece.

"You gonna let me make you a midnight omelet?" he asks, turning the stove knob with a practiced twist. "It's been a while."

It has. "Senior year?"

"Sounds about right." He cracks eggs into a bowl, adds a splash of truffle oil, and starts whisking. "I've been experimenting with this stuff. Not sure how I feel about it yet. You game?"

I nod. "Sure. Thanks."

Dad couldn't boil water when he found himself a single dad raising a three-year-old, but he learned fast. By the time I was old enough to remember, he could whip up anything. It's one of the few things, apart from mermaids, that he seems to genuinely enjoy.

His knife blurs as he chops onions and mushrooms. "How's the new volunteer working out?"

"Lili," I say before I can stop myself. Her name feels weird in my mouth, like I'm giving something away. Since meeting her, I've gone out of my way to keep her at a distance, to remind her that this idea of rewriting history is pointless. And yet, she keeps showing up. She ran alongside the boat the entire tour when I expected her to quit after a few photos. She spent days helping me with the new script, trying to get me to rehearse, even though I hate performing for tourists.

Except maybe her.

She laughs when I start to get angry, argues back when I try to aim my frustration at her, helps me find answers to questions I didn't even think to ask.

And for better or worse, she pushes me to want more instead of just accepting things the way they are.

I should go back to calling her Tourist Girl. Pretend nothing's changed. But it almost feels too late for that. I knew it earlier when I said her name—not just in front of her mom, but alone in that study, when she suddenly looked afraid of the answers she'd been chasing.

And when she hugged me, I did the thing I absolutely knew I shouldn't have. I hugged her back. She felt soft and strong in my arms, sweet like I could breathe her in for hours without any effort at all.

And the worst part is, I didn't want to let her go.

Dad's still waiting for my answer. I can't say any of that out loud. I shouldn't even be thinking it.

"She's like your truffle oil," I say instead.

He doesn't turn around, but I can tell he's smiling by the slight tilt of his head. "Gotta be careful with that stuff. A little brings out the flavor, but it's easy to overdo."

"Same with her." I hesitate, then settle on: "She's not what I expected."

Dad tosses the vegetables into the pan, and the hiss of butter fills the kitchen. "You want to find someone else?"

I shake my head. "No, it'll be fine." It has to be. Because after yesterday, there's no avoiding her.

We took careful pictures of every page of the book from the McCleave's archives and compared them to some of the entries in her dad's notebook, and there's no doubt left in my mind: It is Kezia's diary. The one that the Whaling Museum has is from earlier in her life, up through just after her marriage. This one looks like it starts right before the war. It's the one she would have kept during her supposed smuggling operations.

If we can make sense of her dad's entries and match them up with pages from Kezia's second diary, we might actually find the answers Lili's looking for. I doubt they'll be the ones she wants, but they'll be definitive.

I don't believe in fate. But it feels like something is pulling me farther into this, farther into her orbit, and I don't know how to stop it.

I do know that I should try.

"Can we talk about the mermaid tour for a minute? I had some thoughts I wanted to run by you."

Dad scoops grated cheese into the eggs. "I've been wanting to talk to you about that too. Did you get those pictures for the website?"

"Yeah, the new girl"—I shouldn't say her name—"she took them. I was going to sort through them later."

"Good. And you saw the reviews?"

"I did, and I kept them in mind while working on the new script."

He slides a chipped plate in front of me, the same one I've used since I was a kid, and then transfers the omelet onto it. "Let me see it once you have a working draft."

The food looks perfect, but my appetite vanishes. "Why?" I ask, pushing the words past my teeth. "You want to check my spelling?"

Dad turns to face me, leaning back against the counter with his own plate. "I've thought about it, and I agree, removing you from the tour is not the right call."

I blink, my fork pausing halfway to my mouth. "What changed your mind?"

He doesn't answer right away, instead shoveling food into his mouth with mechanical efficiency. When his plate is clean, he finally looks at me. "Wren, the tour is about our family. What's the one thing I always tell guests?"

I frown. "Please don't lick the display glass?"

He doesn't smile. "You're still Captain McCleave's descendant. People recognize that. It's a strong part of our narrative, and I don't want to lose that." He leans forward slightly, his tone softening. "I thought maybe taking you off the tour would be the answer to our problem, but I think it's best if you stay on the boat with Tate."

I study his face to make sure I heard him right. "Wait, really? Because that's what I wanted to talk to you about." I tell him about the changes I made in the new script, about reframing the historical details to coincide with more mermaid mythology. I even offer to ask Tate for help on my delivery since, Lili's right, it needs work.

But when I'm done, he just sets his empty plate down, slowly so it doesn't bang. "Wren, you're not understanding me. I want Tate doing the bulk of the tour. You'll still be there, you can even tell people about McCleave and how he found Nerissa and later Nereus while they're taking pictures during the scene."

While they're too distracted to listen, he means. The mermaid tour is the only thing about McCleave's that's felt like I've had any meaningful impact on. I don't want to just give it up, and I tell him as much.

But he shakes his head. "You read the reviews. What you've been doing isn't working."

"I know." The kitchen feels smaller. Tighter. "And I get that there's a problem, but I think I can fix it if you're willing to let me try."

Dad finishes his coffee and lays a hand on my shoulder as he passes me. "This will work out. You might even like it better this way."

"And if I don't?" I say as he's leaving the kitchen, my voice sharp now, like I can cut into him the way he just cut into me.

He pauses. Just for a second. But it's empty, a reflex, not a hesitation. Then he keeps walking, like I never said anything at all.

The frustration builds in my chest, tightening around my ribs until it feels like I might choke on it. I thought maybe—just maybe—if I actually tried this time, something would change. That if I put in the work, if I gave him a reason to listen, he would.

But it's the same as always.

I grip my fork so hard it digs into my palm, then drop it onto the plate with a sharp clatter. The omelet sits there, perfect and untouched. A waste.

SIXTEEN
Lili

I'd followed Wren out when he left earlier, then stayed outside on the front porch after he was gone. The wood for the new railing is piled up under a tarp in the yard, waiting for Mom to measure, cut, and nail it into place, and then for Goldie and me to paint it.

But I'm not thinking about work, on the house or on the diary, as I hug my knees to my chest and look up. The sun set some time ago and now the sky is clear and full of stars, each one glowing quietly, like a tiny light in a vast, peaceful sea. They are beautiful from this spot, and I hope Dad got to see them on a night just like this. I wish I'd been here to see them with him, but I'm trying very hard not to blame him for that choice, when I know he thought he was so close to the answers he made sure I wanted every bit as much as he did.

The house is quiet when I slip back through the front door some time later. The moonlight follows me inside, streaming through the curtainless windows, bathing the now wallpaper-less room in a pale glow, and the only noise is the faint creak of the hinges as I ease the door shut behind me.

I toe off my shoes, the cool wood of the floorboards chilling the soles of my feet as I tread softly toward Dad's study.

"Late night."

Mom's voice comes from inside the room, sudden but not surprising.

"Yeah, sorry. I was just on the porch and I lost track of time." I walk in to see her sitting at Dad's antique desk, a single lamp glowing beside her, its light casting soft shadows across her face. "You too, it looks like," I add, nodding at the painter's mask around her neck that's covering part of the paint-spattered Britney Spears T-shirt she's wearing.

She gives me a tired smile and lifts it off, setting it carefully on the desk.

"Goldie asleep?"

She nods but doesn't speak. Her exhaustion is palpable in the way her body seems to fold in on itself, even without a word.

"I'm sorry I didn't come right up to help you guys." I move closer, the words tumbling out in a rush. "It's just that Wren and I found something kind of big, in a lot of ways." There's an internal clash of excitement and apprehension that I haven't fully reconciled with yet. Before I can try to explain, I catch the shadows under her eyes and the weary lines on her face. "Mom? Why don't you go to bed?"

She stays where she is, looking around the room before settling on the area rug in front of the desk. "It's the same one he had in his study in our old house. He spent so much time pacing on it."

I hesitate, the sudden shift in topic catching me off guard until I look down at the faded patch she's staring at, the stark evidence of Dad's restless footsteps.

"Back and forth, back and forth, for hours on end. He'd miss dinner, wouldn't come to bed, wouldn't leave that spot for anything." She spreads her hands out on the desk, pressing down. "Forever pacing because he thought the past was more important than the present." She looks up at me then, her eyes heavy with sadness. "He missed so much making that path right there."

An uneasy feeling creeps up my spine, and I step back from the rug instinctively, not wanting to add to the wear.

"We missed you tonight," she says, her voice tinged with something deeper than tiredness. "All these nights lately. It's not just working on the house. You've been doing your part, but we're supposed to be doing it together."

I lift my arms helplessly then let them fall back to my sides. "Mom, I'm trying to do the best I can. I know I'm not here as much as I want to be, but you agreed I could work at the museum and look into Dad's research. Are you telling me you want me to stop?"

The thought alone sends a panicky flutter through me for more than one reason. I know it's not the same, what I'm doing and what he did. I have to make the most of the limited time I have here. Wren's not going to let me take Kezia's diary when I leave Nantucket, and sure we took photos, but there's no substitute for the real thing. I need to bridge the gap between what my dad started and what I hope to finish before I leave.

There's also a little nagging thought in my mind that I want to do this *with* Wren. I don't examine it any more than that.

Thankfully, Mom shakes her head.

"It's okay to look into your past, but your present is happening right now, too. This time in your life won't come back once it's gone."

"I know," I say, swallowing down the lump in my throat. "I'll try to do better. I'll even watch *Spider-Man* or any other superhero movie with Goldie this weekend if she wants."

Even her smile looks tired when she stands. "I think she'd rather go thrifting. I haven't been able to take her yet."

"I can do that," I say, aware that she's exhausted in a way that has far more to do with me than with the renovations. I have to try and do better, which is why I don't follow her up to bed. If I start working on the diary tonight, then maybe I can get home sooner tomorrow.

That worn path in the study rug sends me into the kitchen instead, where I'm immediately confronted by how busy Mom and Goldie have been in here too. All the cabinet doors have been removed and partially sanded. There's still so much work left to do, and for some reason, that thought steadies me. It means I still have time.

Three hours later, sitting at the kitchen table with a half-eaten slice of toast slathered in Mrs. Mayhew's blackberry jam, that hope has all but fled.

Bouncing between Dad's notebook, the books Wren let me borrow from the museum, and the diary photos on my tablet has gotten me exactly nowhere. I've matched up and deciphered a few diary entries, but most of them are just birth and death records, notes about people she visited, or remarks on seasonal plants or weather patterns. Like this one from right before the start of the war:

> *1775 Friday, March 31. Been remarked by a number of aged people that there never was such a moderate winter since their memory but past fortnite more bad weather than all winter months.*

Or this one about the miller and his wife:

> *1775 Thursday, October 26. Rode up to Fulling Mill—one Nichols an Old countryman keeps the mills here—he married at the Vineyard lately brought his family on—he lives in Nat Macy's house near the mill—his wife appears to be an agreeable woman.*

I finish the last bite of jam-covered toast, trying not to feel discouraged. It's only one night. I can't expect to unlock some hidden secret right away.

I'm about to put everything away and head to bed when a single word in one of Wren's books catches my eye and ignites in my mind, lighting up everything around it. I frantically clean the jam off my fingers and swipe my tablet, scrolling through the photos of Kezia's diary until I find the right entry. Then I double- and triple-check Dad's notebook, implications bursting like the fireworks inside me, brilliant and beautiful.

I shoot to my feet, reaching for my phone to text Wren before I realize how late it actually is. I check the clock on the stove; it's after one.

Biting my lip, I start typing anyway.

Lili: It's late and you're probably asleep but I've been reading all night and I think I found something.

I let out a deep breath and put my phone face down on the table preparing myself for a long night of obsessing over my discovery with no one to talk to about it.

But then my phone dings.

Wren: I'm awake.

Warmth tingles over my body.

Lili: I feel like I woke you up.
Wren: You didn't.
Lili: Don't you have to get up super early to open the museum?
Wren: Yes.
Lili: Then why aren't you asleep?
Wren: Because I'm not. What did you find? Something to explain why your dad was so obsessed with the number 43?

I hesitate before responding. I did not think this through. Where do I even start?

Lili: I feel like I need to show you in person.
Wren: I'm not coming back over to your house this late.
Lili: I didn't mean that.
Wren: So you texted me to tell me something you can't tell me?
Lili: No, I just got excited so I texted you.

He's the one who doesn't respond right away.

Lili: Are you still there?
Wren: Yes.
Lili: I should have just waited until tomorrow.
Wren: It's fine. Come in early tomorrow before we open. 6:30 am. Show me then.
Lili: Really? That would be great.
Lili: Just wait. You'll be the one hugging me tomorrow.
Wren: I doubt that.
Lili: So did you have my number saved in your phone?
Wren: Yes.
Lili: Under what name?
Wren: Why does it matter?
Lili: I'm just curious if I've been promoted from tourist girl yet.
Wren: I'm going to bed.
Lili: Fine. Good night, tour guy.
Wren: Night, tourist girl.

SEVENTEEN

Wren

Lili is practically vibrating with excitement when I wheel into the back room the next morning, her energy too big for the space. She's perched on the edge of the table, her fingers tapping against the cover of her dad's notebook impatiently until she sees me.

She glances at her watch with exaggerated precision. "Didn't we say 6:30 a.m.? What is this 6:33 nonsense?"

I don't answer. She's still not wearing the McCleave's polo shirt, but I never expected her to. The blue-and-white checkered dress she has on today is nothing special. Just fabric. Just a pattern. But somehow, on her, it feels like summer itself walking toward me.

I veer around the opposite side of the table. "Who let you in?"

"Your dad. He even thanked me for the new display of Nerissa dolls I put together in the gift shop yesterday." She gathers up her bag and notebook. "I want it on the record that you are the one who's late."

"Some girl was texting me at an absurd hour last night," I say, locking my wheels and opening my laptop.

She grins, her eyes glinting with amusement. "I bet that girl had a very, very good reason."

Then she's dragging her chair—loudly—around to my side of the table, before settling in so close that I can count the faint freckles on her nose.

"You're in my light," I mutter, trying to focus on the screen instead of her.

Without missing a beat, she turns on the desk lamp and pushes the notebook toward me, nudging it consistently. "Come on, open it, open it."

Before I can respond, she leans in again. Her hair brushes my neck, soft and warm, and the faint, sweet scent of strawberries fills the air. She's too close, and it's distracting in a way that makes me uncomfortable.

In one sharp motion, I unlock my brakes and wheel away.

"What's wrong?"

"I need air," I say, my voice rougher than I want. "And coffee."

It's an overreaction. Spending most of the day with her yesterday, then texting late into the night—it blurred the lines in ways I don't want to admit. I woke up tangled after hazy dreams that weren't about the girl who's supposed to be in my head, and now guilt and frustration are running under my skin like an itch I can't quite scratch.

But that's on me. No one else. Which is why, when I glance over my shoulder as I reach the door and see the look on her face, I say, "You coming?"

There are quite a few cafés and restaurants surrounding McCleave's, but when I wheel past Petticoat, Lili points back at it. "Eryn's not working today?"

She is, but I don't feel like sitting across a table from both Eryn and Lili, nor do I feel like explaining that.

"The coffee at Handlebar Café is better." Not a lie, but I still rarely go there, mostly because it's farther from the museum and wheeling over all the cobblestones drives me nuts. I'm beyond annoyed when we get there, and listening to Lili's order just makes it worse.

"Good morning. I'd like a large cold cup with three pumps of classic, two pumps of vanilla. Then an inch of caramel drizzle in the bottom, swirled until it's mixed well, then two half-caf ristretto shots and swirl that, then iced coffee to the line, and a splash of cream to finish, please. Oh, and ice."

As the poor barista trudges off, Lili turns her smile on me only to have it fall when she sees my expression.

"What was that?"

"It's warm out. It's not a crime to order iced coffee in the morning."

I shake my head slightly, laughing under my breath. "Everything about that order was a crime."

She looks around the mostly empty café. "There isn't a line yet. I'd have gone with something simpler if there were other people waiting. And you know what?" she continues. "I like my coffee this way. I'm happy to tip extra for it, so I don't think the barista minds either."

"She minds." I gesture toward the counter, where the barista is aggressively stirring caramel into the bottom of her cup like it personally wronged her. "Even if only on principle."

Lili sighs like I'm being impossible, and when our drinks are finally ready, we move to a table outside.

She watches me over the rim of her cup. "You know there are things in this world that you're wrong about."

"Not many." I eye her coffee. "You, on the other hand . . ."

She pushes it toward me. "Try it then."

I sip my Americano. "No."

"Why not?"

"Because you're supposed to be showing me some huge thing you discovered."

"Oh, yes!" She pulls her coffee monstrosity back. "Okay, so one of the books I borrowed from the museum was a copy of the Eliza Mitchell diary, because you said she was the earliest source that claimed Kezia had a smuggler's hole somewhere near Quaise." She pulls the book from her bag and begins flipping through the pages before sliding it over to me and tapping on one of the paragraphs. "This is the section where she actually claims to have seen inside it."

I've read this before, but I scan it again now to appease her.

Many have wondered whether Kezia Gardner did indeed possess a concealed passage by which she might convey contraband to the water under cover of night. I was very anxious, as well as curious, to find out about there being anything of the kind. One day, I went out a Black Berry Picking alone, as was my usual custom. I managed not to be seen, and I went where the entrance might be found. I crawled in and found just as had been told me quite a storage place, and in the center I could stand nearly straight. All was timeworn and very much decay'd but I saw all that I needed to convince me of the crafty business she had that provate room arranged for. No doubt she was a very capable woman, but lacking very much in principle.

I finish reading, waiting for her to explain how this is supposed to prove anything. "Okay?"

She's still grinning as she opens her dad's notebook and hands it to me, leaning to point out a passage on the left page that appears to quote Kezia. It's difficult to read and Lili is apparently too impatient to wait.

"Never mind, I memorized it. It says: '1775 Tuesday, July 18: The blackberry brambles along the south pasture grow thick with fruit, though I dare not go near. One breath of their sickly sweet ripeness and my throat begins to tighten.'" She barely pauses before adding, "And before you ask, I already found the same exact lines in Kezia's diary. I can't make out all the words exactly but *blackberry*, *throat*, and *tighten* can't be anything else."

She shoves her tablet onto the already-crowded table, the photo of the diary entry pulled up and ready. "Kezia wouldn't have hidden anything near blackberries because she was allergic to them!" Lili collapses back against her chair, pure satisfaction written all over her face.

I reread all three sources, struggling with her dad's handwriting and the damaged page in the diary, but eventually I have to concede that she might be right. "I think I see the words too, barely, but yeah."

"Wren." She grabs my shoulders and gives me a light shake. "It's okay to be excited. We just proved she couldn't have had a smuggler's hole where everyone else claimed!"

I huff out a laugh before I can stop myself. "Okay, but you're talking about one account. There are others."

Her grin doesn't dim a single watt. "The Mitchell account

predates the other sources. Isn't it possible that everybody else took their stories from hers?" She knows she's right as she holds up her ridiculous coffee for me to cheers. "Come on," she says when I don't immediately lift my own cup. "This is good for you too. Think about it: The Whaling Museum cites later accounts for the smuggler's hole in their Kezia exhibit, and McCleave's can challenge their sources! Don't tell me you don't love the idea of that."

I do, but even if the smuggler's hole is a myth, it doesn't erase the rest of accepted history. If there's more to find, and that's an ocean-sized *if*, it's going to take more work and, frankly, a lot of luck. But I still raise my coffee, because she already proved me wrong once and part of me wants to see if she can do it again. "To sticking it to the Whaling Museum."

I watch as she leans back, eyes bright, completely lost in the thrill of discovery. She owns this moment, like she never doubted for a second that she'd make it happen.

It's hard not to be impressed.

Lili catches me staring, her smile turning curious. "What?" she asks. "Surprised a Tourist Girl could put something like this together?"

"Yeah," I say, still watching her. "But I won't make that mistake again."

Her teasing expression falters, like she wasn't expecting me to actually answer. Like she wasn't expecting me to mean it.

I wasn't expecting to either, but I can't take it back. I can, however, put a smile back on her face.

Reaching across the table, I pluck her cup right out of her hands and take a sip. The sugar and caramel hit first, thick and cloying, like someone melted a candy bar straight into a cup. I choke it down, pushing the drink back toward her.

Lili's surprise turns to laughter. "Well?"

I set the cup down with a shake of my head. "Like I said, a crime."

EIGHTEEN

Lili

Of all the days for Goldie to wake up sick this summer, today is the worst. And she knows it.

Mom presses the back of her hand against Goldie's flushed forehead, her eyes squinting with worry as my sister does her best to hold back tears. The thermometer beeps, and Mom lets out a soft hiss of air. Goldie's chin quivers, and I can practically hear her fighting the urge to sob.

"But I don't want to miss the water fight!" she says, voice wobbling as she stares at Mom, pleading.

The Fourth of July Nantucket Water Fight started nearly fifty years after a local resident bought a 1927 American LaFrance ladder antique fire truck and challenged the fire chief to a water duel using only a historic hand-pumper from the Gardner Street Fire Hose Cart House. The whole town got involved and it's been an annual event ever since, one that I've been hyping Goldie up for all week.

The plan was to join the crowds, soak each other in the water fight, and then race down to the beach later for fireworks under the stars. I'd been looking forward to it from the second Mom agreed we could spend the summer here.

I hug myself around my stomach, feeling a knot form as I follow Mom out into the hall. "Is she really sick?" I ask, trying to keep my voice light.

Mom shows me the thermometer. "She's not going anywhere."

The knot pulls taught. Goldie had been too little to come when Dad used to take me. She barely remembered what the water fight was until I started telling her about it. Last night she'd been so excited she could barely fall asleep. "Maybe she'll be better by tonight?"

Mom looks doubtful. "Even if she's better by tonight, I wouldn't feel okay about taking her to the beach with other people."

I know she's right, but hearing Goldie sniffling in the bedroom is heartbreaking. "Then maybe just here, in the yard, picnic style. I don't want her to have to miss the fireworks too."

Mom glances toward the bedroom door, like she's weighing it. "We'll see. Right now, I'm going to sit with her. Why don't you go into town and meet up with Wren and your friends? Maybe you can still have some fun today."

Wren had surprised me when he said he'd have a water gun with my name on it if I wanted to try to find him. I think he meant he intends to soak me with it, but I could try to get him first. The idea doesn't stop me from feeling awful that Goldie has to miss out. And Mom too.

"Go," Mom says gently, nudging me toward the stairs with a subtle tilt of her head. "Have fun for all of us. I'll text you if she feels better and we can do anything at the house." When I still hesitate, she says, “Hurry, before I change my mind and make you watch a superhero movie marathon with us.”

For 364 days of the year, Nantucket feels like a place frozen in time. Gray-shingled buildings, the cobblestone streets, and the salty ocean air are all as constant and unchanging as the tide. But today is different. History is alive, splashing through the streets, turning the postcard-perfect town into a chaotic, joyful battleground. Red, white, and blue bunting hangs from lampposts, while streams of water arc through the air, glistening like liquid rainbows.

The fire truck reigns supreme in Main Street Square, blasting its hose into the crowd. The old hand-pumper stands proud, with volunteers working the handles as kids with squirt guns dart between them. A little girl in a pink tutu shrieks with laughter as a bucket of water tips over her head, soaking her from curls to sneakers. No one is safe in the splash zone, not me, not tourists, not the guy in a suit running barefoot down the street. The scent of melting ice cream, sunscreen, and soaked pavement mingles with faint music, “Born in the U.S.A.” thumping in the background. The water fight isn’t about monuments or records, it’s about the people who lived here, who laughed and fought and made it their home. It’s about taking something pristine and letting it get a little messy, a little loud, and a little ridiculous.

And today, it’s perfect.

I spot Wren sooner than I expect, lying in wait by a refill cooler. It’s the only cobblestone-free area on the street, and he’s staking out the territory like a predator, ready to target anyone who tries to cross. He and his white T-shirt are somehow still remarkably dry.

Seems like something I should help him with.

Aiming my neon green water gun in his direction, I cross the street to approach from behind.

"Hey, Tour Guy!" I call out. I wait for his eyes to collide with mine and for him to take in my satisfied grin before I squeeze the plastic trigger.

I'm still crowing my victory when he snakes an arm around my waist and swings me around in front of him like a human shield just as a group of tweens comes spraying past us.

I laugh, plucking the damp fabric from my skin when he lets me go. "I still got you first."

He shakes the water from his dark hair, grinning at me. It's a good look on him. "I got you better."

"So this is how you stay dry? Grab and hide behind unsuspecting people who get too close?"

"Nah, just the ones who should know better."

There's more than just a challenge in his eyes when he stares at me, but before I can decide what he means, he glances past me. "Where are your mom and sister?"

I tell him about Goldie.

His brows furrow. "Poor kid. You know, if you want to grab another T-shirt from McCleave's for her later, I've got some extras in my truck."

"Thanks," I say, taken aback by the kind offer. "She'd like that."

But then he ruins the moment by shooting me again and making me laugh so hard I miss my shot when I try to retaliate.

That's when Eryn calls out to us from across the street.

Wren immediately stops shooting. He doesn't even point his

water gun in her direction. But as soon as I lower mine, he takes one last cheap shot at me.

"Gotta stay alert, Tourist Girl," he says under his breath, grinning as he nods at Eryn.

She takes his hand and holds it before turning to me. "Lili, hi!" She gives me a quick, wet, one-armed hug, and then pulls back, looking sheepish. "Sorry! Elliot was waiting for me earlier like some psycho with a water bucket, so I'm absolutely drenched."

"I don't know who Elliot is," I tell her.

Wren looks at her like he doesn't know either.

"He's a new hire at the café that I've been training. He's the one who made those maple bacon sticky buns that I brought for lunch the other day," she adds, sounding sort of proud. "Anyway, the water fight is already wrapping up—how are you two not soaked yet?"

I got here late, but I'm not nearly as dry as Wren is, and I shoot him a mock glare. "He did his 'grab a tourist and hide behind them' thing."

Eryn looks between us. "His what?"

"You know, where he—"

"Where's Tate?" Wren interrupts. "I lost him a while back."

Eryn glances at me again before answering. "I think he's still off hunting his little brothers on the one day of the year he's actually allowed to do that. He said he'd meet up with us in front of the museum after. I guess we could head over?"

I take a step back in the opposite direction. "I should probably get going too."

"Where?" Wren asks quickly enough to surprise me. "Your mom told you to stay out, right? We're going to get pizza at Steamboat

Wharf and then Tate knows a spot on the beach that's not too crowded. You should come."

Eryn only hesitates for the briefest of moments before chiming in too. "Yeah, come." She releases Wren's hand to link her arm through mine. "The pizza isn't great so the company should be."

After meeting up with Tate and drying off in the parking lot, we all pile into Wren's truck. He doesn't comment when Eryn immediately changes his playlist, maybe because the drive is so short and we're pulling up in front of the pizza place before the first song is even over.

Steamboat Wharf Pizza is a cute little redwood paneled building near the beach, definitely a grab-and-go kind of place. There aren't any tables, just a long counter directly inside wide-open double doors, but the air is thick with the mouthwatering scent of garlic and freshly baked dough.

The tourists are everywhere, spilling out from the entrance in long lines, their chatter a mix of excitement and impatience as Eryn and I hop out of Wren's truck. I catch Wren's eye for a moment before he settles his attention back to her.

"You're sure you don't want me to wait?" he asks, handing her some cash and eyeing the crowd with a small frown.

She leans through the window to give him a quick kiss. "Somebody else will get our spot on the beach if you guys don't hurry."

Waving them off, she joins me in line, smiling into the warm breeze until my hair gets whipped directly in her face.

"Are you okay? Oh no, did I get your eye?"

She doesn't look like she's in pain exactly, just confused. "I'm fine. Um, your hair smells like strawberries."

"Really? Still?" I grab a strand to check for myself. "Wow, that's good stuff. My mom got me this shampoo and lotion set last Christmas and I've been using it since we got here. Nice to know it lasts even through a water-gun fight."

Eryn's smile is a little tight.

"Sorry, not a strawberry fan, huh?"

"I am, it's just . . . nothing, never mind." Then much quicker, she says, "It's just that sometimes Wren smells like that too lately."

The bottom of my stomach starts to drop out when I think about how closely Wren and I have been working together recently, literally. And if Eryn noticed, does that mean Wren did too?

Suddenly, she drops her head and laughs. "Tate's probably been giving him some strawberry candy or something. Please can we forget I said anything and talk about something else?"

I'm not eager to linger on it either. "Well, we had our first research breakthrough the other week. Or did Wren already tell you?"

Eryn shakes her head and I start telling her about blackberries and the smuggler's hole, but pause when I notice her eyes glazing over.

"I guess maybe it doesn't sound like much, but it's actually kind of a big deal."

"I'm sorry," she says, her voice sincere. "History was my worst subject in school and I just haven't gotten over that. But if you're excited, then I'm excited for you."

I laugh lightly. "Thanks, but we don't have to talk about history. I get enough of that during the day." That's a white lie. I could talk about it all the time, but most people aren't like me.

I push the thought of Wren out my mind as we step up to the counter to order.

We have to walk a little over a block to the beach once we have our pizza, and since I'm going to spare her more history talk, I ask her about baking instead.

Eryn beams like a lighthouse at sunset when she talks about the differences between sourdough and yeasted bread, how rough puff saves time but lacks the delicate layers of traditional puff pastry, and why she prefers Italian buttercream over American for its smooth texture. She's got that perfect mix of knowledge and excitement, and it's clear that baking isn't just a job for her, but a craft she's always refining.

I'm kind of speechless when she's done. "And why aren't you in pastry school somewhere, or, I don't know, off winning *The Great British Baking Show*?"

Her cheeks turn pink as she smiles. "I've thought about it, but pastry school doesn't really fit in with everything else. Wren would never want leave Nantucket and we've been through so much that I can't imagine a future without him in it."

I hesitate. "Does he know that you want to go? Maybe he'd be more open than you think."

"Oh, no," she says offhandedly. "It's fine. I do love it here and the café is great, and I even like being a mermaid. I don't really need anything else."

But I can't help but notice that she seems a little less bright as we step out onto the sand.

NINETEEN
Wren

The beach buzzes with life, the sound of laughter and the crackle of sparklers blending with the steady, rhythmic rush of waves slapping against the shore. We've found a quieter spot farther down, tucked behind a brush of grass that offers at least the illusion of privacy. Above us, the last traces of daylight are slipping away, leaving the sky a vast, endless stretch of black, waiting for the first spark of color to ignite it.

Tate spots the girls first, or more precisely, the pizza boxes they're carrying. He jumps to his feet, kicking sand in his haste, and laughing when I shout after him in annoyance.

It's good to hear him laugh that easily. The past few weeks have been a little strained between us, but tonight? It feels like we're okay again. I never told him I'd tried—and failed—to convince Dad to change his mind about pulling me from the tour. I haven't mentioned it to Lili either. As far as she knows, Tate's been helping me practice. I doubt either one of them will bring it up tonight, but eventually, I'll have to. For now, though, I focus on their familiar shapes, drawing closer.

I pick out Eryn easily, her silhouette etched against the fading light as she repeatedly bats Tate's hand away from the pizza box. Then Lili, smoothly reaching up to pluck his captain's hat off his head and tossing it like a frisbee into the grass.

I'm still watching her, a half smile playing on my lips, when Tate plops down beside me. He follows my gaze, then looks back at me with a sly grin. "You know your girlfriend is the one on the left, right?"

I roll my eyes at him. "Don't be an idiot."

"I'm just saying." He shrugs, a teasing glint in his eyes. "You looked a little lost there for a second. And it's not the first time I've noticed." He pulls his hat back onto his head, his smirk fully fading. "Might want to be careful. Could be someone else gets confused, too."

I brush the sand off my hands. The cool night air does little to calm the warmth creeping up my neck. That's not what's happening, not with me and not with anyone else.

When Eryn reaches us, I grab her hand, pulling her down beside me. I don't even glance at Lili when she sits across from us.

Tate, now fully in food mode, doesn't notice either way. A whale could suddenly beach itself right in front of us and he wouldn't care. He laces his fingers together and stretches them out in front of him before snatching the pizza box out of Lili's hands as she's opening it.

"Seriously?" she says.

He shoves an entire slice into his mouth, accordion style, and grins at her.

Lili deliberately lifts her eyes to his hat. "Didn't that used to have a golden anchor pinned to it?" Her voice is smooth, laced with playful mischief. "Oh no, did it fall off in the grass?"

"What!?" Tate chokes out, because if there's one thing that could possibly distract him from his stomach, it's his hat. Or maybe his boat.

"She's kidding," Eryn says quickly, taking pity on him.

Still, Tate doesn't relax until he checks, yanking his hat off and then sighing with relief before giving Lili a mock salute. "I'm starting to see you now, Tourist Girl."

The nickname hangs in the air, and in the rising moonlight, Lili's green eyes meet mine, brief and sharp, like the quick crest of a wave before it crashes. She drops her eyes to the pizza box and leans forward to grab a slice.

I don't plan to spend any time tonight analyzing why exactly I don't like Tate calling her Tourist Girl.

Eryn leans slightly into my side, her face lifted toward the sky, waiting for the fireworks to start.

Tate's and Lili's voices filter through the darkness, a steady rhythm of banter. He makes her laugh a few times, a light and airy sound, though I can tell she's trying not to. I wonder if he'll ask her out after tonight. He'd talk nonstop about his boat, oblivious to how even the topic of being out on the water makes her ill.

"Am I leaning on you too much?" Eryn shifts her head, tilting up to catch my eyes.

"Hmm? No, you're fine."

"You just went really stiff." She pulls back slightly, her eyes searching mine, waiting for an explanation.

Guilt crashes over me. What would it matter if he asked her

out? Maybe they'll bond over food or something non–ocean related, and find they have a ton of things in common. But even as I think this, I notice that Lili is methodically plucking off her pizza the black olives that Tate insisted on, and that I have a similar pile of olives next to me.

"I'm fine," I say, forcing my muscles to relax, refocusing on the moment. I watch as Eryn smiles softly at me, then up at the sky, her face lit by the first burst of fireworks.

The air booms and crackles as colors explode in a kaleidoscope of light reflecting off the water and shimmering across the shore. I've never cared much about the Fourth of July show, but I lift the arm not bracing me, inviting her to lean in more fully. She does, her body fitting easily against mine, and I pull her closer, a gesture so automatic it feels like breathing.

While I try to focus on the fireworks, it's Lili's laughter that draws my attention again and again. It's light but constant, like the flickering of fireflies, and impossible to ignore.

After the finale crescendos some time later, Tate's voice pulls me back to the present. "Looks like Cinderella's done with the ball." He nods toward Eryn, who has slumped against me, her breathing slow and steady.

I run a hand over her arm, shaking her gently.

"Did I fall asleep again?" she murmurs, blinking as she checks her watch. "I'm sorry, I always do this. I had to be at the café at 4:30 this morning." She yawns, jaw cracking as she stretches. "And again tomorrow."

Tate and Lili join me in reassuring her it's fine as we begin to gather our things.

There's a moment when Lili pauses, her brow furrowing. The

blanket is folded under Eryn's arm, Tate is throwing away the last of the trash, and I'm still sitting in the sand. "Stupid question, but where is your wheelchair?"

Tate's head snaps up, eyes darting around. "Wait, where is it? You don't think . . ." His eyes bulge. ". . . grand theft wheelchair?"

"Wheelchairs and sand don't really go together," I tell her. "I left it in the truck, but I've got my trusty pack mule over there to help me get here and back."

"That's Mr. Pack Mule to you," Tate says, squatting down in front of me so I can grab a hold of his shoulders. He hoists my legs up piggyback style, then takes off at a run. "I'm calling shotgun!"

When we pull up to Eryn's house after dropping Tate off, I watch through the rearview mirror as she gives Lili a hug in the backseat before stepping out of the truck.

"Still on for lunch tomorrow?" she asks, turning to me.

I nod, reaching out the window to take her hand and tug her closer. My eyes trace the familiar contours of her face, and I remind myself that her hand was the first to find mine when the doctors told me I'd never walk again, and that throughout that first year, when all I wanted to do was give up, she never once let me let go.

She tucks her hair behind her ear, lowering her head slightly, as if my gaze is too intense.

I lean in and kiss her, holding it long enough to feel her cheeks warm under my touch and see her flush when I pull away. I'm not usually big on public displays of affection, but I needed to remind myself that I'd be every kind of fool to risk losing her.

She steps back, dragging out the contact of our fingers so that it looks like I'm reaching for her by the time we let go. I'm still staring after her as she turns then hurries inside her house.

Until Lili's voice breaks my focus.

"You don't mind if I sit up front, do you?" she asks, already climbing up between the seats before she finishes talking.

I do mind. The front seat of my truck is decently large, but I was less aware of her when she was behind me.

She sighs in the relative silence as we drive, smiling softly to herself.

"Something funny?" I ask.

"Not funny, just good. Today felt like stepping back into a memory. The water fight, the fireworks." She smiles brighter even as her eyes lose their focus. "It was the first day since my dad died that it didn't hurt to think about him."

I don't answer right away. Our parents, our losses—they're not the same.

"You don't mind that we missed an entire day of researching?" I ask.

From the corner of my eye, I see Lili turn. "I didn't even think about that." There's a hint of surprise in her voice, as though the realization just struck her. She checks her phone.

"Any word on your sister?"

Her voice sounds heavier now. "Goldie wasn't up for going outside to see the fireworks. My mom's hoping she'll fall asleep before they run out of *Avengers* movies to watch."

"Maybe you can bring her back next year," I offer, not sure where the words come from.

Lili lets out a humorless laugh. "My mom was pretty adamant

that this is a one-time thing. That's why I've been pushing so hard on the Kezia stuff. I don't get another shot here."

I slow the truck to a stop, pulling back on the handbrake, an impulse rising that I probably shouldn't act on. "It's not that late. We could still get some work done if you want."

Her voice comes out quiet, hopeful. "Really?"

Then I remember. "No wait, the museum is closed."

"Don't you have keys?"

"Normally, but Tate is opening tomorrow, so I gave them to him."

She leans back against her seat, visibly deflated.

"We could just work here." The words slip out before I can catch them. "Like that night when we were working on the tour speech?"

"Did you show it to your dad yet?"

I shake my head. "I'm still going over a few things."

She gives me an exasperated look but doesn't push. Instead, she seems to consider my offer. "I guess there's no reason we couldn't work for a little while."

My pulse spikes, a mix of nerves and . . . relief. Quickly followed by the sinking realization that this is the opposite of what I should be doing. "No, wait. I forgot we left everything at the museum."

She rummages through the bag that she brings everywhere and doesn't see how my whole body tenses. If I'd just kissed my girlfriend goodnight, gone home, and gone to bed, I wouldn't be watching Lili's hair fall in front of her face, resisting the urge to brush it back.

I don't want this—these thoughts, this constant awareness, the growing desire to be around her and know what she's thinking.

The only thing keeping me from driving straight to her house is the knowledge that this is all on me. Lili isn't stealing glances at me or wondering what I think about a song or a book. To her, I'm a research partner, maybe a friend, and her new friend's boyfriend.

And I am that. Eryn's boyfriend.

I am.

"Should we go to our tree?" she asks, straightening with her tablet and notebook. "You know, where we worked on the tour speech?"

My hand grips on the steering wheel. "I hardly think we can lay claim to it after one night."

"Well, I don't remember the street names."

I do. It's disturbingly easy to navigate there, almost as if I've been waiting for a reason to go back.

I turn down a quiet street lined with thick trees and park under their canopy. She hands me her notebook and unlocks her tablet. "I've been looking over a few specific entries in her diary. The pages are in extremely poor condition, but beyond that, the handwriting looks different." She lifts the center console, scooting into the narrow middle seat to give me a better view of the screen. "She normally writes very precisely, same letter height, same word spacing, but these"—she swipes through several photos and back—"are all almost messy. I mean, look at this one."

I grab my glasses, willing my attention from Lili to the tablet in her hands. Thankfully, I see her point instantly, and happily shift into academic mode as I pinch the screen to zoom in. "It is different."

Lili tugs on her bottom lip, alternating her gaze between me and the tablet. "It's still her though, right? I mean, it looks like her handwriting, just—"

"—strange, but yeah, it's still hers. Look at the swoops on the *O*s and the angle on the *E*s." I indicate the letters, and she sighs in relief beside me. "And it's one of, what, five pages in the entire diary that your dad didn't even attempt to transcribe?"

Lili nods intently. "I noticed that too." Then she looks up, all but brimming with excitement. "I guess it's up to us."

TWENTY

Lili

A couple of hours later, I'm beginning to understand why my dad might have skipped these pages. The passages we've been able to partially transcribe are all from somewhat heated entries regarding escalating tensions between the American and British forces:

> *1776 Friday, February 9. The Congress have ordered that no Nantucket vessel be supplied with provisions unless they have a permit signed by three Justices of the Peace of Barnstable. Stephen Paddock has been off to get a number signed and came on today with them. Paddock tells that the Americans have got possession of Dorchester Hill, which commands Boston.*

> *1776 Saturday, March 29. Hear there is an Act of Parliament to burn sink and destroy all American vessels.*

1776 Tuesday, July 16. Sturgis Gorham came here this afternoon, had just come to the Island. Brings the Declaration of Continental Congress, declaring America to be free and independent States. Horrible! I wish they and all their well-wishers had been strung 50 ft in the air before they had been suffered so far to bring about their wicked and ruinous plans. I believe the only motive they have in view is to aggrandize themselves, they care not for their bleeding country; the Lord reward them according to their works.

Her handwriting gets even messier after that, her increasing anger evident with each barely discernible stroke of her quill. I'm getting to the point where I'm starting to dread what she might write next.

I don't realize I'm voicing the thought out loud until Wren takes off his glasses and rubs the bridge of his nose. "A lot of people were upset about the war. That doesn't mean they did anything more than write about it. But I don't think we're going to get anywhere tonight. The light isn't great, and I feel like we might need the originals to figure out the rest of these words."

He's right. I've had the same thought for the last twenty minutes now, but hadn't wanted to admit it. I can't shake the feeling that we're close to something though, something even my dad didn't know, and that need to dig that I inherited from him is hard to ignore.

Reaching up, I switch off the bright overhead light, then take the tablet and turn that off too. There's still moonlight spilling in through all the windows, but the sudden darkness feels intimate.

"We might not find what you want. You do know that."

Goose bumps ripple over my skin at the sound of Wren's voice, low and quiet in the dark. "Mitchell lied about the smuggler's hole."

"Yeah, she did. But smuggler's hole or not—"

"—even Kezia's own words aren't helping us right now," I finish for him, and let my head fall back against the seat.

He's silent for a moment, then softly says, "What do you want, Lili?"

"Right now I'd settle for a magnifying glass and a good two-thousand-lumen lightbulb."

I loll my head in his direction when he doesn't say anything. My eyes have adjusted to the moonlight, and his serious expression makes me sit up straighter. "You know what I want."

He shakes his head. "To prove Kezia Gardner wasn't a smuggler?"

"Yes."

"I just wonder sometimes."

"Did you just admit to thinking about me?" I say it lightly, trying to brush off the tension building between us.

"More than I should." His voice is a grumble, barely audible, making me question what I truly heard. Then, louder, he says, "I know you want to figure this out, and you made me want answers too. But do you wonder *why* you're doing this?"

I'm completely taken aback by that, so much so that I can't answer right away. He lets the silence stretch, and I don't know if I'm grateful for that or not.

Finally, he says, "Your dad, this was all his obsession long before it was yours, right?"

"Yeah, but it's my history too."

"Okay, but how much are you willing to give up for it? Do you really want to spend the rest of your summer in a mermaid museum, wasting all your free time with me, staring at an old diary that we may never fully understand? Or worse, we will, and it'll confirm what everybody but your dad already believes?"

"Whoa." I laugh a little and push my bangs back off my forehead. "Look, it's late and we're tired, and I think we both need a break from the past."

He doesn't let it go. "It's a fair question."

"We have different opinions on that."

"We usually do." He pauses. "So?"

I think about the path my dad wore down in his rug and shake my head. "I don't feel like I'm giving up all that much. I like the museum and trying to read this diary with you. Maybe I'm not getting to spend as much time with my mom and sister as I thought I would, but they understand." Mom does, sort of, and Goldie will too once I get to share everything we find with her. "And I'm not obsessed in the same way he was. Don't get me wrong, I want to know, but I wouldn't sacrifice everything else in my life to find out." Then, something slips out—something I've never admitted to myself before. "Like he did."

I glance at Wren, gauging if he really wants to hear this. He's looking right back at me, brows furrowed slightly, waiting for me to continue.

Finally, I say, "My dad was adopted. Did I ever tell you that? His parents died when he was a baby, and it was actually friends of theirs who adopted him. Really nice people, but he never thought of them as his family. They took him away from the island and he spent the rest of his life trying to get back a piece of what he lost.

I won't pretend it wasn't an obsession; it was. He wanted to learn everything he could about his parents, and his grandparents, and everyone that came before them." I stare down at the notebook in my lap, running my fingers over the worn leather. "And when I started showing an interest in our family history, I became interesting to him, too." There's a note of surprise in my voice that even I hear. I've never thought about it that way before, but I know instantly that it's true. "His obsession ruined our family, I know that. I used to blame my mom when I was younger, but he was the one who wouldn't stay. This is where he wanted to be, even if we couldn't afford to uproot and be here with him." I shift to face Wren, tucking my legs under me. "And now I'm here, because . . . I don't know, it makes me feel like I'm closer to him somehow." My voice falters slightly. "Is that pathetic?"

I feel Wren's gaze on me, intense, and for a moment, I can't help wishing it was his hand instead. "*Pathetic* isn't a word I'd use to describe you."

Heat pulses through my chest, not just from his words, but from the way he says them—deep yet soft, almost like a caress. At least, that's how they feel.

Actually, I'm feeling a lot of things right now, and I'm not sure I should be feeling any of them. I know I shouldn't be encouraging either one of us to open up like this, but I can't seem to stop that either.

"Will you tell me about your mom?"

"What, I owe you now because you told me about your dad?" His gaze trails over my face, and I shiver.

"No," I say quickly, "but you're not the only one who wonders sometimes."

He takes a long breath. "What do you want to know?"

"Is she still alive?"

His answer is immediate. "I don't know."

"When was the last time you saw her?"

"She left when I was three."

He's not offering any additional information or elaborating at all. He's making me ask for every detail.

"Has she tried to reach out at all, or have you tried to talk to her?"

"No."

"What about your dad?"

He doesn't answer, and I realize he probably wouldn't even know.

"You know you could just tell me what happened instead of making me drag it out of you."

He stares at me, a slight smile curling at the edges of his mouth. "I could."

I inhale through my nose. Even now, he's pushing my buttons. But before I can ask another question, he starts speaking.

"She was a tourist visiting the island with her family during the summers until she met the boy who made her want to stay."

A tourist. No wonder he wasn't warm and friendly when he met me.

"My dad, he was gone from the start, would have followed her halfway around the world if she'd let him," he says quietly, almost distant. His fingers tap once on the steering wheel, then still. "But then my grandfather died and the museum became his responsibility. By then I was already on the way and I guess she felt trapped. Trapped by this island, trapped by a man whose novelty quickly wore off, and then trapped by a baby that would forever tie her to both of them.

"She made it three years," he continues, his voice light, but his knuckles whiten on the steering wheel. "I'm sure she surprised even herself. My dad would have given up everything here and gone with her, anywhere that he thought she'd be happy. He didn't understand for a long time that we were a big part of what she wanted to leave behind."

When he finishes, I'm left with no words—nothing to offer except the empty space between us.

His eyes drift to the windshield before settling on me. "Did that answer your question?"

I nod, but another one lingers. "Do you remember her?"

"No. But I've seen pictures. She was pretty in that way a lot of tourists are." He pauses, then adds, "Pretty like you."

I blink, caught off guard. "I can't tell if that's a compliment or not."

He doesn't answer and I don't think I want him to.

"Would you ever want to find her?"

He doesn't break his gaze from mine. "No." Then he leans back, making me realize just how close we've gotten. "I don't need to chase after the love of someone who chose, long ago, not to give it to me."

TWENTY-ONE

Lili

"Lili, Lili! Wake up!"

I've always been a light sleeper, the kind of person whose eyes pop wide open in the middle of the night when the neighbor's dog barks once from inside their house. So when a deep male voice calls my name, inches away from my face, I nearly jump through the roof.

Of his truck

Wren's sunlit truck.

Oh no.

And I'm touching him, I'm practically snuggled into his side with his arm draped around my shoulders.

In an instant, I jerk back to my side of the truck, pulling the center console back down between us.

In unison, we both dive for our phones. I only have one missed message.

Mom: I'm exhausted and about to fall asleep in here with Goldie. Do you mind taking my room tonight? Oh and I'll explain about all the towels tomorrow.

I sigh in relief. She doesn't know I didn't come home.

Wren, however, is frantically scrolling through his phone, and I'm still close enough to see his screen.

Dad: It's late. Are you staying at Tate's?

He opens another conversation.

Tate: Your dad called looking for you. I told him you were crashing at my house. Where are you?
Tate: I'm worried here, man. Did you go back and pick up Eryn? Text me.
Tate: I'm not messing around here. Call me now.
Tate: If you're dead I'm going to be so mad.
Tate: I'm texting Eryn.
Tate: I made it worse.

He mutters something and taps Eryn's thread.

Eryn: What's going on? No one knows where you are.
Eryn: You're scaring me right now.
Eryn: I'm picking up Tate. We're going to drive around and see if we can spot your truck. Please be okay.

His thumbs fly across the screen, tapping out a response.

Wren: I'm here. I'm fine. I fell asleep working on the research project and only just now checked my messages.

He drops his phone down between us, running both hands through his hair. Neither of us speaks.

I can't believe we fell asleep.

Wren hasn't mentioned me to Tate and Eryn yet, but what will they say when they find out we were together all night? I press my face into my hands. "I'm so sorry."

"It's not your fault." But he won't look at me, and his hands are still tangled in his hair.

"I remember being tired but not falling asleep." And definitely not on him. "Do you?"

Another head shake. "Are you okay? Your mom?"

I shake my head. "She doesn't know."

Wren's phone dings. He grabs it so fast I don't see the screen. He taps something in response, then starts the truck.

"I'll take you home."

My hand shoots out to cover his when he reaches for the gear shift. "You can't. If I show up now, my mom will know I didn't come home. Right now she probably just thinks I left early." I lower my hand. "I can't go back until this afternoon."

He fists his hand on his knee. "Tate and Eryn are meeting me at the museum. I can't show up with you before I've had a chance to explain."

My brain is racing at this point, searching for a way out of this mess for both of us. "Drop me off somewhere on the way—a café or something. I'll just come in later like I always do."

His gaze locks onto mine, his expression serious as he takes me in. "In the same clothes you wore yesterday?" He breathes out, muttering a curse. "And I smell like you."

"You what?"

"I smell like you." His voice is louder now, but tight with frustration. "You were pressed against me all night. Your perfume—whatever it is—on my clothes, my skin."

I might've argued that he was holding *me* to *him* all night, but it's a pointless distinction in the moment. After what she said last night, Eryn will 100 percent notice.

My voice is hollow, sick. "What do we do?"

He shifts into drive. "The only thing we can do."

We don't say a word as he drives, and neither of us reaches for the stereo. There's nothing to say. I text Mom, implying that I slipped out early this morning for work without outright lying to her. I don't feel good about it.

That ill feeling only spreads when Wren parks in front of the museum.

He's moving immediately, putting his chair back together and sliding out and into it. "Let's go."

I stumble as I get out, legs not cooperating. I feel like a zombie, shuffling after him, and my stomach churns at the thought of facing Eryn. I'd rather deal with my mom's disappointment than her hurt.

We round the corner, and there they are—Tate sitting atop the gift shop counter, and Eryn with one arm wrapped around herself and the other up near her mouth, pacing until she catches sight of Wren, and then she's running to him.

She throws her arms around him before he's stopped moving, falling into his lap with practiced ease.

It takes a second for his arms to come up around her and cradle her head with one of them.

"I'm sorry I scared you."

I linger back, trying to remain unseen, but Tate spots me. Unlike Eryn, he wasn't in a hurry to embrace his missing friend. And now that he sees me, it's almost like he's not surprised as his head drops forward.

"I'm just glad you're okay."

"Eryn—"

"I was so worried when Tate texted."

"Eryn—"

"And then we couldn't find you, and—"

"Eryn!" It's the third time Wren has had to say her name, and there's finally enough force behind it for her to listen. "I'm fine, but I need to explain."

"Explain what—?" But then she stills and her eyes find me.

She slides off his lap.

Wren reaches a hand out for her but she steps out of his reach. "I want to explain. I just need you to stop for a second."

She looks like she'd rather have the mermaid skeleton come to life and chase after her.

Unlike when we were waiting in line for the pizza and she was mostly embarrassed to bring up a wholly unsubstantiated doubt she had, this time it's right in front of her with rumpled clothes and uncombed hair. And a scent that she'll probably never enjoy again.

The eye contact Wren makes with me is so brief that I almost miss it, but I understand it immediately.

He's not going to play this off as a series of innocent but unfortunate events. He's not going to make what happened sound reasonable or even understandable. He's going to tell her the truth.

We weren't working the whole time, not even most of the time. We were playing with fire last night. And unintentionally or not, I woke up in his arms.

It's not that I want him to lie to her, but the whole truth is only going to hurt her. And him.

So when I see him take that deep breath before it all spills out, I make a choice.

"It's my fault."

Everyone turns to look at me. Even Tate lifts his head. "After we dropped you guys off, I got it in my head that we could still get some research in since it wasn't that late. Wren wanted to come here." Not a lie, since he was the one who mentioned the museum. "Only Tate had the keys, so I thought we could just work in his truck." I look everywhere except at Wren, but I can feel his gaze boring into me as I dig my own hole deeper and deeper, all while trying to keep him as far from it as possible. "I don't think he thought he had a choice; I certainly didn't offer him one. The next thing we knew, it was morning." Now, I look at him, meeting his stare head-on with what I can only hope is an apologetic expression. "I'm really sorry, Wren." I should never have put him in this position.

"I'm sorry to you guys too." I glance between Eryn and Tate. "But nothing happened, please believe that." Wren's eyes narrow when I turn to him. "And I know you wanted to take me home first and explain everything on your own, but I couldn't let you do that. This was all my fault, start to finish. You shouldn't have to take the blame I deserve."

I hold my breath after that, waiting for Eryn to say something. It feels like a full minute goes by before she speaks.

"It sounds like it wasn't anybody's fault. And I believe that nothing happened, of course I do." Then she's moving toward me, and she doesn't stop until she's hugging me, maybe a little more stiffly than she did yesterday, but she doesn't pull away. Instead, she says something beyond mind-boggling. "Thank you for coming with him and explaining everything."

My throat is too thick to speak, so I just nod.

"I'm just relieved that everyone's okay. We didn't even know we were supposed to be worried about you too." Her expression falters for a moment. "Oh no, your mom. Is she freaking out? Does she even know you're okay?"

I'm finding it incredibly hard to talk when faced with this much unreasonable kindness, so I'm grateful when Wren answers for me.

"Her mom fell asleep early and now she thinks Lili just slipped out before she woke up."

Eryn looks relieved. For me.

"Well, at least that's something. I wasn't sure if we were just the first stop on the whole apology/explanation tour."

It is seriously a gut punch when she smiles at me like I didn't just spend the night in her boyfriend's arms.

Then, after a few more words, she kisses Wren on the cheek, but there's a brief hesitation before she pulls away. "Maybe keep a permanent set of museum keys with you from now on."

I've stayed silent throughout all of it, and I have no words when Tate tugs on my sleeve. "I could use some help in the back room."

I turn to follow him, but not before catching Wren's eyes over Eryn's shoulder.

He almost looks sorry.

And I can't decide for what.

TWENTY-TWO
Wren

As soon as Tate and Lili slip into the back room, a heavy silence settles over Eryn and me. It feels palpable, like an invisible wall between us. The hum of the museum's air conditioner fills the space, but it only amplifies the tension.

"Did you have to call out at the café?" I ask, my voice low, not wanting to disturb the fragile stillness.

Eryn adjusts the strap of her bag, glancing briefly at the clock on the wall. "I asked Elliot to cover for me. He didn't mind."

Right, the new guy she's been talking about. "That was nice of him."

A small smile touches her lips, and I can't be sure if it's for me or him. "I told him I'd help him perfect his bear claw recipe on Wednesday." There's a brief pause before she adds, "I figured you wouldn't mind since you and Lili were going to be here working."

So on our only mutual day off, Eryn and I will each be with other people. And for some reason we're both pretending that's fine.

I start trying to flip the scenario in my head. What if it were the other way around? What if Eryn had spent the night with Elliot, had fallen asleep with his arms around her?

Would I be angry? Hurt?

I honestly don't know.

"Eryn?" I say her name softly. She hesitates before meeting my gaze. "Are we okay?"

Her brows knit together. "Why wouldn't we be?" But it feels forced, as though she's trying to convince herself as much as me.

I sigh, my shoulders tensing. "I don't know. Doesn't something feel . . . off?"

She smiles, but it's shallow, not reaching her eyes. "I think we've just been busy. We're fine."

The words fall flat between us. I shake my head slowly. "I'm going to tell Lili I can't help her anymore." My throat tightens around what feels like a confession. I haven't been much help to her anyway, and last night only proved how much more drawn to her I've become—too much for comfort.

Eryn's smile falters for a moment, a flicker of something unreadable crossing her face, before she straightens. "I think you're overreacting. Don't you enjoy having someone to geek out over history with?"

I do. More than I should. "Yes, but—"

"Then don't quit." Her voice is firmer now. "We'll figure it out, we always do."

But we won't talk about it.

That used to feel like a relief, a reprieve from the constant probing questions everyone else threw my way after the accident. Being with Eryn meant I didn't have to explain, didn't have to relive every painful moment.

She never asked about physical therapy or what it was like to wake up in a body that no longer felt like mine. She didn't push me to talk to my dad when our visions for the museum clashed—she probably didn't even know. She's aware that my mom left when I was little, but nothing like what I told Lili last night.

And I'm no better when it comes to her life. I don't know why I sometimes see her waiting tables at the café instead of being full-time in the kitchen, or if she's upset about that. I don't know if her parents still fight the way they did when we were in high school. We've gotten so used to existing in a space where deep questions are off-limits that we don't even think about them anymore.

That used to feel right, or at least easier. Right now it just feels like an excuse.

I look at her, really look at her, and wonder if she's ever thought about what it would've been like if things were different. If we hadn't kissed on the beach that day, if I hadn't broken my back days later. Overnight she became the girl whose new boyfriend was in the ICU, fighting to hold on to his life.

What choice did she have?

What choice did I have?

I want to reach out, to touch her hand, to find some reassurance that we're still solid, still us. But my hands stay at my sides, clenched into fists, holding back the words that would unravel everything.

"We'll figure it out," she repeats, softer this time.

I nod, but my chest tightens. We've built our relationship on the foundation of avoidance, and I'm starting to feel the cracks.

⁂

Whatever Tate and Lili are talking about cuts off abruptly when I enter the back room. They aren't doing inventory or anything else that I can see.

"Eryn take off?" Tate, for once, doesn't have a snack, and he looks awkward, unsure what to do with his hands.

"Yeah. She said she's making orange-flavored morning buns and she'll save some for us if we all want to swing by at lunch."

Lili looks pained hearing this, but Tate just scoffs.

"Wow, are you the luckiest—" But then he shoves his hands in his pockets. "Never mind. I think you know exactly what you are right now."

Yeah, I do.

He starts backing toward the door. "Guess I gotta go do the things."

"What things?" Lili asks, her voice edged with something close to panic at the prospect of being left alone with me.

"You know, the things. I don't just walk around here looking pretty."

I hold the door for him.

"Right. So, I'll see you two *night owls*"—he pushes the word through his teeth as he holds my gaze—"for buns at noon?"

Lili doesn't respond, but she'll go. I'm not letting her skulk around, blaming herself for something that was more my fault than hers.

"Buns at noon," I say.

And then it's just me and Lili again. She pretends to stack books on the table, her movements too deliberate, too staged. I watch, giving her a minute to drop the act and face me, which, thankfully, she does.

Slamming a final book down, she squares her shoulders. "Okay, fine. You're mad."

"I never said I was mad."

She snorts. "Well, you usually are, so it's a fair guess."

I stare at her, taking in her appearance for the first time this morning. Her lips are extra red from how much she's been biting them, and her hair has tumbled loose from the hasty braid she pulled it back in while we were driving here. She looks like she just woke up in the best possible way, and after last night, I know exactly how soft her skin is.

Unlike her, I was still awake, barely, but enough to feel it when her head gently settled onto my shoulder and her tablet slipped from her hands. And when she curled into me, I was aware of wrapping my arm around her. I only meant to hold her for a moment. I even rationalized it by telling myself that I could more easily wake her if I was holding her. I was still rationalizing when I fell asleep too.

So, no, I wasn't mad last night, and looking at her now, I'm not sure I can summon anything close to that emotion. But I *should* be mad at myself. Instead, I'm thinking about how close we were, how easily we fit together. And how wrong it feels to want that again.

"You don't have to say it," she continues. "I know you're mad that I steamrolled your apology out there and stole your chance to fall on your sword. And you know what? I'm not sorry for doing it, because thanks to me, you still have a girlfriend."

"And that's what you want?"

I don't know who is more surprised by that question, me or her. I wasn't planning on asking it, but now that it's out there I know I won't take it back.

She opens and closes her mouth a couple of times. And then I catch the faintest hint of fear in her face. "Wren." That's all she says, but it's enough to shock me back into reality.

I mutter a curse under my breath.

Lili nods as if she can see the wheels turning in my head, that I'm trying to reel myself back in. My anger finally bubbles up, a delayed reaction, but there nonetheless.

"I never asked you to say anything to Eryn."

"No, but I could tell you were about to do something idiotic."

I lower my lids to half-mast. "I'd love to hear what you think idiotic sounds like."

A spark lights in her eyes, relief maybe, or something more. "You were going to drag her through every single thought you had last night, everything that could have happened, and all the nothing moments that did." She crosses her arms. "I told her what actually happened. You were going to destroy her over something that only exists in your guilty conscience."

I don't have an immediate response to that. I didn't have a plan when I arrived here and saw Eryn, I just knew I wasn't going to lie to her. I do feel guilty about last night. Maybe I didn't cross that big line, but I pushed it, more than once, and unless I'm mistaken, Lili pushed it too.

"So that's why you did it? You took all the blame so that Eryn and I wouldn't break up?"

Her arms slide down to her sides, and when she answers, I can hear the weariness in her voice. "I did it because Eryn doesn't deserve to be hurt over nothing."

I don't challenge that statement out loud, but I don't look away from her either, and my silence says a lot.

She breaks the stare first, glancing at the books she stacked. "I don't think we need to talk about this anymore. We don't open for another hour and a half, so I'm going to make sure the gift shop is ready for customers. Maybe you can—"

"Stay back here? Yeah," I say, fighting to keep my voice even. "And maybe . . . we should ease off the research for a while."

She goes perfectly still for a moment before giving me a quick nod.

TWENTY-THREE

Lili

All day at the museum, Wren and I avoid each other as much as possible. Every glance seems too loaded, too full of unsaid things, so we both just keep our heads down. And as soon as my shift is over, I don't stay to pore over Kezia's diary with him for a few more hours like I normally would. I just leave.

When I get home, the house is unnervingly quiet. The usual soundtrack—the rhythmic hum of saws, the buzz of sanders, and the '90s music Mom loves to blast—is all absent. It's as though all the life we've poured into this house since coming here has been sucked out.

I call out but no one answers. Even the simple click of a door opening upstairs is missing. I shoot off a quick text, but it remains unread. It's only after I notice the car is gone that I let a small thread of concern unspool in my chest. Maybe Goldie's still sick, and Mom took her to the doctor? The thought lingers, but I can't decide if something feels truly off or if it's just my own guilty conscience lingering.

After popping up to my room to finally change into fresh

clothes, I find myself out on the porch, sitting with my legs pulled up to my chest, waiting. The air is warm, but cooling as the sun sets. Time drags, and I stare out at the gravel road and listen to the wind as it rustles through the trees. An hour passes before I finally hear the distant rumble of Mom's car engine.

"Hey," she says as she climbs out of the car, a takeout bag dangling from her hand. Her voice carries a mix of exhaustion and surprise, like she's still catching her breath from the day. "I didn't think you'd beat me home, or I would've left a note. Hope you haven't been waiting long."

"Not long," I say, the words coming out a little too casual, but my gaze drifts to the empty passenger seat. "Goldie's not with you?"

"She was up before me this morning, fever gone, and too antsy to stay cooped up in the house. I checked with Mrs. Mayhew and she invited her over to explore some of the things her husband left behind." She steps up onto the porch, but then freezes, her eyes narrowing in sudden concern. "Please tell me you haven't used the upstairs sink?"

I frown, confusion crossing my face. "Yeah, I washed my face?" And brushed my teeth and everything else I would have done that morning if I hadn't woken up in Wren's truck and panic hadn't pushed all those thoughts right out of my head.

Mom shoves the takeout bag into my arms, then bolts through the door and upstairs, muttering under breath, "Please, please, please be okay."

By the time I get upstairs, she's standing in the bathroom doorway, leaning slightly, her face drawn but carrying the relief of someone who's just escaped a disaster. A weary smile pulls at her lips. "False alarm. Everything's fine."

"Okay," I say, my voice hesitant as I try to peer around her into the bathroom. "What was almost not fine?"

"The fifty-plus-year-old pipe that burst up here yesterday."

My mind reels for a moment, the guilt from earlier taking a backseat for the moment. "Wait, what?"

She sighs, pulling me back toward the stairs as she speaks. "Just use the kitchen sink for now, okay? Graham said there shouldn't be any issues until the parts I ordered come in, but I don't want to take any chances."

"Fine. I won't use the bathroom. But who is Graham?"

She glances over her shoulder at me, looking slightly surprised that I don't know. "Mr. Callaway, from the church."

"The architect?" I vaguely remembered Mrs. Mayhew introducing us to a well-dressed guy with a hint of salt in his pepper-black hair and laugh lines around his eyes that made him look older than he probably was. I guess maybe I saw them chatting together last Sunday too, but I didn't know they had much more than casual exchanges. "When did he go from Mr. Callaway to Graham?"

Mom cuts me a look at my teasing tone. "When he saved my butt and all the floors upstairs in this house yesterday." She steps into the kitchen, and I follow, watching as her hands rest on the counter. She stops for a second, then laughs softly. "I guess I can laugh about it now, but I was in full panic mode when it happened. Everything I tried to do just seemed to make it worse. I was up there with buckets and every towel in the house, trying not to wake Goldie." Her voice flattens as the memory plays out. "Did you know there are only five plumbers on the entire island, and all of them were either at other houses or off when I called?"

"You should have called me," I tell her, almost annoyed that she didn't. I don't know anything about plumbing, but I could've at least helped empty buckets. She shouldn't have had to deal with that alone, though clearly she didn't.

"Well, I called Graham instead," she says, turning to inspect one of the new cabinet hinges. "He must have rounded up half the church, including one of his sons, because he showed up with a small army after I called him. And then he stayed to wring out towels with me long after everyone else left."

"Wow, that was . . . really nice of him."

Mom stops pretending to look at cabinet doors. "It was a hectic situation, and we should all be glad to have a friend here who knows something about repairing the plumbing in these old houses."

I stand there watching her, wondering if there's more behind her smile than just gratitude. "Graham it is then." I hold her gaze, and she's the one who looks away first. "And I'm glad we have a *friend* here who'll help like that."

She shifts slightly, a quiet laugh escaping her as she rubs her forehead. "Don't say it like that," she says, but there's a faint twitch at the corner of her mouth, something reluctant and almost amused.

I widen my eyes. "I didn't say it any particular way." Except I kinda, maybe did. It wouldn't be the worst thing in the world for her to meet someone who's handy in one of the few ways she's not and who's kind enough to spend what is a pretty big holiday around here sopping up floors.

"I'll have to say thank you on Sunday," I add, the teasing gone now. The situation could've turned into a real nightmare if they hadn't been able to fix it. My own morning keeps replaying in my mind, and I can't help but imagine how much worse it could've gone if Eryn had reacted differently. I know I was pushing boundaries with Wren last night, emotionally if not physically. And unlike with the floors in our house, damage was definitely done.

Mom pauses in the act of unpacking the food. "Graham never said, but it was my fault. I'd been messing with the sink earlier in the day even though I don't know what I'm doing. It was going great until it wasn't." She pulls out another container, the plastic crinkling in her hands. "I told myself I wouldn't touch the pipes, but after all this time here, I started thinking that if I was just careful enough, nothing would go wrong." Mom keeps talking, oblivious to how still I've gone at her words. "And what happened? I nearly flooded the whole house."

I opt out of taking my bike when Mom sends me to get Goldie; it's not too far to walk, and right now, I need to feel the ground under my feet. The crunch of gravel and the soft give of the dirt beneath my sneakers. By the time the Mayhew house comes into view, I've managed to piece myself back together, at least on the surface.

The house is similar to ours—saltbox style with traditional gray siding and white trim—but it's been better cared for over the years. The shutters are freshly painted, the lawn neatly trimmed, and a row of vibrant hydrangeas lines the walkway. It's the kind of place that looks like it would be used in a "Visit Nantucket" ad.

I draw a deep breath, preparing my polite smile and hoping Goldie won't be too hard to extricate. Exhaustion from last night is catching up with me, and all I want is to get home. Just as I'm crossing the yard, the front door swings open, and my sister steps outside, calling back over her shoulder, "I will! And thank you!"

She stops short when she sees me. "What are you doing here?"

I cross my arms. "Hi to you too. Glad you're feeling better."

She rolls her eyes and drags her feet across the grass toward me. "Hi."

"Better."

"But seriously, what are you doing here?"

We start walking back toward our house. "I got home early, so Mom sent me to get you for dinner."

"Ooh, you got home early. Are we supposed to throw a parade?"

I blink at her, taken aback. "What's with the attitude?"

She shrugs.

"Anyway, I'm going to be home a little more from now on." Who knows how long this break from doing research with Wren will last. I watch Goldie to gauge her reaction. "I thought you'd be happy."

Another shrug.

"We can go thrifting now."

That perks her up. "Now?"

"I mean, not *now* now; Mom's waiting with dinner. But I don't have to work tomorrow."

"We can go back to Mrs. Mayhew's! She has the coolest stuff; you won't believe it." Goldie is already turning, and I have to catch her arm to stop her.

"You just left. And I'm sure she has her own dinner to eat."

"She likes it when I come over." Goldie jerks her arm free with a little more force than necessary, considering I'm barely holding it.

"Fine, whatever, but we're not going back right now. I told you we'll go somewhere—"

"—tomorrow. Yeah, I won't hold my breath." That's a lot of sarcasm for most ten-year-olds, but Goldie is a pro. She doesn't even look at me when she says it.

"Hey." I stop walking, and she takes a few more steps before reluctantly stopping too. "What is with you?"

"How do I know you'll even be around tomorrow? You weren't here yesterday. Or last night."

Ice trickles down my back. "What do you mean?"

"I'm not stupid. I know you didn't come home."

That ice pierces through to my insides. "Why didn't you say anything to Mom?"

"Because now I know something that you don't want her to know."

"You're going to blackmail me?" Who is my little sister right now?

She smiles at me coldly, and I shiver. "We're going thrifting tomorrow."

"I already said I'd take you. You don't have to do it like this."

"This way, you can't break your promise. And I want to show you Mrs. Mayhew's house too."

I shake my head and start walking, quickly passing her. She hurries to catch up.

"It's not gonna be terrible," she tells me. "Just wait until you see inside."

I don't answer her.

"Where were you last night anyway? With Wren?"

"I was doing research and accidentally fell asleep."

"If that's true, then why didn't you just explain it to Mom?"

"Because I didn't feel like getting into it. And I don't feel like getting into it with you either."

"Are you still looking at Kezia Gardner's diary?"

I'm not even going to ask how she knows about that. "Yes."

"Can I look at it?"

"No."

She's silent for a minute, and I have a strong suspicion that she's considering forcing me, but she doesn't.

"I could help."

"No, you couldn't. Dad, me, and"—I hesitate for some reason, not wanting to say Wren's name—"a museum expert are struggling with it. What could you possibly do?"

"I just wanted to see it," she mumbles under her breath. "Why is it so important anyway?"

She's deliberately walking slowly to drag this out, and I'm seriously tempted to just leave her behind. Instead, the words gush out of me. "Because Dad died before he could prove that she wasn't the villain everyone said she was, so now I have to prove it for him. And it's really hard, and I feel like I don't have enough time. The time I do have, I'm constantly being pulled between you and Mom and the museum, and now things with Wren are more complicated, and I don't know if I can do it all, okay?" I gasp after it all pours out of me.

"Okay," she says quietly. Then, "I won't say anything to Mom. You don't have to come with me tomorrow."

We stay quiet until we reach the door. "We can do one or the other—thrifting in town or Mrs. Mayhew's. Which is it going to be?"

Her face scrunches up as she thinks. I'm surprised this is such a hard decision for her. Thrift stores are like her Disneyland. Finally, she sighs. "Mrs. Mayhew's."

"You're sure?"

She doesn't look giddy about it the way I expected, but she does look determined. She gives me one firm nod.

"Okay then, tomorrow it is."

TWENTY-FOUR
Lili

When I wake up the next morning and turn over in my bed, it's to find Goldie awake and staring at me with her practiced creepy doll smile on her face.

"Ah!" I scowl and roll back over to face the other side. "Mom told you not to do that to me anymore."

I hear her sit up in bed. "I haven't done it since Arizona. You should be thanking me."

"No," I say, my voice muffled from my pillow.

And then my bed is moving, jerking under the weight of her bouncing on her knees. "Come on, get up. You promised to come with me to Mrs. Mayhew's today."

"Goldie! Stop!"

The bouncing slows. "Okay, but get up. Please."

It's the *please* that drains my irritation away. That and the fact that I'm witnessing weeks of pent-up impatience from a ten-year-old. Honestly, I should be thanking her for only a creepy smile and jumping on my bed. I'd have been way worse at her age.

"Fine, but stop so I can get up."

She climbs off and I take my time sitting up, doing the whole yawn and stretching thing, noticing that Goldie is already fully dressed and even has her shoes on.

"Lili." My name is a whine coming from her.

"I'm moving."

Her huffed response says not fast enough.

"What is the big hurry? It's not like we're gonna show up at this woman's house this early anyway."

"Her name is Mrs. Mayhew. And Stan and Ollie wake her every morning at five a.m. anyway."

I pause in the act of digging through my nightstand that doubles as a dresser. "Who?"

"Her cats. They're Maine coons and both weigh over twenty-five pounds. She brought Ollie with her the first day we met her." I can hear a bit of accusation coming from my sister that I didn't remember this.

"Fine, whatever. Do I at least have time to take a shower?"

"Why? We have to get through some old boxes and everything's really dusty."

Great. "Are you sure you wouldn't just rather go thrifting in town?"

Goldie can't nod her head fast enough. "Positive."

Keeping her dust comment in mind, I grab my least favorite pair of jeans and a T-shirt that I usually wear only when helping Mom paint something, then I twirl my finger at my sister to turn around so I don't flash her while getting dressed. She does a good impression of someone whose bones are melting as she begrudgingly turns.

I make things worse when I insist that we eat breakfast. Never have I ever seen a kid scarf down Fruity Pebbles so fast. I, on the other hand, eat at a normal human pace, which gives Mom a chance to come down and join us.

She kisses us both on the head on her way to the fridge. "Well, this is a nice sight." Then she sees the full pot of coffee I've already made and gives me a second kiss on the head.

Goldie blurts out our plans for the morning with way more excitement than a kid should have at the prospect of digging through someone's old stuff.

It's not like I planned on being so absent, it just happened. But the fact that something so little is bringing her this much happiness just makes me feel guilty all over again for putting her off so much.

I hurry to finish the rest of my breakfast, then, with an apologetic look to Mom, leave the dishes for her to do. One more thing this house doesn't have is a dishwasher. I don't think she minds, though, and seeing the way that Goldie is bouncing in the doorway, she certainly understands.

"Go," she whispers to me. Followed by "thank you."

Mrs. Mayhew has indeed been up since 5 a.m., which she cheerfully informs us of when she pushes open her front door.

"Ollie just could not wait for his breakfast this morning, could you, my boy?" The big cat she's holding licks his lips while another seemingly identical cat winds between her feet. "Yes, you too, my sweet Stan. Now let's move back so our guest can come in." The cat in her arms meows. "Yes, you are right, Ollie, *guests* plural." Then she looks at me as though noticing Goldie isn't alone for the first time. "Lili! It's so nice to see you again."

"Nice to see you too, Mrs. Mayhew. I hope it's all right that we just dropped by like this."

"Of course, I told Goldie she's always welcome and now you know you're always welcome too. The boys and I just love company, don't we?" She bends down to scoop up the second cat, then jiggles them both until they meow.

My sister grabs my arm and tugs me in after her, and I choke back a gasp once we step inside.

Cat houses, dozens of them in all shapes and sizes, and so many scratching posts. The furniture is covered by pillows with cat faces crocheted on them, blankets with little paws stitched onto them. A mirror shaped like a cat head rests above the fireplace, and every single surface everywhere is covered with cat figurines. In contrast, there are empty shelves angling up and down all over the walls that I don't understand until Mrs. Mayhew lowers her cats to the ground and Stan and Ollie immediately dart up them like ramps. I'm not even allergic to cats, but I feel the need to sneeze just looking at everything.

"So," she says with a grin at me. "I hear you've been spending quite a bit of time at that museum I recommended."

I turn away from a floor-to-ceiling cat tree shaped like a pirate ship, complete with tiny portholes for the cats to peek through, miniature sails for them to climb, and even a crow's nest at the top. "Yes, thank you for that. Wren has been a huge help."

She beams. "He's such a sweet boy, isn't he? You tell him he's still got my MacKenzie-Childs black-and-white casserole dish."

I don't know what that means but I guess Wren will. "Sure, I'll let him know."

Goldie nudges me to move forward. "Come on, I want to show

you something." Then to Mrs. Mayhew: "Can I show my sister what I found yesterday?"

Mrs. Mayhew is in the middle of scolding one of her cats for biting the other one and waves us off. "Of course, sweetie. Just mind the Swarovski cats on the desk."

Goldie leads me through the living room, then down a hall that has just as many framed cat photos lining its walls as it does people photos, and pushes open a door that leads into what looks like a library.

As soon as we're inside, I turn around to face my sister. "You could have warned me that we were about to enter the house of a thousand cat figurines."

"There are only three hundred eighty-one cat figurines," Goldie corrects before moving to a specific bookshelf. She runs her finger along the spines, yanks a book out, and quickly hides it behind her back.

"What's your favorite book in the whole world right now?"

I resist the urge to roll my eyes. "That's an impossible question. You have to at least narrow down by genre." Then I frown at her. "Wait, are you holding a first edition of *Anne of Green Gables* or something? Because that would be pretty cool."

Goldie grins and shakes her head.

"I'm supposed to keep guessing?"

She nods, still grinning like a maniac.

"*The Hobbit*? *The Lion, the Witch, and the Wardrobe*?"

More head shaking.

"Anything by Jane Austen? What then? Am I at least warm?"

"Older than Jane Austen. At least I think. When did she write stuff?"

"Early 1800s."

"Okay yeah, before that."

I frown. "You have something that was written in the eighteenth century?"

She bites her lips and nods.

I throw my hand out and make a half circle in the room. Everything I see looks like cats. I'm trying to think of the oldest cat book I know and I'm coming up blank. "I don't know, *Puss in Boots* or something?"

She starts to shake her head again but must sense that I'm getting tired of this game. "Fine, I'll give you a hint. Her initials are K. G."

"K. G.? And it's a her, from the eighteenth century?"

Goldie looks ready to burst.

"What? What am I not getting—" And then I feel the blood drain from my face. "Kezia Gardner. Are you trying to tell me you found another one of Kezia Gardner's diaries?"

"Not exactly." Goldie whips the book out from behind her back, and the next second she's shoving it into my hands.

I stare down at an obviously faux leather cover that's starting to crack and lift away from the corners. And then I sigh. "Goldie, this looks like a photo album from the 1980s. You're about two hundred years off."

"Just look inside," she insists, leaning closer.

I flip open the cover, expecting to see yellowed photographs or postcards from decades earlier. Instead, my eyes land on handwriting—unfamiliar but unmistakably old. I scan it quickly, not comprehending anything until the name at the top snags my eye.

My breath catches in my throat.

The world seems to shrink around me, focusing solely on the inked letters. My heart pounds as the lines sharpen, revealing the name I've been obsessing over since finding Dad's notebook: *Kezia Gardner*.

I run my fingers lightly over the plastic-covered page. The room around me fades away, replaced by the weight of history, the whispers of the past echoing in the strokes of each letter. And there's a date at the top: *1776 Sunday, December 22*. She would have received this letter mere days after the most recent diary entries Wren and I transcribed, where she wrote about the increasing restrictions for Nantucket vessels and strongly condemned the revolutionary cause. I close the album with shaking hands. Because there's another name on this letter, and I recognize it too.

Slowly, I sit down in the nearest chair, the magnitude of what I might be holding sinking in.

Goldie watches me, her earlier excitement now tinged with concern. "I thought you'd be more impressed," she says quietly. "I know it's kind of hard to read, but that's her name at the top, isn't it?"

I nod, barely able to process her words. "Where did you find this?" My voice comes out quieter than I intended, almost reverent.

"Mrs. Mayhew's husband collected a lot of old stuff about Nantucket," Goldie explains, her voice a distant hum in my ears. "I started going through it to help her sell it, but then I found a bunch of letters and stuff like this—"

I grab her arm, the urgency bubbling up. "More letters? You found more letters to Kezia Gardner?"

She twists free, her excitement reignited. "There are a lot of boxes in the attic. But it's cramped and dusty up there so I didn't look long. Maybe."

I stare at her, my brain barely processing the information. Each word she says adds to the growing storm of thoughts in my head. The only clear, solid thought is a name: Wren.

I carefully set the album on the table beside me and pull out my phone.

TWENTY-FIVE

Wren

It takes Eryn less than ten minutes to dash into her house and shower off the last bit of her mermaid makeup following our early—and thankfully only—mermaid-sighting tour of the day.

When she gets back into my truck, she leans over to give me a quick, almost perfunctory kiss. A hollowness hits me when I realize I can't remember how long it's been since it felt like more than that from either of us.

"Aren't we going to eat?" she asks when I don't start the engine right away. "Because the brunch crowd is going to be intense if we wait much longer."

I'm not thinking about food though, and I think she can tell. She meets my gaze.

"The weekend is over. It's done and dealt with. I'm not interested in rehashing any of it and I don't need you to feel like you have to overcompensate with me. We're fine. Let's go eat." She gives me a smile that's as close to normal as she can make it, but it falls just short enough to speak louder than her words.

"Tell me something, Eryn." My voice comes out quieter than I intended.

She pauses mid-buckle of her seatbelt, her hands stilling as she looks at me, waiting.

"Do you remember our first kiss?"

Her expression turns puzzled, not because she doesn't remember but because I've never asked her this before.

She makes a halfhearted lunge for my phone when I pull it out.

"What? You're the one who posted the video. Did you take it down?"

"No, because it was cute at the time, and it was the start of us." But she stops trying to grab the phone away from me. "Fine, but just know it'll be super embarrassing."

We have to scroll pretty far back in her feed through lots of mermaid and baking content, far more of the latter than the former, before I tap the thumbnail showing me walking toward her on Brant Point Beach—because I could still walk then—just after sunset with a pizza box in my hands. "Electric Love" by Børns plays as the lighthouse looms in the background. I angle the phone so Eryn can see the screen.

We were fifteen at the time, and we both look young in the video, especially me. Shirtless, barefoot, and with my hair so overgrown that it was starting to curl at my neck. I looked like I didn't have a care in the world, and back then, it was true.

Eryn looks almost the same. Her straight black hair was shorter, but otherwise she's even dressed almost the same today, in a cropped white tank and cutoffs.

"Do we really want to watch this now?" She looks over despite her words.

The music is too loud to hear what we're saying, and the golden hour had come and gone, so there are quite a few shadows too, but to my surprise, I remember it all too well. "I was asking you why your phone was set up to record."

"And I told you I wanted some pictures of you, me, and Tate, but obviously, I never invited him."

It was just the two of us alone on the beach, and for whatever reason, I had started to get that feeling like something was off. I should have just asked her if something was wrong, but that level of maturity was beyond me at that point. I went for the dumb joke instead.

I smile, watching myself try to be cool. "There I am, telling you they were out of pepperoni, so I got sardines instead. You were so disappointed, but you still told me it was fine." I laugh and shift the phone closer to her. "Look at the way you're frowning at the box."

"I didn't want to make you feel bad."

I lift my gaze from the screen to stare at her profile, saying softly, "No, you never did, did you?"

The moment is coming then; I'd know it from the look on her face now, even without the musical cue in the video. I remember telling her I was kidding about the pizza, and just as I was lifting the lid to show her, one of my best friends since kindergarten grabbed my face and kissed me.

Beside me now, Eryn covers her face. "I can't believe I did that."

I couldn't either. I didn't have a clue that she liked me that way. In the video, she pulls away then runs out of frame and I immediately take off after her. End of clip.

The comments under the video are full of heart eyes and plenty of romantic movie–level speculation on what happened when I caught up with her.

I put my phone down. There's no footage of what happened next, and we would've never posted it if there were.

I'd frozen when she first kissed me. There was nothing I expected less in that moment than Eryn's mouth on mine, so I did the worst thing I could've possibly done in her mind.

I didn't kiss her back.

In hindsight, I should have seen something like that happening. We spent enough time together, and despite Tate and half the school constantly teasing us, I'd just never looked at her that way, and before that night on the beach, I didn't think she looked at me that way either. I'd kissed a few other girls by that point, so it wasn't the kiss itself that threw me, it was the girl whose lips were pressed against mine. Eryn wasn't any other girl, and in my head, I'd always categorized her as the non-kissing kind. My brain couldn't make the switch fast enough.

She hadn't run far, so I caught up to her where the tide was sliding over our feet. She had her arms wrapped tightly around herself, and I remember how close to tears she was.

I'd never seen her cry before, not really, but I knew instinctively that I didn't ever want to be the cause. My brain still wasn't ready to move her into the kissing category, but I didn't know what else to do.

So I kissed her.

It all just kind of happened after that. Me and Eryn.

And then I got hurt days later and everything changed. I barely saw how *I* was supposed to fit into my new reality, let alone how she would. But she surprised me then too.

She didn't panic and run; she didn't even gradually fade away like most of my other friends. She stayed. She was there for my dad and me even when I tried to push her away. And once I realized my life didn't end with my wheelchair, she was still there.

And I . . . I know we wouldn't have made it without her.

I take her hand now, startling her out of her remembered embarrassment, and tell her, "I can't imagine these past four years without you."

She tucks her wet hair behind her ear with her free hand. "Me either."

Her smile has real warmth to it this time, but it fades when my phone dings and we both see the text that comes through.

Lili: Whatever you're doing, stop and call me right now.

TWENTY-SIX
Wren

Eryn sees the text from Lili when it flashes on my phone, but doesn't react the way anyone else in her position might.

She doesn't frown or sigh, she just sits back and in a normal voice says, "I hope everything is okay."

"I'll just be a second," I tell her, lifting the phone to my ear.

Lili answers on the first ring.

"Wren. Where are you and how quickly can you get to my neighbor's house?"

"What's going on? Your voice is all high and shaky." I make eye contact with Eryn, who is leaning in, trying to hear.

"Everything is fine, but you need to come over now. Not my house, my neighbor's house."

"Is something wrong with Mrs. Mayhew?" I'm reaching for the gear shift before I've even finished speaking.

"No, she fine, the cats are fine." I hear her inhale like she's trying to steady her voice. "Wren, I found something. And I'm honestly afraid to look at it too closely without you. It might be—"

There's another pause. "If it's real, then I'm holding a letter written to Kezia Gardner dated December 22, 1776."

"Did you say the twenty-second?"

"Yes. Tell me I'm wrong about what good King George passed that day."

I clutch the phone tighter. "The Prohibitory Act." It was the tipping point for the Revolutionary War when Britain barred any country from trading with the US, on pain of forfeiture of the ship and all goods to the Crown.

There's absolute silence from Lili's end of the phone.

"Who's it from?"

She doesn't answer.

"Lili, who was writing to her?"

"It's from Edmund Harrington."

I close my eyes.

"Do you recognize that name?" she asks, almost in a whisper.

"Yeah, I recognize it. He, um, was an American-born merchant and customs official who worked for the British government. He was a Loyalist through and through."

"Well," she says, her lighthearted words immediately undercut by the break in her voice. "That doesn't look good for my girl, does it?"

"Did you read it?" When she doesn't answer, I soften my voice. "Lili, did you read it? And remember I can't see if you're shaking your head."

There's a watery laugh coming from her end of the phone. "No, I didn't read it. Edmund has terrible penmanship and"—she clears her throat—"there are a lot of creases. Someone folded and unfolded it many times. It'll take some time to transcribe it."

Which means it was reread again and again. Kezia wanted to make sure she didn't miss a thing. If it's real.

"It might be fake. Or about nothing. Or about literally anything else."

I hear her sniff. "See, I know it's bad when you start being nice to me."

I am acutely aware of Eryn sitting quietly beside me during this conversation and, while there's no judgment coming off from her, there's plenty going on within me. Because I want to rush over to Lili, to be there for her, and dig into this thing until she's smiling again. Hearing her break on the phone like this is killing me.

I glance over at Eryn. "I can't meet you right now, but I'll try to call you later and—"

Eryn takes the phone right out of my hand. "Lili? Yeah, he'll come. No, it's fine. I hope you guys can find something helpful. Sure, okay. Bye." Then she's pushing her door open.

"Wait a minute, what about going to eat?"

"I'll come by the museum later," she replies. "This sounds kind of urgent, doesn't it? And I'm not sure that I got all the seawater out of my hair."

"Yes, you are. Why not just come with me?"

"Because I have no idea who Edmund Harry-whatever is or why you looked so upset hearing his name. I'd just be in the way, and bored. Go," she says again, this time from outside the truck. "It's better this way, trust me."

Several minutes later, I see Lili pacing in front of the dirt road that meanders off to Mrs. Mayhew's home. She's chewing on her lip and squeezing her elbows, but the second she looks up and spots me, it's like all the tension leaves her body.

And slams right into mine.

She crosses the front of my truck to the passenger door. I lean over to push it open for her, tracing her features when she sweeps her bangs to the side and smiles at me like I'm the best thing she's seen all day too.

I swallow. "You okay?"

She nods a little too quickly. "I said I wanted answers, right?" She squeezes her fingers around a puffy leather photo album in her lap. "So why do I feel like I'm adrift on the ocean and there's this huge wave waiting to capsize my raft?"

"Because you might be holding something that condemns your ancestor." I keep my tone gentle. At this point I've invested in Kezia's story too. Lili even had me doubting myself a little after she debunked the Mitchell account.

"I want it to be fake," she confesses.

"I know."

Her voice is barely audible when she lowers her head and adds, "But I don't think it is."

"Hey," I say, reaching out to push her fallen hair back from her face. It's the first time I've been the one to reach out and touch her. My fingers graze the side of her cheek as she turns to look at me with eyes that have gone shiny. "Let me see."

She lets me ease the album from her grip, and then we're both holding our breath as I open it.

The shiny, plastic film encasing the letter catches the sunlight at first, forcing me to lift the album up at angle to see it clearly.

The letter is written on paper yellowed from age with slightly frayed edges and a tear on the bottom right corner. The ink has faded to a brownish-black, typical of how iron gall ink from the time would have aged. I try to keep my breathing under control as I carefully turn the protected page over. The wax seal I'm both hoping and dreading to find isn't there, but the roughly round stain it left attests to the letter once having been sealed.

Lili is fidgeting beside me, waiting for a verdict that she knows she's not prepared for. "Is it—?"

I shake my head, not an answer, just a delay. "I don't know," I finally tell her. And then, because I know she won't be satisfied with a simple yes or no—which history rarely gives us—I let her in on where my thoughts are.

"Without testing the paper, I can't say for sure how old it is, but McCleave's has documents from the same time period and, with allowances given for the amount of handling, I wouldn't argue with the date on the front."

"What about the name?" Lili presses, and not just with her words; she's leaning into me to better see the letter.

"I'd have to do some research and compare the handwriting with other known examples from Edmund Harrington. I'd just be speculating at this point."

She slumps beside me. "So either it's real or someone from the same time forged his signature?"

"It's real as in it's old, but as to whether or not Harrington wrote it . . ."

I turn the other plastic pages and see a few other old letters. It will take time to transcribe them, but from what I can make out of the names, they're all to Kezia from friends and family, including one from her famous cousin, Benjamin Franklin, about sending her a pair of snuffers and some candlesticks.

"I can't believe Mr. Mayhew just had these in a photo album," I say, showing Lili. "Anything of note in any of the other letters?"

"Not that I saw, but they are all addressed to Kezia. Well except for an older copy of the Ewer map in the back," Lili says. "I guess maybe he just stuck that in there?"

The final "page" shows what does at first look like the famous Ewer map of Nantucket from 1869, which is universally considered one of the most detailed and significant maps of the island from the era. Unlike earlier efforts, which often provided only rough outlines of Nantucket, Reverend Ferdinand Ewer captured the island with remarkable precision, including its harbors, inlets, and settlements. McCleave's even has a copy hanging in the gift shop, albeit with several additions indicating where our various exhibits were "found." I'm about to turn back to the Harrington letter when other details—unfamiliar details—start jumping out at me.

"I don't think this is the Ewer map."

"What? Yes, it is. Look at the—" But she cuts herself off when I carefully slide it out and unfold it.

"Ewer based his map on Henry Walling's trigonometrical survey of the state, but added details that made his map invaluable not only to navigators and merchants but also to military planners and smugglers."

Lili stares at the map, seeing but not understanding. "Okay, and don't take this the wrong way, but so? Both of those maps were created years after Kezia died."

I shift the map closer to her. "*They* were. *This?* This looks a lot closer to the map J. Hector St. John de Crèvecoeur published in 1782, but with far more detail." There were subtle differences though, like a decorative coastal hachure border around the coastline and a rope-twist pattern at the map's edges.

"I don't know that one."

"Whatever it is, if Mayhew had it in here with all these other letters to Kezia, then it's possible, even probable, that she had it too." Maybe it means something, maybe it doesn't, but the letter from Edmund Harrington dated the same day as the Prohibitory Act is potentially bad enough for her dad's theory.

"Wren." Her voice softens. "It's okay. Whatever it ends up meaning."

She says that, but I can tell she's far from okay. She's got more than Kezia's reputation hanging in the balance here, and that reminder instantly sobers me.

"There's more. Boxes of who knows what. Goldie made it sound like you could fill a museum with the things Mr. Mayhew collected."

My heart, which has been racing since I opened the album, pounds from more than just that possibility. Even in the middle of all this new evidence about Kezia—and likely not good evidence from Lili's point of view—she's thinking about what this all might mean for me.

I've got to get out of this truck and quick, because if I stay pressed up against her any longer while she's looking at me like I'm the only person on the planet who she wants beside her for this, I'm going to end up hating myself for what I do.

I slide fully back to my side of the truck and shift into drive, heading up the road to Mrs. Mayhew's house.

I rock the truck a little harder than necessary when I hit the brakes, but Lili doesn't complain. She's excited too, even if it's tinged with uncertainty, and is out of the truck in a moment, ready to dash up those three simple steps and the many more inside without a second thought.

I don't get out of my truck.

Lili makes it halfway across the yard before coming to a halt and slowly turning back to me. We make eye contact through the windshield, and then she's letting her eyes close for a moment or two before walking back toward me and resting her hands on my open window frame.

"Where did you say these boxes are?" I ask, going for cool and collected instead of raw and frustrated as I stare up at the two-story house that I've been in only a few times—through a back door similar to the one at Lili's house—and whose first floor I've never seen beyond. It didn't occur to me that I'd need access to more than that.

"The attic, or I guess it's more of a crawl space." Lili looks directly at me. "I'm sorry. I saw the letters and I didn't stop to think about anything else when I called you."

It's not her job to have to worry about stuff like that. I still remember a time when I didn't have to think about it constantly. I'm usually very careful about the places I go. I know where I fit and where I don't, so it's not often that I'm confronted with places that aren't designed for people like me.

"What if Goldie and I helped rock your chair back and up the first set of stairs? I think we could—"

"No, you couldn't." My voice is hard. "You and your kid sister aren't gonna lift me and my wheelchair up anything."

"We could try," she says, sounding both apologetic and defensive.

I almost laugh at her. "And then what? Hey, maybe you could carry my feet and she could grab my hands and you guys could just drag me up one step at a time? Yeah, that's a great idea. And then, after that, it'll be super easy to get into the attic. Do you wanna run inside real quick and find out if it's up more steps or one of those fun, pulldown-ladder types? Because if it's a ladder, maybe you could just tie a rope around me and then you guys could hoist me up. That could work if you get the old lady to pull too." I start to push my door open then as though I'm getting ready to get out, but Lili straightens and locks her arms to keep it from opening more than a few inches.

"I said I was sorry; you don't have to make fun of me for trying to figure out a way to fix this."

"Then don't make it so easy."

Her face flushes but she keeps her voice mostly steady. "You're not mad at me, you're mad at the situation. I am too, but you don't need to take it out on me just because I'm the only one here."

I look at her and think back to that first day she walked into my museum. I didn't see it then, the gut punch she would be to my life, but I can't escape it now. "Not mad at you?" I don't try to hide how incredulous I find that statement. "All I do is think about you, and that's not supposed to make me mad? It makes me insane!"

She lowers her arms from my door and stares at me like I'm suddenly holding a weapon.

"I can't get away from you, and when I try, all it takes is one call and I come running. And for what? A tourist girl who doesn't know the first thing about my life?"

"I know plenty about you." Her eyes are shining again and her voice breaks. "And we both know you don't see me as just a tourist anymore."

"But I need to." I lean through the window, forcing her back a step. "You think I want to do this to Eryn? She's amazing and sweet and for whatever reason, she loves me. And that's been good for me for years. I was fine, and I could have kept on being fine until you showed up and ruined that for me."

"I didn't do anything to you."

No, she didn't, but I can't seem to stop lashing out at her anyway. "I was with Eryn when you texted, but the second I heard your voice, I wanted to be where you were." I slump back against my seat. All these thoughts have been building in my head for weeks now, and they all boiled down to that one admission.

I hate myself for making it.

She looks as stricken as I feel, and I know that there's no coming back from this. I meet her gaze, drink in the clear green color that has been painting my dreams emerald and sage, for what I have to hope is the last time. I don't yell or even raise my voice.

"Before you, I thought I had the girl I could be happy with. Now I know the best I can do is try not to let her see how much I want to be with someone else."

I stop to breathe then, too fast and too hard, because I didn't want to say that, I didn't want to know that, and based on the tear that slips down Lili's cheek, she didn't want to know it either.

"I may not be able to give Eryn everything she deserves, but I can be loyal, I can not break her heart. I can be better than my mother was to my dad."

TWENTY-SEVEN

Lili

I hug my arms around myself as Wren backs down the road, turns, and drives off without looking back. I didn't even get a chance to say anything, to defend myself or explain.

Or tell him not to go.

I turn away and angrily brush the tear from my cheek. That's when I see Goldie push open the screen door and step out onto the porch. There's no way to know how much she overheard, but Wren hadn't exactly been quiet.

Whatever she heard, she knows enough to be silent now as I walk over to her and hand the album back to her.

"Please thank Mrs. Mayhew for letting me see some of her husband's collection, but I can't look at anything else right now." Then I turn and start back down the steps.

"You're leaving? What about the other letters? There's so much stuff, Lili. We could spend days going through it all together."

I completely ignore the hopeful pitch in her voice as I continue walking. "You can't understand this, but right now, the last thing I care about is the past."

She hurries after me, trying to keep pace with my quicker stride. "Please? Just for a little bit." When I show no sign of slowing, she leans in a little closer, her face hardening. "I could still tell Mom that you didn't come home the other night. She won't let you go back to the museum."

I laugh but my chin also trembles. "Go ahead. I don't think I'll be going back anyway."

She stops walking then. She played her trump card and lost. I guess I did too.

I quicken my pace. This wasn't supposed to happen this way. It's true I hadn't exactly thought much about anything after I texted Wren, at least nothing practical. I wasn't ready to process the blow that this letter from a British official to Kezia was to my dad's theory, so instead, I'd focused on Wren. I had imagined the look on his face when I first showed him the letter, the way he'd stare at me when I told him there was more, and the hours we'd get to spend close together poring through everything.

I've been telling myself I don't want more than that from him—nothing that would hurt anyone in the long run. But with each step, that belief weakens.

Because this *hurts*.

Because he *does* have someone else.

She *is* the one he's with.

And I'm just supposed to be the tourist he's tolerating for the summer in exchange for free help at McCleave's.

It's all so much worse now, knowing what he had no right to ever tell me. For weeks, I've been reining in my emotions, pulling myself back each time my heart leaned toward his. I could barely admit my feelings to myself. I would *never* have said anything to him.

For Eryn's sake and for his. And for mine, because it was so much better when all I had were my own impossible, unacknowledgeable feelings. Those I could handle. Those I could deny. Those I could pretend didn't exist.

But I don't know how to get away from this when according to him, it's my fault that he can't stop thinking about me. I'm to blame for his feelings. I'm the reason his relationship with Eryn will always be a little bit worse.

I stop abruptly, my foot hovering over the first step of the rebuilt porch in front of my house. He blamed me, accused me, and left without giving me a chance to defend myself—or to point out that it was his actions that caused the most damage.

I turn before the plan fully forms in my mind, heading not back to Mrs. Mayhew's and the answers that will now have to wait, but toward the shed and the bike I left parked inside.

The first time I walked into McCleave's Museum at the start of the summer, I'd been nervous and hopeful, and maybe just the tiniest bit scared—even before I saw the mermaid skeleton. This time it's an entirely different emotion fueling my steps.

I ignore the other visitors and thankfully avoid Tate's notice as he checks out a family in the gift shop. No one tries to stop me as I stride toward the Employees Only door and push it open.

I know he's in there before I even see him at the long worktable where we've spent countless hours sitting side by side trying to put Kezia's story together. He's not looking at her diary now. He's not looking at anything except a blank surface, and when he lifts his head and our gazes meet, I almost lose my resolve.

Almost.

"Lili? What—"

I shake my head and walk closer, stopping when only the table separates us. "No, it's my turn to talk." I take a breath. "You said a lot of really unfair things to me."

He drops his head forward again. "I know."

"Good," I say, but his visible lack of animosity now doesn't change anything. "Because I didn't deserve almost any of it. I am sorry about the house and the stairs and for not thinking. I'm not going to stand here and pretend that I understand anything about what that's like for you. But I was trying to help figure out a way for us to still do what we were there to do, and the way you shot me down was— Wren, it was cruel." My voice automatically starts to soften and I have to fight to push it back up. "I think I've earned a little bit of understanding from you by now. Because there are about a million different ways you could've reacted, and you chose the one that you knew would be the most unkind, and then you turned it into this whole other thing without even giving me a chance to react." I pick up speed because there's no way I'm going to risk him interrupting me now.

"And yes, I know I'm here doing the exact same thing to you, but too bad. You do not get to blame me for whatever feelings you have for me, not when you're the one with a girlfriend. You're the one who's not available, you're the one who I'm not allowed to want, because if I do, then I'm the bad guy." All my righteous anger is no match for the actual heartbreak I feel saying this to him. "I don't want to be that person, and up until today, you'd been making that really, really hard for me."

Now would be a great time for him to yell at me or even blame me again, to call me Tourist Girl and mean it the same way he did that first day we met. Anything to chase away this lump in my throat.

He's certainly breathing hard enough that I expect it, and when he opens his mouth, his voice is hard. It's his words that aren't.

"Come here."

I frown because I really need to feel a certain way right now and I don't trust my reaction to anything less than anger from him. "What?"

His eyes lock with mine. "I said, 'Come here.'"

I shouldn't be going anywhere near him, but my legs have other ideas and I'm rounding the table before I can decide if getting closer to him is the worst idea I've ever had. As soon as I'm within reach of him, I don't have to walk anymore.

Those exact same arms that I casually admired that first day in the museum gift shop are around me, pulling me closer until I have no choice but to stumble into his lap. And when he slides his hand up my neck and to my jaw, lifting my face to his, I could've stopped breathing more easily than I could've stopped what happened next.

"It's not your fault," he says, and I feel his breath ghost over my lips. "It was never anybody's fault but mine." His gaze drops to my mouth, and I know I need to pull away now as his thumb brushes my skin, before either of us forgets why this can't happen.

Because I can't think beyond his arms and his face and how little it would take to feel his lips against mine.

Oh please don't do this, don't want this, don't grab his shirt and lift your mouth that final fraction of an inch. Please. Please.

And that's when we both hear the door open. And that sudden shocked breath that reminds us that there has always been only one truly innocent person in all this, and she now knows exactly how guilty Wren and I are.

TWENTY-EIGHT

Wren

There are moments in life that sear their way into your mind so deeply and so painfully that you can recall them with excruciating clarity until the day you die, maybe even longer than that.

The split second when I was about to surface from my very last cliff jump and instead felt the worst physical pain I could imagine when Tate landed on me and my body literally snapped in half, my spinal cord shredding apart like a stick of string cheese, is one of them.

Seeing Eryn's face as I hold Lili in my lap, so close to kissing her that we're sharing the same breath, is another.

I think I'd rather break my back again.

The color drains from Eryn's face in an instant as Lili jumps up, but her expression takes longer to process what she's seeing. It lingers blank and stunned on her face like a casualty of a relationship that's dying before her eyes. And when it finally crumbles, it's like that small movement took all the energy she had, leaving her locked in place with her white-knuckled hand on the door.

"Eryn." I say her name, a broken, scraping sound. There are

no other words, not when I can still feel the heat of Lili's body pressed against mine. But that one word is enough to shock her back into life. And when she turns from me and literally starts running, I curse my broken back all over again because I can't chase after her.

It's quiet until the door slowly clicks shut, and for long moments after. I can't look in Lili's direction, and I know without checking that she isn't looking at me either. The last thing we want to see is each other.

Finally, her tear-thick words break the silence. "I'm so sorry. Oh, Wren, I'm so sorry."

I close my eyes to block her out. I can't hear her apology now, when the screaming voice in my head is accusing me of being exactly like the person I've always despised most.

"This is all my fault. You tried to leave me alone and I came right after you. I'll tell her. I'll tell her everything and she'll understand that it wasn't your fault and that I'm, I'm—" Her words just stop because she can't even convince herself at this point. Yes, she came back, but if she hadn't, there's a big part of me that knows I'd have gone after her.

And I'm the one who told her to come to me. I knew exactly what I was doing as I watched her walk around the table; I'd imagined it enough times. I wanted her for so long that in that moment, I didn't think about anything else. And when she got close enough to reach, I took her.

My hands flex out at my sides, trying to release the memory of her skin sliding against mine. I shut my eyes again as I'm hurtled between one achingly perfect moment and the clawing agony of the one that followed, desire and dread, happiness and horror. And beneath it all, the beating truth that trickles like poison down my throat.

Regret that Eryn didn't come through that door even five seconds later. Because my resolve had been hanging on by a thread.

Because then at least I'd have had that one perfect moment before this hell dragged me under.

And Lili is still talking like anything we might say right now could fix this. "Please," she's saying in a broken whisper. "Please tell me what to do."

As though I have an answer, as though hers is the real offense here when we both know that for those eternal seconds before she ran, Eryn never took her eyes off me.

"Wren," she says again when I don't answer her. Then again, finally moving in front of me so I have no choice but to see and hear her. "Wren?"

I stare at her face, tear stained when before it had been sweetly flushed. "Just go, Lili."

And mercifully, she does.

My solitude is short-lived though. Not five minutes later, Tate pushes through the door. He's not holding a bag of pretzels or gnawing at a piece of jerky; he's not even chewing gum so far as I can tell. He's not cracking a smile either.

He stares at me, and I stare back.

"You don't have to say it."

He raises his eyebrows but not his voice. "Wren, tell me I didn't see what I think I just saw."

I can't answer him.

Tate takes half a step forward, then stops as though he doesn't want to come closer. "Tell me you didn't." That's all he needs to say.

He's my best friend, so he probably saw this—Lili—coming before I did. He even tried to warn me.

"I didn't mean for any of this to happen."

For a split second I think Tate is going to take a swing at me. But it's only words he lets fly.

"You didn't mean it? You didn't mean it! Then you don't do it! You think about other people and you don't hurt them." He whirls away from me only to turn back so quickly it's like a dance spin. "How could you do that? I mean how could you let it get to that point?"

I don't know. I only know I did and now I've ruined everything.

His lip curls back and I can see him fighting the uncharacteristic urge for physical violence.

"I don't know what to say to you right now except you're an asshole for what you did to Eryn. And for what you did to Lili too."

TWENTY-NINE

Lili

By the time I get home, I feel wrung out. I step listlessly up the front steps and into the house. I've cried harder in my life, much harder, but never from a place of shame.

Guilty tears burn far more bitterly than grieving ones.

I did this to myself. And worse, I did it to someone else too. Somewhere on this island I'd so desperately wanted to come back to, there is a girl crying because of hurt I knowingly inflicted upon her.

Because I did know. With every step I took toward Wren in that back room, I knew I was walking closer to something that wasn't mine, no matter how much I wanted it to be.

I can't be sure if he'd been fighting within himself during those final few seconds of our almost kiss. Maybe he would fully have let me go in another heartbeat, all on his own. Maybe he would have realized that he didn't want to throw away years with Eryn for a fleeting moment with me. Maybe the feelings for me he thought he was struggling with paled in comparison to what he has with her.

And maybe he would have let me down gently, apologized for leading me on because of his temporarily confused thoughts.

Maybe I'd have been the one to run off while he and Eryn went on to happily ever after.

Or maybe I'm just a worse person than I thought, because I'm fantasizing about a reality where I can escape my guilt and become the victim, when the truth is I'm anything but.

I close the door behind me with a bang and I'm thankful that the house remains quiet. Goldie must still be at Mrs. Mayhew's and Mom must be in her room. All I want right now is to crawl back into my bed and hide from the mess I made at the museum and the twisted thoughts in my own mind.

But I don't make it halfway up the stairs before Mom steps into view at the top and I freeze because I'd swear, based on the look on her face, that she knows exactly what happened today.

"Mom?"

She studies me for a second without any of her usual warmth, then turns her back to me, saying, "Come into my room, Lili. Now."

There's no way she knows. How could she? But my heart isn't listening to logic, and it hammers like a cannon in my chest with every step I take after her.

She's staring out the window in her bedroom, so small that it fits only a twin bed and a tiny reading chair. I linger half in, half out of the doorway until she gestures to me to sit on the bed. The frame squeaks when I sit, and dread begins to inch up my legs, like quicksand I can't escape. Somehow, she knows.

"What you did today was hurtful in more ways than you know."

The tears that I thought I'd used up on my bike ride home replenish in an instant. "I know."

"Do you?" She finally turns to face me. "Because I just spent the last hour comforting a girl who doesn't understand why you keep choosing everyone else over her."

My thoughts are so tear soaked and bitter that I don't understand her at first, and I almost ask her why Eryn came here before realizing she's talking about my sister.

"Goldie?" I'm so relieved that she doesn't know about the actual horrible thing I did that day that I flop back on the bed. "I went with her to Mrs. Mayhew's like I promised, but something came up and I couldn't stay as long as she wanted. I told her I'd make it up to her, and I will. I do want to see everything." But while my brain is pulled in another direction, for once, Kezia Gardner is going to have to wait.

"Hey!" Mom's uncharacteristically sharp voice has me sitting back up in a second. "To you it may seem like no big deal, but she is ten years old and you are her world, and the fact that you keep showing her how unimportant she is in yours is crushing her." Mom spins away, pushing her hair from her face before turning back to me again. "I had these conversations for years with your dad about you, and I can't believe I have to do this again with you because you're now the one who refuses to see that there is a little person who just wants to be with you."

I am struck silent by the mention of Dad.

"All summer you were the only thing she's talked about. 'Wait till Lili and I do this' or 'Wait till I show Lili that.' Only you were never here." She exhales audibly before adding, "If you only knew how little she wanted, how small a thing from you could have made her happy." She shakes her head. "She was so sure she'd found something that you couldn't say no to, and more than that, that there was finally something she could do with you."

I say nothing. I can't find my voice, knowing that I've hurt yet another person I care about and I didn't even notice.

Mom doesn't know how low I am in that moment and continues to lay into me.

"I've let you run off to that museum since the day we got off the ferry because I trusted you to find a balance." She sits beside me and lifts her hand to push my slightly sweat-damp bangs back to better see my face. "Lili. You are so much like your dad that sometimes it scares me. Oh, there's a lot of good you got from him," she adds when I close my eyes. "You've got his passion, his determination, and his resilience." She brushes my hair back again, the soft gesture tempering the sting to come. "But you've also got his single-mindedness, which can make you neglectful and even selfish at times."

My chin quivers.

"Honey, I am not saying any of this to make you cry, but I need you to understand that this situation with Goldie is important and could have lasting effects on your relationship with her. So." She lightly slaps her hands to her knees. "Here's how things are going to go, starting tomorrow. You may only volunteer at the museum three days a week; the other four you spend with me and Goldie. I'm fine if you want to go out with Wren or your other friends a couple of nights a week too. But maybe invite Goldie sometimes too?" She nudges my shoulder when I don't so much as lift my head. "Lili?"

I can't help it. I start to cry, big, body-racking sobs. And the whole thing just pours out of me, the early clash between me and Wren, the totally uninvited attraction that grew into something more, something that I thought was only dangerous to me because it was obviously one-sided, until maybe it wasn't, and then the horrible, awful almost kiss when Eryn walked in.

I'm not even sure if she hears everything through my tears, but she must catch enough because she hugs me close.

"And she was your friend too, not just his girlfriend?"

I nod miserably. "She's the only person who's treated me like she liked me from the moment she met me." I pull away from Mom's embrace; as good as it feels to be comforted, I know I don't deserve it. "And I'm sorry about Goldie too. Honestly, I didn't even realize that I was hurting her. I will fix it, no matter what it takes, I will." My throat tries to squeeze shut again. "But I don't know what to do about Wren and Eryn."

Mom doesn't try to hug me again. "I don't think there's an easy answer."

"I feel horrible for hurting her, but I also feel horrible because I don't feel as horrible as I know I should."

"Because you like Wren?"

I can't face the question, so I ask one of my own. "Did you ever like a guy with a girlfriend?"

She nods. "More than once."

"And did you ever . . . ?"

She stares at me with sympathy on her face. "Lili. I think you are going to have to ask yourself some hard questions here. What do you want after today? Eryn's friendship, or as much of it as she can give you now? Or Wren? Because I don't know if it's possible to have both."

I genuinely like Eryn and don't want to lose her friendship. And Wren is . . . I still don't know. After today, could he still have feelings for me? If given the choice, would he choose me over her? Would I want that, knowing what it would mean to Eryn?

Do I even deserve to be chosen?

I feel like crying all over again.

Mom stands up. "It's hard stuff, making mistakes and then having to deal with the consequences. And this was a big mistake."

"I know."

"But I'm telling you now, don't start running from them, because that is a hard habit to break. Your dad did that, and I have to believe he'd tell you the same thing right now if he could."

I flinch slightly, not liking the full picture that all my inherited tendencies from him are making. Because the truth is, I know he wasn't a perfect man. Like with my feelings for Wren, I know there are memories of Dad that I've been trying to push away.

Like getting a postcard in the mail when I would have given anything to hear his voice.

Like the fact that he stayed here and never let me visit, no matter how many times I asked.

Like the fact that he died before telling us that he was even sick, forever robbing me of the chance to say goodbye or ask him if I could have done something, *anything*, to make the last seven years different.

Mom turns to leave, but I call her back.

"I'm like you too, aren't I? A little?"

She smiles then, warm like sunshine. "I certainly hope so, because I'd love to take at least some of the credit."

She leaves me then, a mix of regret and hope and fear slumped on her bed, but she's right about one thing, at least. I'm not going to run.

Right now, a huge part of me wishes I'd never come back to Nantucket. I'd have never met Wren or hurt Eryn, and I'd have never gotten so consumed with finishing Dad's research into Kezia and would have been there for Goldie without even having to try.

I know I'll have to find a way to apologize to Eryn even if she can't forgive me, but I can't think about Wren anymore right now. Goldie is where I need to start. I still have a chance to do something good before summer ends.

THIRTY
Lili

The sun is cresting the rooftops, its golden light brushing the edges of the sky, when I find myself heading back to McCleave's later that week. Goldie has her face lifted up to the early morning warmth, eyes closed as she pedals without a care in the world.

"So does this mean you forgive me?" I've been asking her the same question for days of nonstop sister bonding, and she always gives me the same answer.

She keeps her eyes closed. "Maybe."

"And what exactly do I have to do to get more than a maybe?" I joke, but my voice carries a note of longing.

"Be a better sister."

My foot slips off my pedal and the bike wobbles before I can straighten it again. She didn't even say it harshly, but she didn't have to.

I watch her profile, thinking how grown-up she suddenly looks. "There are so many things I wish I could do over from this summer."

She rolls her eyes. "I know, I know, Tour Guy."

I reach out to tap her arm until she looks at me. "Yes, things with him. But with you, too." I inject a note of softness into my voice, so she can hear how serious I am. "Goldie, I don't ever want you to feel like you and Mom aren't the most important people in my life. I got caught up with a lot of things and I didn't notice what you were trying to tell me. I know Dad used to do that with us, and he missed out on a lot because of it. I don't want to be that way with you, and I'm really sorry."

Goldie pedals her bike as she looks at me, gauging me, and then she says, "Okay."

"Okay?" I almost laugh at her single syllable response. "That's it? You're not gonna make me grovel or be your servant for a week to earn your forgiveness?"

She screws her face up. "I'm not nine anymore."

No, she's not, and I think we both know she's letting me off easy.

"So you liked that Wren guy, huh?"

Or maybe not so easy. "Yeah."

"Doesn't he have a girlfriend?"

I lower my head until I'm staring at the road under my tires. It comes out like more of an exhale when I say, "Yeah."

"Well, I think he should've picked you."

My throat gets tight as I look at her, caught between a smile and tears. "His girlfriend is actually really great."

"So are you." Before I can react to the sweetness I absolutely haven't earned from her, she's standing up on her pedals and racing ahead of me.

I ride the high of Goldie's words until we're standing in front of the museum a few minutes later and I'm clutching my bike handles like a lifeline. The air is cool and crisp, but heat prickles along my skin.

Goldie skips beside her bike, her excitement palpable, as we guide them to the rack. "I can't wait to see the mermaid. And you said they're adding a boy mermaid too? Do you think they'll let us see it?"

I shrug, trying to match her enthusiasm. "I guess we'll find out. Can you lock the bikes while I make sure there's someone here to let us in?"

She grins in response. "On it!"

The truth is, I'm dreading seeing Wren again. It's only been a few days since I was here, but I still don't know how to make things better. Or if that's even possible.

That realization slows my steps as I reach for the door, only to have it swing open before I can touch it.

Tate leans against the frame, wearing a T-shirt with an outline of Rhode Island next to one of Nantucket, with a caption that says, *That's not an island.* That's *an island*. He's eyeing me like he doesn't think I should be here.

I don't exactly disagree, but I made a promise to my sister and I'm not breaking any more of those, so I eye him back. Neither of us says anything.

Goldie skids to a stop beside me a few seconds later. "Okay, we can go in now."

"Oh, can we?" Tate turns and stares at my sister, causing me to tense and inch a hand protectively toward her. I'm not about to let him take his apparent anger with me out on her.

He looks her over. "So you're the sister?"

She stares back. "And you're some guy I don't know."

I press my lips together to muffle a laugh, then drop my guard. Goldie's just fine all on her own.

He continues looking at her, then offers her an Oreo from the mini pack at his side—he doesn't offer one to me—and asks, "How do you eat yours?"

She answers by shoving the entire cookie into her mouth.

"Efficient," he says, before popping his own cookie into his mouth.

They smile at each other. And just like that, they're friends.

Tate stands back against the wall for us to pass. The museum won't open to the public for another couple of hours, so none of the backlights have been switched on yet. The gift shop is partially dark too, with just a few display-case lights adding a glow to the room.

Goldie doesn't need light though. She spots the table of Nerissa T-shirts and immediately starts grabbing at them, begging me to buy her a new one.

"I'm an unpaid volunteer," I remind her, easing the fabric from her hands and smoothing out the folded shirts.

"With an employee discount," Tate says, piling more into her eager arms.

Goldie grins at him. "What's the most expensive thing in the gift shop?"

Tate smiles back, twisting to face one of the large blown-glass figurines on the shelf behind the register.

I looked at the price tag once and nearly choked, and still break into a sweat every time I have to dust it. "No!" I say, before he can point it out. "You can have one shirt, *one*."

Goldie makes a grumbling sound that fades as soon as Tate offers her another Oreo.

"There's nothing that amazing in here anyway. We keep the real mermaids locked up." He pulls a keyring from his pocket. "Wanna sneak a peek at the new one before anybody else gets to see it?"

They take off so fast that I nearly drop the T-shirts in my hands. "What happened to wanting to spend more time together?" I call after her.

"I see you all the time, I live with you. Right now, I want to check out the mermaid with this guy!"

I faintly hear him tell her his name as I start to refold the shirts, only to jump as another, much closer voice speaks from behind me.

"His younger brothers taught him all the kid tricks," Wren says. "That, and he always has snacks."

His voice is casual, light, but it still makes my pulse stutter. I force my eyes down to the shirts in front of me, trying to focus. My hands are moving too fast now, my fingers shaking a little as I try to keep folding.

It's not that I mind Goldie picking Tate over me. It's more that I was planning on keeping her glued to my side today so I wouldn't have to deal with being alone with Wren. Just me and him. The last time we were together, things shifted, and I don't know how to shift them back.

"All his kid tricks seem to cost me money." I lift a T-shirt then gesture to the register. "Want to"—I stop a split second before saying "check me out" and instead say—"ring me up?"

Thankfully, Wren doesn't react to my halted sentence and moves behind the counter, reaching down to power on the register.

We wait for the boot-up sequence to start.

"My sister and I—well, mostly Goldie—talked with Mrs.

Mayhew about donating portions of her husband's collection to McCleave's, and she's happy to give you whatever you want."

Wren's gaze drops to the counter, shoulders tensing. "Yeah, she called to make the offer herself. My dad agreed to let me look, but we can't promise her anything in terms of displays. Mostly I'm hoping to sort out anything of financial value for her future."

I nod, aching over the helplessness I know he feels having to say that.

"But thank you," he adds, his voice carefully even, as though he's trying to smooth over his frustration with his dad before it spills out. "I've offered several times to help her, but she never would have accepted if your sister hadn't found those letters."

We're quiet for a moment too long, and I wonder if this is how it's always going to be between us—forced politeness and awkward silences. "Yeah, I mean, you're welcome." The words feel like stones in my mouth. I clear my throat. "Do you know when—" I start, but Wren interrupts me.

"Tate is going to pick up the boxes later this week and bring everything here for me to go through." He pauses. "I didn't know if you'd want to be around for that."

My gut tightens. Yes, I want to be there, but the thought of being so close to him again, of working side by side, weighing every word like it might crack something else wide open, fills me with dread. And now I'm worrying that there was something in the way he spoke just now that means he thinks I should say no, or at least is hoping I will.

Everything with Wren and me aside, I can't forget why I sought him out in the first place, or the promise I made to find the answers my dad couldn't. I need to know if that letter we found is real and whether or not there's more to find. And I can't do that on my own.

"I still don't know for sure who she was. I can't walk away until I do."

"Yeah, I don't think I could either." He almost smiles, but it's the kind of smile that feels like a wave breaking too far out, barely touching the shore before it pulls back. Then his gaze lowers to the computer screen almost gratefully when the login prompt appears.

The clacking of the keyboard is the only thing I hear as I fold and refold the shirt even though I know it's going to get tossed into a bag. The POS software initializes, running its checks, connecting to the barcode scanner and receipt printer with a few soft beeps. The familiar sounds should settle my nerves a bit, grounding me in the perfectly fine and professional routine.

Instead everything echoes miserably.

"Is this really how it's going to be between you and me from now on?" I lift my gaze to Wren's. "Because I don't think I can keep doing this."

Wearily he says, "You can go find Tate and your sister."

"You know that's not what I mean."

"What do you want me to say, Lili?" His voice cracks, just a little. The sound of my name on his lips feels different now, rougher, like it's been scraped against something sharp.

I flinch but I can't stop myself. "I don't know, but I hate feeling this way and I hate that I hurt Eryn and you. And I know it doesn't change anything, but I'm so sorry."

At first I think he's going to blow me off or even tell me to leave again, but he doesn't. He looks right at me. "I'm the one at fault here. You didn't do this"—he raises his voice when I open my mouth to interrupt him—"and I'm the one who has a girlfriend."

My heart pounds painfully at the present-tense reference to Eryn. I just assumed they broke up, but only now am I realizing how naive that was. And how wrong it was for me to subconsciously hope they had.

"Or maybe I only *had* a girlfriend. I still don't know."

My heart clenches, but I keep my face neutral. "You haven't talked to her?"

He grabs a pen and twists it in his hand. "I keep trying, but she's not ready to talk to me yet."

His head is tilted just slightly forward, and it's painfully obvious what he wants. "You want her to forgive you." I have to fight the urge to cry.

"I don't want her to hate me."

"I don't think Eryn could hate anyone."

His smile doesn't touch his eyes. "She might make an exception for me." Then he drops his head before lifting it again. "It's hard to explain, but we've been together for four years."

"That's a long time." Especially considering they aren't even twenty yet.

"It's more than the years, it's everything that happened during that time." His features twist and his breathing grows heavier. "I didn't want anyone around after my accident, but she knew I needed her, so she was there, no matter what. She's always been there for me, and I—it's not like I owe her, but it would feel like a betrayal of some kind to give up on us, when she never did."

He falls silent after that, pinning me with an intensity I can't escape, like he's willing me to understand something he barely understands himself. "Before you, that had never been hard to do. But, Lili, if—"

"No, don't, please." I close my eyes as if that will somehow stop his words. I take a step back until almost the full length of the counter is between us. He's not moving toward me or even reaching out in my direction, but I still feel the need for the added physical distance between us. "I don't need you to say anything else. In fact, I'm asking you not to." My eyes trace over him, instinctively taking in the way his dark hair curls just a little at the edges, the conflict in his eyes as they dart away from mine. And then his jaw. It's tight, a warning, like he's on the edge of saying something that would ruin us both. "I understand, more than you know, but I can't hear you say it, okay?" I don't think I could handle that.

I hurry off in search of Tate and Goldie before the ache in my ribs becomes any harder to breathe through. I know I don't have a right to want Wren to choose me, but it still hurts to know he won't.

THIRTY-ONE
Wren

The day dragged after Lili and her sister left. The museum felt empty despite all the guests, especially when Tate wandered off too. We've exchanged a few words, but as long as Eryn is avoiding me—and by extension, him—things aren't going to be okay between us.

Eryn hasn't answered my texts or voicemails, and every time I try to catch her at the café, her coworkers give me the same excuse: She's busy, can't leave the kitchen. I keep going back, though. I don't know what else to do.

And I miss her. I miss the way she would smile at me like I was the only one in the room who mattered. I miss how excited she got watching someone try a dessert she made for the first time. But more than that, I miss the space she used to occupy in my life, a space that now feels eerily hollow. It's as if I've forgotten how to breathe.

That night, I stay later than usual at the museum. I don't want to rush home, where the silence is too loud and my thoughts are too heavy. So, when I finally leave, it's well past closing. I drive by the café, hoping to catch a glimpse of Eryn through the windows, but instead of seeing her inside, I spot her outside—her shoulders hunched, the soft amber light of the streetlamps casting a warm glow around her. She's wiping down the tables, but her movements are sluggish, almost mechanical. She drags her hand across the surface of the table with an exhaustion I've never seen in her before, her face drained of its usual spark, a hollow look in her eyes that cuts deeper than I'd expect.

Then, a guy steps out of the café. Elliot, I'm guessing, since I don't recognize him. He's wearing an apron and holding something small between two fingers as he approaches her. I see her look up, and for a split second, her entire expression softens. He says something low, probably teasing, but it's enough to make her crack a small smile before she leans in to take the bite he offers her. When she grins at him, clearly impressed with whatever he gave her, his face brightens, and before he can stop himself, he sweeps her up in his arms, spinning her around like something out of a movie. She laughs, and I feel a strange ache in my chest as I watch them. The sight is both beautiful and brutal. She looks genuinely happy, and it's not the kind of happiness I've seen from her in a long time.

He sets her back down, almost sheepishly. I can tell by the way he steps back that he realizes it might have been a little too much, a little too sudden. His hands linger awkwardly at his sides, his grin a bit more bashful now.

She laughs again, shaking her head in that way she does when she's letting someone off the hook. But then, her gaze trails over his shoulder, and her smile falters. Her eyes catch mine through the windshield, and the warmth in her expression disappears in an instant, replaced by a tight, unreadable tension.

She stares at me for a moment longer while my hands grip the steering wheel and my pulse grows too loud for the quiet of the cab. Elliot finally says something to her, inclining his head toward the door, and without a word, she nods and follows him inside.

I drive off after that, turning down side streets and bumping over dirt roads, staring out at parts of the island that I rarely see anymore. It's maybe an hour later when I pull into my driveway. I'm both surprised and somehow not to see Eryn sitting outside on the curb.

She's still in her Petticoat uniform, brushing dirt off the back of her shorts, standing stiffly, which lets me know she's been waiting awhile. Even so, I take longer than usual to get out of the truck, as if metaphorically dragging my feet might make the moment last longer, unwilling to face what's waiting.

I wheel over to her, stopping a little farther away than I would have before.

"I can't stay long," she says, her voice barely a whisper, "and I'm not ready to talk."

Any hope I had evaporates the moment I hear the rawness in her voice. The way it cracks at the edges cuts through me like a knife.

"I just needed you to know . . ." She pauses, struggling to get the words out, her voice thick with emotion. "I'll still be the museum's mermaid for the boat tour and for the upcoming exhibit reveal if you need me."

"You don't have to do that," I protest. I hadn't even thought about the exhibit. But she doesn't owe me anything. She doesn't owe anyone anything.

Her eyes drop to the ground. "I don't want to let anyone down who already bought a ticket," she murmurs, her voice trembling. "And your dad depends on me."

I swallow hard. “This isn’t about my dad or a stupid exhibit. It’s fine, Eryn. You’re not . . .”

I see the way she flinches when I speak, her whole body tensing, and the pain of that reaction hits me harder than anything else she could say.

“There’s so much I need to say to you,” I continue, my voice quieter now. “I don’t know if you listened to any of my voicemails or—”

She starts to shake her head slowly, dropping it lower with each pass.

“Er, can you at least look at me?”

She winces at the shortened form of her name, but to my surprise, she does meet my gaze, tears shimmering in her eyes.

“Eryn.” I’m the one who sounds broken now. “I’m so sorry—” But I cut off my own words when she visibly braces as though trying to shield herself from what I might try to say next.

So I stop.

And when she turns to leave, I let her go.

I carry her expression with me as I head inside, making my way to my bedroom next to the kitchen. It used to be the dining room, until Dad walled it off and converted it for me after the accident. My old bedroom upstairs is just a storage room now. Dad’s hunched over the kitchen table, the two pieces of the FeeJee mermaid laid out in front of him.

“Head fall off again?” I stop in the doorway. “That’s the third time this year. Why not just retire it?”

“It’s one of McCleave’s original exhibits. I just need some time to figure out a better support structure.”

Right, except there's never been a good way to attach a monkey skull to a fish body, and after more than a century of repairs, some more destructive than others, it's not looking good.

"Do you even have the tools you need here?" I ask, already knowing the answer.

He looks up at me, exhaustion dulling his expression. "I ran out of coffee at the museum."

I eye the beer bottle beside him, and he grunts in response. "Late for you too. And did I see Eryn outside?"

It's not really a question, given the large window to the front yard beside him, but I still hesitate, unsure how much he saw or heard. "Yeah."

"She didn't come in?"

Obviously not. "She had to go."

He nods slowly. "Guess she didn't want to get us sick, huh?"

That's what I told him to explain her absence for the last few days, but I knew he didn't buy it. I wheel fully into the kitchen. "She's not sick, which you clearly know."

"I know something's wrong," he shrugs, "but I don't think it's the flu. A lot of people who are usually like salt in the sea with you are suddenly nowhere to be seen. The new girl's cutting her shifts, Tate won't leave the janitor's room, and now Eryn shows up crying. It's not looking too good."

"It's not feeling too good either, but I don't really feel like getting into it right now."

He doesn't move. "I have two theories. Wanna hear them?"

"No," I groan.

He holds up one finger. "Something happened with Eryn and

Tate, maybe he told you about it, and now nobody's talking. Doesn't exactly explain the new girl's absence, though."

I lift my head wearily. "Lili. Her name is Lili."

He sighs. "So it's the second theory then."

I don't say anything.

"Oh, son." Two syllables, yet they pack so much sympathy and disappointment together. "Did something happen?"

I shake my head. "But I wanted it to, and Eryn knows." It sounds bad when I say it out loud, somehow worse than when it was happening.

He rests his forearms on the table and drops his head, not saying anything. He's not looking at me either, although it's a different kind of not looking than Eryn was doing outside. His silence isn't a shield; he's listening, and he's thinking.

"I never thought I'd be capable of hurting someone who loved me. I never wanted to be like *her*," I murmur. Even though we haven't talked about my mom in years, I don't need to elaborate. He knows exactly who I'm referring to.

Dad pushes the precious specimen to the side with one arm like it means nothing as he reaches back into the fridge with the other, grabs two beers, and sets them on the table. I don't drink often, and I've never shared a beer with him before, but I guess we're cutting through a lot of tape tonight.

I take the bottle, feel the cold condensation against my palm, and he takes his, opening it with a dull pop that echoes in the quiet kitchen.

"One time only, you understand? There's a reason I don't like talking about the past."

I nod quickly, but I'm not sure what I'm about to hear.

He takes a long swig, draining half the bottle before he speaks again. "You know the fields down by the Hawthorn's place, the hills heading toward the Wyer's Valley?" He doesn't wait for me to answer. "This time of year, they light up with fireflies, so many it's like walking through stardust. As kids, we'd go chasing after them, trying to catch them in jars or our hands to watch them glow. I never caught one . . . until Kerry."

Even now there's a light in his eyes when he talks about her, a tenderness that both hurts and captivates me. I want to not understand, but I have those memories with her too. Instead of shoving them away like I have in the past, this time I let one sweep over me.

I feel my tiny legs struggling to toddle up that hill, stubby hands reaching, my little fists clenching. I can almost feel the softness of the fireflies' wings between my fingers now as the cool summer night wraps around me. And I remember my mom—her hands, larger than mine but delicate, gently coaxing my hands open.

Her face is clear in my mind, lit up with awe as she watches the glow of the fireflies disappear into the night sky. "Some things can't be caught," she said to me, and even in that perfect moment, I remember her sadness and my own as she dropped my hand.

"She was happy at first, I know she was," he continues. "We'd go swimming in the ocean every night and she'd let me chase her through the tall grasses that sprung up along the shores. And when I caught her—" His smile turns softer now, private. "Well, that's how we got you."

My bottle is dotted with condensation, but I haven't taken so much as a sip, and I don't now, no matter how much I'd like to numb myself.

"I knew, even then, what kind of life she wanted, just like I knew I could never give it to her. I tried to pretend I didn't see her fading, and she let me. Until she couldn't anymore. Because just like those fireflies, the ones in jars or trapped inside hands, if you didn't let them go, they'd die."

"And you let her go." I can't stop the bitterness that seeps into my voice or the way my fingers tighten almost painfully around the neck of the glass bottle. I'm about to push away from the table when he says something I never expected to hear.

"I didn't let her go, Wren. I just opened my hand."

It's the closest he's ever come to condemning what she did, and I'm struck silent hearing the vulnerability in his voice, the quiet regret.

He drains the rest of his beer, then stares at the empty bottle for a long moment, his fingers tracing the label. "There's nothing worse than being with someone when you know they don't really want to be with you. I lived that life for three years, and it's taken me sixteen more to realize it would've been kinder for her to let me go from the start. I'm not saying I regret it, and you're the reason I don't, but all these years and I still don't know how to let go inside." He forces his hands apart with obvious effort. "It'd be easier if I could hate her, I know that. But every time the fireflies are here, I remember the girl she was, and how, for a time, I got to call her mine."

I haven't forgotten the fireflies either, and while I don't think I'll ever stop being angry at her for leaving us, I don't think I can blame him anymore for choosing not to hate her.

His voice drops lower now so that I have to strain to hear it when he continues. "You said you didn't want to be capable of hurting someone who loves you, but Wren, we all are. The difference is what you do after. If you want Eryn, then you do whatever it takes to win her back." His head stays tipped forward, but his eyes lift and hold mine. "But if you don't, then it's far kinder to be honest with both of them sooner rather than later."

I feel pinned by his stare, absolutely frozen in place.

"Do you love Eryn?"

I would have answered that question without hesitation a month ago. Now, I can't find the words as I finally break free from his scrutiny.

"I'm not gonna say this right. I don't know how, so I'm just gonna say it." Dad takes a deep breath. "Accident or not, you are worthy, do you understand me? Don't let your own hang-ups or the mistakes that your mother or I made make you think otherwise." He hits his fingers against the table, drawing my gaze and making sure he has my full attention. "I'm not saying what you did was right. You know it wasn't, and you have to do everything in your power to make it right with the people you hurt. But after that, Wren, you have to be able to forgive yourself. And then you have to think about what you really want, not just what you feel like you should want."

THIRTY-TWO

Lili

"Another early morning?"

Thanks to the shower curtain, I only hear Mom when she walks into the bathroom all three of us have to share, which means that even getting up this early, I can't cry in the shower in peace without someone coming in to brush their teeth.

"Yeah. I'll be out in a second." I step back under the spray and let the water rinse away the tears I've indulged for too long. Wren told me to my face that he can't choose me. He and Eryn have too much history, too much invested in one another.

I let my face crumble one more time behind the safety of the shower curtain, before turning the knob to full cold, giving me the icy spray I need to pull myself together.

"Lili?" Mom asks when I stifle a yelp.

"I'm fine, the water just went cold." I turn off the tap and reach my arm out to grab a towel before wrapping it around myself and opening the curtain. I step out of the tub and start to comb my hair in front of the sink.

"Oh, these wretched pipes. Graham's bringing by some new

fittings for me to try, but I'm worried we'll still have to replace most of them."

In our reflection in the mirror, I see that she doesn't look nearly as put off by the idea as she should.

"Graham again." I smile at her.

She pauses to fold and rehang her hand towel. "Yes, Graham again. And he's invited us over for lunch after church on Sunday."

My smile falters just the tiniest bit. "Okay. He does know we're leaving, right?" But what I'm really asking is if she's changed her mind about how soon.

She smiles wearily. "He knows. He's offered to come by in a couple of weeks with his son and help us box everything up. Including your father's desk, if you'd like to take it. I don't think it'll fit in your dorm, but I can keep track of it more easily off this island than on."

I nod wordlessly. Then swallow and say, "So it's two weeks then?"

She looks around the bathroom, thinking of the spaces beside and beneath this one before murmuring her assent. "The front porch just needs to be painted, and then the plumbing still needs attention, but otherwise there are only a handful of things left to button up. In fact, there are some rooms that are already ready for you to photograph for the rental listing."

She stops when she sees my stricken expression, then runs a hand over my arm and pulls me into a hug. "The house will still be here after college, if this is where you really want to be."

I'm holding my towel up, so I can't hug her back, but I rest my head on her shoulder, and she doesn't seem to mind when my wet hair instantly soaks through her sleep shirt. "I'm not ready yet."

"You haven't talked to Eryn, have you?"

I shake my head against her shoulder. One of many unfinished things spinning through my head.

"Have you tried?"

Another shake.

She lets me go and turns back to the sink, watching me through the mirror. "Sounds like something you need to do sooner rather than later."

I hug my towel tighter and sit down on the closed toilet. "She might not want to talk to me."

Mom spits and rinses, wincing at the loud groaning from the pipes. "Maybe she doesn't, but you should at least try to apologize directly to her."

I give her my most pitiful look.

"She works at that café next to the museum, right? The one you said has the most amazing cinnamon roll things?"

"Who has amazing cinnamon rolls?" Goldie squeezes into the bathroom, yawning. Another problem with this old house—the plumbing is loud enough to wake the dead, so even my little sister is getting up at the crack of dawn now. "I want cinnamon rolls."

Mom and I exchange a glance through the mirror, and my rounded, threatening eyes do nothing to keep the words from spilling out of her mouth.

"There's this special bakery in town that Lili knows. Maybe she can take you this morning."

There's no shutting this down once Goldie is on board. Her

sweet tooth is legendary, and even though I try to explain that morning buns are more like croissants than cinnamon rolls, the fact that they're frosted has her determined. And my fate sealed.

"Don't suppose you want to go somewhere else with a shorter line?" I say to my sister outside of the Petticoat Café. They've only just opened, but the line of people queued up outside already numbers in the dozens.

Goldie sneers at the suggestion. "You said that the morning buns here are better than anything we used to get from Desert Bloom Bakery."

I had said that.

I sigh, glancing back and forth between the end of the line and inside the shop. I don't see Eryn at the counter, but she's the only one who makes the morning buns, which means she must be in the kitchen. I gnaw on my lip.

"What's wrong with you?" Goldie asks.

"I'm trying to decide how much of a coward I am."

"You're not a coward." She says it like it's the most obvious thing in the world. And since I really want that to be true, I nod.

"Okay, then are you all right to wait in line for us for a few minutes? I kinda have to go talk to somebody around back."

The look she gives me is heavy with suspicion, but eventually she nods too. "Fine, but if you try to blow me off, I will make you be my servant for *two weeks* before I forgive you."

I feel like she's only half kidding as I circle around the side of the building. Eryn once told me to knock on the back door of the café anytime the line out front was too long and she'd slip me whatever I wanted herself. I know this isn't what she meant, not at all, but I've been delaying this long enough. A wooden door, faded to a weathered blue, stands before me, its surface rough beneath my fingertips. I lift my hand and rap my knuckles gently against the wood.

She deserves my apology, even if I don't deserve her forgiveness.

A few moments later, Eryn pushes the door open. She's smiling at first, her eyes bright and warm, but that all dims as soon as she sees me.

She has a light dusting of flour on her cheek, the fine powder catching the sun, and a streak of frosting smudging her apron. She's clearly been here since long before I even stirred awake, pouring her energy into her recipes, probably trying not to think about Wren, or me, or the mess we left in our wake.

And now I've brought it all back to her doorstep—literally.

"Please don't shut the door," I say quickly, though I know that Eryn isn't the type to slam doors, no matter how much she might want to.

She exhales, a deep, measured breath, and calls inside to someone, her voice steady as she instructs them to start laminating the next batch of dough, whatever that means. The sounds of the bustling kitchen fade as she steps out into the warm morning air with me and swings the door shut behind her with a soft click. "I have to be quick."

I nod, her distant tone squeezing my throat tight, threatening to crush the words I've rehearsed over and over. I remind myself that I can't fall apart now, not like I did in the shower. Breaking down in front of her would be gross and unfair, forcing her into the role of comforter when she's the one who's been hurt.

I start talking before I feel ready, the words tumbling out raw and unfiltered. Nothing planned, nothing careful or articulate. "I'm not looking for forgiveness, but I need you to know how sorry I am. You were the last person I ever wanted to hurt, and I only wish I could go back and be half the friend to you that you were to me."

Eryn dips her head forward and her hair slips free, partially concealing her face. It's a small motion that feels like a barrier she's trying to put between us. "Why did you do it?" she asks, her voice steady but strained.

I blink rapidly at her, not expecting a direct question at all. Especially when I don't have an answer. "I don't know. I only know I shouldn't have."

"I thought you were my friend."

"I was," I say, a hint of pleading breaking through before I can push it back.

"But that changed."

Because a friend wouldn't do what I did.

"When?"

"Eryn." I give her another desperate look. I'll tell her whatever she wants to know, but this seems cruel, to both of us.

She doesn't look away even as I squirm. "Tell me."

"I don't know. At first it was like I was just wearing Wren down. He put up with me because he didn't have a choice, and I put up with him because I needed his help. He hadn't told me the whole story about his mom yet, so I didn't understand why me being a tourist was so intolerable to him, but—"

"He told you about his mom?"

I hesitate, then nod, feeling as though I've somehow just admitted to something worse than a near kiss. "But I decided that I could prove him wrong, if not about all tourists, at least about me. Whenever there was a moment I could tell he was thawing toward me, it felt like a win. Honestly, I thought that was all I wanted, just for him not to hate me. It wasn't until we started working on his new tour script and making real progress with our research that I started to wonder if it might be more than that."

"You were helping him with Tate's speech?"

"No, his new speech, you know, because he didn't want to give up the one part of working at the museum he likes . . ." Based on the look on her face she obviously didn't know about this. My voice falters. ". . . so I've been helping him write and rehearse a new one for himself to pitch to his dad."

She goes so still that, if I didn't know better, I'd think this revelation hurt her more than everything else combined.

"Since when?"

I glance past her to the closed door, wondering how much time we have left before she's called back inside. This is not what I thought we'd be talking about. I just wanted to apologize and then, I don't know, but not this. "My first week here, but none of that matters, does it?"

Her hands slide up to grip her elbows, wrapping her arms protectively around herself. "It matters because that afternoon in the back room may have been the first time you meant for something to happen, but you and I know it wasn't the first time you both wanted it to." Her fingers squeeze into her skin. "And I want to know when that started."

She's right, and that's what makes shame splash like bile through my insides. "On the Fourth of July, when we fell asleep in his truck. That was the first time I let myself think about acting on those feelings. We never—we just talked. Nobody has ever understood how important this project was to me, but Wren did. It started to mean something to him too, and then it became easier to talk about other things that we cared about too. That's how he told me about his mom. And I talked about my dad." I squeeze my eyes shut, not wanting to see her when I admit this next part. "And I started to not care as much about the past when we were together."

I chance a look at her. She's standing in exactly the same position, arms folded around herself, head held high, eyes dry, but there's something fragile about her now, like she's holding herself together with the barest of threads.

"I don't understand how it could've changed so quickly. How do you go from arguing to—to—" Her words choke off. "We were never like that. He's always been sweet to me. I don't think we've ever been in a real fight." Her features go blank, and then, almost to herself, she adds, "And the worst part is that deep down I knew."

My brows pinch together. "Knew?"

"There were all these little signs and moments where I'd catch him staring at you or you at him. I started to feel like the intruder."

My chin quivers before I can stop it. "No, I'm the one who shouldn't have been there."

She looks back at me again. "But you were. Every time I turned around you two were huddled together. I thought it was just glances. Elliot and I have had glances." She stops abruptly then starts up again a moment later. "You've been so nice, and Wren would never hurt me." Her voice is barely a whisper, but I hear it crack.

"Nothing ever actually happened between us," I say, but I can't argue when she responds.

"Everything happened."

The back door of the café opens, and a guy's head pops out, his smile coming easily at the sight of her. "Eryn, the buns are done proofing."

"Okay, thanks, Elliot. I'll be right in." She waits until the door shuts before turning to me again, and I can tell she's fighting to hold back her emotions. "I don't know what I'm supposed to do now."

"You don't have to do anything. I hate that I hurt you this way and that I messed things up with you and Wren."

"You didn't do it alone."

"I know that, but—"

"Lili. I don't think I want to keep talking right now. I don't hate you." She pauses. "I don't even hate Wren. I just have a lot I still need to think about. When I'm ready to think about more"—she makes a vague gesture between the two of us—"I'll let you know."

And then she's gone.

THIRTY-THREE
Wren

"So where do you want them?" Tate hoists a large file box into the back room, interrupting my lunch. His voice is casual, but there's a coolness in his tone that pulls my attention away from my sandwich.

Lili bursts in a beat later, slightly out of breath, her cheeks flushed. She must have run after him.

"Is that—?" Her eyes widen, darting between the box and Tate's face, a hint of hope lighting up her expression.

"Box one of twelve," he answers, then shifts his focus back to me. "And I'm gonna drop it here if you don't tell me where to put it."

"On the table," Lili and I say in unison. Our eyes meet for a fleeting moment, a spark of connection amid the ever-present tension between us now.

Tate groans, not from the weight of the box, before trudging over to the table and lowering it with a thud. He starts walking back to the door, then stops and eyes both of us. "A little help?"

We hurry out after him.

The boxes make a daunting stack once we have them all

together on the table. I expect to see Lili smiling, but she's just staring at them and twisting one hand in the other.

"This is going to take a long time to go through." She looks at the clock on the wall and twists her hands tighter. "I only have fifteen minutes left on my lunch break before I'm supposed to be back in the gift shop."

Tate glances between the two of us and eventually mumbles that he'll cover the gift shop this afternoon.

"Thanks," Lili says quietly. She doesn't sound like she means it.

"But you owe me, Tourist Girl." Tate gives her a mock solute as he backs out the door. "And you two kids better not play too nice."

My jaw clenches at his parting barb, while Lili turns away to hide her flush.

I know Eryn is talking to him again, or at least she's gone back to making him lunch, based on the Petticoat Café bag he had earlier, but beyond the occasional word or two, he and I haven't spoken.

I want to tell Lili not to let him get to her, but she's already moving toward the boxes, her shoulders tense.

"Okay to start with the one on top?" she asks, her voice slightly strained.

"As opposed to the one on the bottom?"

"Yes, as opposed to the one on the bottom." There's a ghost of a smile in her voice, even if her face doesn't show it. She lifts the lid off the box and looks inside.

The hours pass, filled with the rustle of paper, the scrape of cardboard, and the occasional grumble of disappointment before we both push back from the table, the final box emptied.

Lili had the idea to sort things into piles, the largest by far comprised of less-obvious fakes, followed closely by weird cat stuff that got inadvertently packed and needs to be returned to Mrs. Mayhew. There are some interesting items in the historically significant pile, but far fewer in the Nantucket specific pile. And nothing beyond the letters and the map, which I spent the last few days authenticating while Lili transcribed a copy, that connects to Kezia Gardner.

"I don't understand." Lili picks up a porcelain statue of a cat in fisherman's garb, her brow furrowed. "Where are the other letters?"

"Maybe he only wrote one." I shrug, the tedium of the last several hours with almost nothing to show for it making my response clipped. "Maybe she destroyed the others, or time did that for her."

Her sharp glance changes my tone.

"Or maybe we just haven't found them yet," I offer. "The Mayhews aren't the only people on this island with boxes in their attics. Maybe they're just hiding in someone else's."

But her expression falls further, and she sinks into a chair, staring at the piles as if they hold answers we can't see. "Since when are you the optimistic one?"

I almost say *Since I met you*, but instead I settle on, "Someone has to be."

There's silence after that while I continue searching for Mr. Mayhew's personal ledger that will hopefully establish provenance for some of these items.

"Wren." Her voice is quiet, almost a whisper.

I turn, thinking she's finally found something. But she hasn't moved.

"How long have we been doing this?"

I check my watch. "The museum closed an hour ago."

"No, I mean all this. Kezia Gardner."

I don't know what she's getting at, but I answer anyway. "Since the start of summer, I guess. Why?"

She slides the album in front of her and flips to the first letter, the one we've read a dozen times already and still can't make sense of. "Do you know what I've figured out about this?" Her voice hardens. "Nothing. It's all rambling. No reference to the war, the Prohibitory Act, nothing of importance. Look at how he starts it: 'I hope this letter finds you in the best of health, as I remain, for the most part, in a state of tolerable comfort. It is no small matter that the wind has lately shifted with a rather peculiar disposition. I am not entirely certain of its cause, yet it brings to mind a most curious reflection on the state of my window shutters today, and though they have been in place for some time, I find them not so secure as they once were. It is likely of little consequence, but they may require adjustment before long. The clock upon the mantle also strikes with a rather unusual chime.'

"And it goes on like that for dozens of lines, talking about absolutely nothing. Why send something like that, much less preserve it well enough for us to be reading it two hundred and fifty years later?"

"I don't know," I admit, my frustration mirroring her own now. "That's why we have to keep looking."

Her gaze flickers, and she lets out a sad laugh. "You sound like my dad. He'd say there is always another book or another map or another piece of evidence and all we have to do is keep searching."

I give her a tired smile and reach into another box. "In that respect, I'd say I agree with him."

Her expression darkens, and she shakes her head, a deep sigh escaping her. "In that respect, and so many others, I wouldn't."

A tightness grips my chest as I push toward her, moving around to her side of the table. "What is that supposed to mean?"

"It means everything, all of this. I think my dad was wrong, and that maybe he even knew it, which would explain why he never let me come here." Her voice cracks the slightest bit, but she shakes it off. "Maybe he realized that he wasted his life on this and couldn't bear to look me in the eye when I found out he chose nothing over his family." She sucks in a deep, steadying breath. "Maybe he sat at his ridiculously expensive desk, looked over his collection of books and notes, and realized he had nothing to show for it except a worn-out rug."

"So, what, you want to quit?" I can hear the disbelief in my voice, the panic pouring out before I can mask it. "Just like that?"

"No, not just like that," she counters, her voice thick with emotion. "I've been through his notebook backward and forward and I don't know if there's anything left to find. I hoped that maybe there'd be something in one of these boxes today, but there wasn't. I just don't think I can keep doing it, or . . ." She takes a deep breath. "Or keep seeing you."

A ringing starts in my ears.

"Think about it. What have we actually accomplished?" She glances at a spot not ten feet away, where I once held not a box in my lap, but her. "I think we've done more harm than good, and maybe it's time we walk away."

One of my legs starts to spasm as I tense up.

"Wait, just hold on a second." Blood pounds in my head, making it impossible to think clearly. "We had a deal. You were supposed to help me find something real for the museum, and I was supposed to help you figure out the truth about Kezia. Well, we're about to dump another"—I bite back an expletive—"mermaid skeleton in the lobby, and this is when you want to give up?" Both of my legs bounce now, the soles of my shoes hitting the footplate with a loud, rhythmic thud. "Where's my real piece of history? Isn't that what you promised me?"

"I'm sorry you didn't get much out of this," she says, and I can tell tears aren't far away. "But I think we both know this is the right thing to do."

"What if I don't? What if I say you haven't held up your end of the bargain?"

"Then I'd say please, because I can't stay here and watch you and Eryn try to go back to the way things were. You can't ask me to do that."

"Eryn," I breathe, and the panic surges again. "This isn't about Eryn."

But it is. I know it is. Everything is about her. The guilt. The feelings that churn in my gut, twisting, making it hard to breathe. I press both hands down on my legs as they bounce harder. "Don't do this now, okay? Not now. What about the number forty-three in your dad's notebook? Or the rest of the diary pages he didn't transcribe?" I'm reaching, but I can't think of anything else to keep her here.

"You're not hearing me," she whispers. "I haven't been staring at a notebook or diary all these weeks, I've been staring at you." Her face flushes but she keeps going, "I'm not allowed to have these feelings for you, but I do, and I don't know how to make them stop."

I lean forward, gripping the edge of the table to steady myself, but I can't. How can she leave now? We're so close. We just need more time. I need more time. "So that's it? Tourist Girl came, had her fun in the sun, and now she's ready to let everyone else deal with the mess she's leaving behind?"

"Don't say that." It's maybe the most broken I've ever heard her sound when what I need is for her to get mad.

"Prove me wrong," I say, when what I really mean is *Don't leave.*

A tear slips down her cheek, but she brushes it away quickly, like she's trying to hide the hurt. "Call me a tourist then. It's what I am. But you know I'm right."

Nothing about this feels right.

She pushes to her feet. "I hope things work out for you, Wren, for the museum and everything else."

"Sure," I say, my anger burning like a shield, when inside it feels like I might never be warm again. Spinning my back to her, I grab the album before she can reach for it. "This stays, by the way. I get whatever we find, remember? You're welcome to keep your employee shirt though. I know how you tourists love your souvenirs."

THIRTY-FOUR
Wren

I cut the engine as my tires sink into the sand at Brant Point Beach. The moonlit waves softly lap at the shore, while Lord Huron's "Wait by the River" plays its melancholy, dreamy notes on repeat. The wooden lighthouse looms in the distance through my windshield, but I stay in the truck, my gaze unfocused. I've seen it up close many times before.

The original Brant Point Lighthouse, built some 250 years ago, used to stand nearly six hundred feet from where the current one stands. Fires and storms claimed the first five iterations, each lasting only a few years. Later versions fared slightly better, with the current lighthouse, the tenth to hold that name, going strong since 1901.

Maybe it's not as tall or grand as that first brick lighthouse, but it's stood in this exact spot for well over a century. Staring at it now, it seems indestructible in a way that almost nothing else is.

A gentle tap on my window jolts me from my thoughts. The girl outside doesn't wait for an invitation before opening the passenger door and sliding in.

"I wasn't sure if you got my message," I say.

"You said you'd be waiting here every night until I did." Eryn stares out at the lighthouse too. I can't tell if the memories it brings up for her are sweet or bitter now. Right down this beach is where she kissed me for the first time. We've shared countless other kisses since then, and so many nights sitting just like this, with the breeze carrying the same sweet scent of wild roses and salty sea air through my half-open window as it does now.

She reaches for the controls to turn off the song, but I tap her wrist with a finger.

"Let it play?"

She seems puzzled, since I've never stopped her before, then somehow sad, as she lowers her hand. "You like this."

I nod.

"You never played it for me."

I don't have an answer for her. "I should have. I should have told you that I don't like pepperoni on pizza, that fireflies make me think of my mom, and that sometimes I think about setting fire to the museum because I can't stand what it's become."

I hear her quick inhalation but otherwise she doesn't react. "Would you really—"

"No, but sometimes I like to imagine it."

"What would you do if it was gone?"

I gaze out at the lighthouse again. "I'd build my own."

The lead singer croons on in the otherwise quiet cab, singing about lost love, grappling with regret and the consequences of his own actions. Maybe I should have let her turn it off. It's starting to feel too much like a confession.

"I am sorry, Er. Sorry for everything."

She remains silent, and I open my mouth, ready to seize the opportunity to say more, but she stops me.

"I think about leaving the island all the time. Sometimes I'll stay up for hours looking at apartment listings in Paris."

"Pastry school?"

She nods. "I keep filling out applications that I never send, but I want to. I really want to." She lowers her head. "And the reason I'm waiting tables again? Teresa caught me looking at different schools and is making me work out front over the summer as an incentive until I apply to one."

I settle back against my seat. "You've been planning to leave all summer?"

"Not planning," she hurries to say. "Just imagining."

It sounded like more than imagining. "You never said anything."

"Would you have come with me?"

"To Paris?" I can't keep the incredulity from my voice.

"That's why I never told you." Pain pinches her brow. "You don't ever want to leave Nantucket, and I didn't want to leave you."

There's a heavy implication in her use of the past tense. She *didn't* want to, not *doesn't* want to.

"What do you want now?"

She levels her gaze at me. "What do you want?"

"I don't want an ocean between us, I know that." But that's not what she means. "I want to go back and do things differently."

"Okay, but how far back? Back before Lili? Back before I kissed you for the first time right out there?" She points down the beach. "How much do you wish you could change?" She shakes her head, but there's uncertainty there, as if she doesn't know the answer herself. "I'm going to ask you a hypothetical question. If you had been the one to walk in on me and Elliot, what would you have done?"

"Did something happen with you and Elliot?"

"Just tell me how you would have felt."

I know exactly how I would feel because I'm feeling it now. "I would be shocked and confused, and I guess hurt."

"Not angry?" she presses. "Not furious? You wouldn't want to hurt Elliot or break into a million tiny pieces because your heart was ripped from your chest?"

She seems to accept my silence as an answer and her eyes grow misty. "It did hurt, so much. You knew where things were going for weeks, and you didn't stop it. That hurts maybe more than everything."

I lower my head.

"But my heart wasn't ripped from my chest either, and it should have been." She pauses as though she wants to be very careful about what she says next. "Wren, I don't think the love that we have for each other is the right kind of love for two people in a relationship. Maybe it used to be, I don't know, but I don't think it's been that kind of love for a long time."

The words hang in the air between us, and I feel a sharp pang in my chest—not from the hurt of her saying it, but from the relief. I've had these same thoughts, even though I couldn't bring myself to say them out loud. Maybe I thought if I didn't say it, it wasn't true. But now that she's said it—*she* said it—it feels different.

I turn away from her and stare at the hint of my own wrecked reflection in the window. "Do you ever think what might've happened to us if I hadn't gotten hurt?" Beyond my own reflection I see part of hers, and I can tell she has. I inch a hand toward hers and she meets it with a brush of her own. "I can't help but wonder if the accident is what made us both hold on to something that likely would've faded away otherwise."

She sucks in a shaky breath because finally, one of us has acknowledged it. "I still care about you."

"Me too." The same sad smile touches both our faces. I look down at the tiny point of contact between our fingers. "I should've loved you better. You deserved better."

Her voice is a whisper. "I did."

I'm tempted to reach over and fully grab her hand, because I don't think I can bear to let her pull it away. What even is my life without Eryn in it?

Her voice is still quiet, barely louder than the ocean a hundred yards away. "I need to go."

I don't grab her hand. "Stay? Just for a little while." And I don't know if I mean in my truck or Nantucket itself. Both feel too selfish to voice out loud.

She hesitates and shakes her head. "All of this still hurts, Wren. I hope it won't forever, but for now . . ." She reaches for her door, then pauses as it inches open.

I'm slumped against the steering wheel watching her, hating this, but also knowing that it's right. "You should send in those applications. Bring some of Nantucket to Paris."

She gives me another smile, this one slightly less sad than the first. And she squeezes my hand. "Be happy, okay?" It's as close to forgiveness as she can give me, and the final reminder that she always deserved better than me.

"You too."

THIRTY-FIVE

Lili

The first time I stood in my dad's office, I'd been overwhelmed by a kind of reverent longing. The smell of old books and ink, the faint lingering scent of his cologne that I imagined more than actually detected, the organized chaos of papers and artifacts—it all felt sacred. He spent so much time here, pouring himself into the past, and more than anything, I wanted to be a part of that with him. Back then, I'd been so determined, so sure.

Now my hands aren't whisper soft, brushing across the surfaces like they're afraid to disturb his world. Instead, I plop into the desk chair, letting it squeak under my weight, and set a cardboard box on the desk with a dull thud.

My notebook, stuffed with loose pages and photocopies, is the first to go in. Then the pictures—images of the diary, copies of the letter and the map—followed by Dad's notebook and, finally, the stack of postcards he sent me. Each item lands with a quiet resignation, as though they themselves are ready to be packed away.

It only takes a few minutes to fill the box. But I stand there for much longer, looking down at its contents while the lid hovers in my hands. This is supposed to be the easy part—the end. I've finally realized what I want. Once the lid goes on, the box can be sealed, and I can be free. No more worn paths in the rug, no more broken promises, no more relationships destroyed. And yet, I hesitate.

"So you're sure, then."

Mom's words from the doorway pull me from my trance, and I press the lid down, as if caught in the act of something I shouldn't be doing. "Yep."

That morning, I told her I was finished with the museum and Dad's research project, asked for a box, and told her we could start packing up the study. She'd complied without a word, leaving me to walk into the room alone, but I knew her silence wouldn't last.

"Do you wanna talk about it?" she asks gently.

I check all four corners of the box, ensuring the lid is secure, then recheck. "There's nothing to talk about."

She steps closer. "Oh, I know that's not true." With a single finger, she inches the lid off and peers inside. "Wow, look at all this."

I track her movements as she lifts the postcards, flipping through them slowly, before setting them aside and opening my notebook. Her hands rest on its cover, protective. "There's still time, you know. You don't have to pack it all away just yet."

"I couldn't find what he wanted. And I didn't like what I did find."

She reaches for my hand, rubbing it gently.

"I thought doing all of this would make me feel closer to him," I tell her. "But it just made me feel farther away. Because now I see exactly what mattered to him, and it wasn't me. So why should I care about any of this?" I push the notebook away dismissively.

Mom bends down, wrapping her arms around my shoulders from behind. "I'm sorry he missed so much. I'm sure he's sorry too." Her hands squeeze, surrounding me in warmth. "But it's okay to care about the things he cared about. You can still be fascinated by your history, love it even, and not love the way he chose to pursue it. You can love it your way, just for you."

She says it so casually, as if separating the two is easy, but it feels impossible to me.

"I think I'm angry at him," I admit, my voice barely above a whisper.

She breathes in deeply. "I can understand that."

I stare at her, a lump forming in my throat. "I don't want to be angry at him."

"It's hard to be angry at someone when they're not here anymore."

I nod, swallowing hard. "And I don't know if he would've changed or apologized if he'd had more time."

She hugs me tighter. "I know." There's a world of unspoken weight behind those words.

We stay like that, the silence and what ifs hanging over us. I glance at the desk, at the mix of my research and his, unsure what to do with the ache in my chest.

Mom chuckles, her breath warm against my hair. "You'll figure it out." She grabs the box lid, holding it lightly. "Have you shown any of this to Goldie?"

Shaking my head, I ease away from her, and move around to the front of the desk to continue packing up the room, starting with rolling up his rug.

Mom's voice stops me, and when I turn back, she extends the lid, her eyes thoughtful. "Maybe you should—you know, before you box it all away."

Goldie is supposed to be painting the last section of the porch railing that morning. Instead, she's lying on her back, staring up at a spiderweb glistening with morning dew in the corner. The paintbrush dangles from her hand, forgotten.

The floor creaks as I step onto the porch. Goldie jackknifes upright, a fleeting attempt to look busy as she lunges for the paint tray. But when she sees it's me, not Mom, she drops the act with a sheepish grin.

Sunlight filters through the slats of the railing, casting dancing patterns on the porch floorboards. It's warm already, the air carrying the faint scent of freshly cut grass. I sit beside her and set the box down between us.

Goldie scoots closer, the spiderweb instantly forgotten. "What's that?"

A streak of white paint is smeared across her forehead, but I ignore that and nod at the matching one on her hand. "That dry?"

She swipes it across her jeans to show me it is.

I lift the lid. "Dad's stuff, my stuff." I hand her his notebook. "Our stuff."

Her eyes widen as she peers into the box, a slow smile spreading across her face. "That's from the letter I found."

I nod, feeling a pang of bittersweetness.

"Did it help?"

I hesitate, caught between a shrug and a nod. "I couldn't figure it out in time."

She lifts the photos, studying each one with care. "Where's the original?"

"At the museum. Maybe Wren will find a way to display it someday." My voice falters.

Goldie's smile fades. "Sorry."

I take the pictures from her hands, setting them aside. "Yeah. Me too."

She rummages through the box again. "So, Dad was wrong then? She was a bad guy?"

"I can't prove she wasn't," I say softly, the weight of my summer's many failures pressing down on me.

I tell her about some of the diary entries Dad transcribed, the letter that seemed to be about nothing, and the map that we can't explain.

"Dad spent years trying to figure it all out. But I was going to do it all in one summer." I scoff. What a joke. "Anyway, I thought you might want to see it all before it gets packed away."

She takes her time looking through everything, then offers me a side glance. "Sorry I couldn't find anything else at Mrs. Mayhew's."

"No, it's great what you found. It was—" I hesitate. "It was what I needed to realize that I don't need to find all the answers. And if I never figure it out, then I'm okay with that."

She nods, then adds more conviction to the gesture. "Dad copied parts of her diary, right? But he stopped too. Do you think he decided he knew enough too?"

I hadn't thought about it like that before, but it's a comforting idea. I always assumed he just ran out of time or into the same potentially damning evidence we did. I like her perspective better. "Yeah, maybe. Maybe he was getting ready to box it all up himself." I run my fingers over the cover of his notebook, the leather darker and softer than mine. "Maybe he thought forty-three was going to be his year," I say, thinking about the number he wrote so often. "And he didn't want to enter a new decade still trying to prove her innocence." He was forty-nine when he died, but maybe forty-three was how old he'd been when he found Kezia's diary. Could be that's all the number ever meant.

Goldie frowns at me. "Forty-three?"

I show her a passage Dad transcribed, pointing to the number scrawled in the margin. "It's something he repeated a lot in his notebook. We could never figure out what it meant in relation to Kezia, and maybe that's because it only meant something to him."

"And Edmund Harrington," Goldie says, letting her attention wander back to the spiderweb.

"What do you mean?" I say slowly.

"Hey, how come the water doesn't break the web? Isn't it heavier than the silk?"

"Hey." My voice sharpens. "Tell me what you meant. What does the number forty-three have to do with Edmund Harrington?"

She looks at me like I'm the ten-year-old. "That's how many lines he wrote in his letter."

THIRTY-SIX

Wren

Dad is officially calling the time of death for the FeeJee mermaid in the taxidermy lab. He pulled out all his old tricks, and even tried his hand at some new ones, but he finally has to admit there's no salvaging it.

"You know my great-great-grandfather bought it from P. T. Barnum himself?"

"I thought he wrestled with it for two days, *Old Man and the Sea* style, off the coast of Japan and, you know, Fiji." I helpfully lift the old piece of etched driftwood that used to be mounted beside the mermaid. "Says so right here."

He makes a dismissive sound in the back of his throat. "Gonna have to find something online for that display before next weekend. I don't have anything else that's close to being ready and we are not having an empty exhibit when we introduce Nereus to the world."

I push back from his work bench. "Scouring the darkest corners of eBay for something worse than the FeeJee mermaid sounds like nightmare fuel. I'm going to leave that to you."

"Thought you wanted to have a say in things like this?"

I keep heading for the door. "Not when all we show around here is made-up."

"Wren?"

I turn back to face him expectantly. He just looks at me at first. He's been giving me space since the night we talked, which I took to mean he'd said all he was going to on the subject of Mom and my relationships. I start to wonder if that's about to change. "Yeah?"

"What would you put out if we didn't have all this?" He gestures to the shelves full of "specimens" in various stages of construction and repairs, some inherited from his predecessors, some cobbled together by his own two hands.

It wasn't so long ago that I would have just shrugged and said nothing. The idea of trying to feature anything real in this place would be like trying to get ramps on all the buildings in Nantucket. In other words, a complete waste of energy.

"I don't know, Dad. But we've got another back room in this museum, and those shelves are a lot fuller than the ones in here."

Tate is restocking the Nerissa T-shirts in the center of the gift shop before we open. He doesn't seem to be going out of his way to keep his back to me, though it's still early, so he might just be too tired to put up the effort. But in that moment, with the morning sun streaming through the porthole windows like spotlights, I decide it doesn't matter.

I'm not quiet as I push toward him. I'm not trying to be.

He doesn't react when I stop on the other side of the table, just keeps stacking shirts. And I'm pretty sure I know why.

"Eryn told you about Paris?"

He cuts a glance at me, then reaches for another shirt.

"If it helps, I told her I wanted her to stay."

"She said you told her to send the application."

I scratch at the back of my neck. "Because it's what she wants, not because I want it."

"I know that." A shirt fists in his hands before he relaxes it. "*Now*, I know that." He looks down at the wrinkled shirt and smooths it out. "She told me about what you guys talked about and realized, I guess." He's still smoothing the shirt when he adds under his breath, "Should've figured it out before you almost kissed somebody else."

There's a hint of a familiar teasing note in his voice, a lightheartedness that I don't at all feel like I deserve. "She never told you either? About wanting to go to pastry school?"

"She did, but she never talked about it like it was real, you know? She'd come sit with me on the boat sometimes, and I'd tell her about my charter company plans and she'd tell me about the bakery she was going to open. Do you know she already has a menu planned out?"

I shake my head.

"It changed all the time, but I knew she wanted it. And I knew there aren't any schools for her around here. Can't take that kind of stuff online either." He sighs. "But Paris, damn, that's far. I looked it up, and you want to know how much a round-trip ticket to France is going to cost me when I go visit her?"

"Half a grand or more." I'd looked it up too.

He nods. "She's gonna be okay." And this time I know he's saying this solely for my benefit. "Maybe better than okay. She thinks you are too. She wants that for you, so I guess I can again too."

The tightness in my chest that I was beginning to think was permanent eases slightly. "Thanks, man."

He nods but doesn't look at me. "I need to eat something. You got any Sour Patch Kids on you?" He doesn't wait for my answer, just suddenly turns away and beelines for a shelf of mermaid-shaped neck pillows that have never sold well due to the scratchy iridescent fabric on the scales. He shoves his arm in between a pile, reaching all the way to the back with an intense look of concentration on his face until, with a triumphant grin, he pulls out a bag of candy. "Ha!"

"Didn't you get in trouble for hiding food around here last month?"

He hops up on the table of T-shirts and stuffs a couple of Kids in his mouth. "Yeah, well, Bethany's not around to rat me out." He holds out the bag to me.

I try to avoid candy since sugar isn't a paraplegic's best friend, but I take one anyway because he is, and this is the first time he's offered to share anything with me in what feels like a very long time. Sharing snacks is kind of his love language. "Thanks. You know, you don't have to waste your money on plane tickets. You could take the *Siren's Call*, or whatever you decide to change her name to, and sail it straight across the Atlantic till you hit France."

He lowers the gummy he's about to drop in his mouth, then stares down at it. "Turns out the boat is a no go. My uncle got back and basically told me he can't afford to sell it to me for the price we agreed on, so."

"That's such a massive load of bull—" I shake my head and will my sudden temper back into check. "You've been deckhand and captain of that boat for years and he pulls this on you now?"

Tate rolls the gummy between two fingers. "He knows I don't have another option, so yeah."

No, I realize, Tate's uncle may not have another option, but Tate does, and it's so clear and obvious to me that I can't believe I haven't thought of it before now. "You know what I think? I think you should go to your uncle one last time and tell him either he sells you his boat now or he can find someone else to captain and take care of it for him."

Tate starts shaking his head. "I can't do that. What about you guys and the mermaid tour? McCleave's needs that boat as much as I do."

"No," I say. "We don't. We're putting a pause on the mermaid tour."

Tate's brows climb halfway up his forehead. "Since when?"

"Since right now. I can't make Eryn do the Nerissa act for me anymore, and, no offense, but I don't want to give up leading the tour. If we lose the *Siren's Call* too, then my dad won't have a choice but to start over with it from the ground up. And this time, I won't let him do it alone."

Slowly, Tate nods. "Yeah, I mean, that makes sense for you guys." He looks up at me. "You know I was never going to take the tour from you. And I'll help however I can with the new one."

"I know, and thanks. But you're still going to get your boat."

Tate's smile is forced. "Yeah. Someday."

"No, today. If he won't sell you the *Siren's Call*, then go buy a different one, a better one. And don't tell me they're too expensive, because I am officially offering to be the first investor in your charter company."

He's already shaking his head. "Wren, man. I can't let you—"

I cut him off. "Tate, *man*, yes, you can. I'm not saving for anything in particular, so let me invest in something I already know is going to be a win."

He stares at me; I stare right back.

Finally, he stands up, suddenly energized. "Yeah, maybe I will go see my uncle. Tell him it's now or never because I'm done waiting for him." His voice is low, determined, and then he half tackles me in a hug, his fist thudding against my back until I grunt in surprise. He pulls away, grinning wide. "Hell yeah, we're going to be a win, you and me and the *Salty Snack*."

I can't help but grin as he punches the air. "Of course you'd name it after food."

"You don't like? I could always go with the SS *Crumbs* or maybe the *Confectioner*. No wait, *Cheddar Buoy*!"

I laugh.

"It's going to be so great. And you will have a permanent spot right by the captain's seat anytime you want it. I'll even get you a skipper's cap."

"Yeah, I'm not going to wear that."

His excitement is still radiating off him in waves but he sobers as he looks at me.

"Maybe you'll even come with me to Paris sometime."

"That depends," I say, matching his tone. "You coming back?"

He looks offended that I have to ask. "Always and forever."

That, at least, is one good thing I still have. "Then maybe I will."

Tate upends the rest of the Sour Patch Kids into his mouth, shaking the bag to make sure he doesn't miss any of the sugar crystals at the bottom. Then he takes a deep breath and looks at me. "So what are we gonna do about you?"

"I have to finish clearing out the FeeJee mermaid exhibit, then figure out the rest of Nereus's discovery story and run that by my dad, then I get to work on the copy for the website." My voice grows wearier with every word.

He makes a face. "Do you actually want to do any of that?"

Not really, but I don't have a choice. "I'll catch up with you later. And thanks for—" *For talking to me again, for making me feel like I have my friend back when I really haven't done anything to deserve that.* "—you know, for sharing your Sour Patch Kids with me."

I start to head back to the FeeJee exhibit.

"Wait, that's it?" Tate lunges around in front of me. "We haven't talked for over a week, and you think you can just help me buy my dream boat and forget the fact that you haven't said a thing about what you're going to do about your tourist girl?"

I don't think I'm ever going to like him calling her that. "She doesn't want to work here anymore, and I can't make her. Her family is leaving soon anyway."

"She told you that?"

I squeeze my push rims reflexively. "Last time she was here."

"Well, damn."

"Yeah."

"She know that you and Eryn are over?"

"Eryn and I only talked last night."

He nods, but I can tell he's thinking. "You think she'd want to know?"

"I was a jerk last time I saw her."

"Well, she's used to that, and it didn't send her running before."

"Yeah, but this time I was trying to be." I meet his eye so he understands the difference. She'd killed me when she told me she couldn't come back to the museum, and I was willing to say almost anything to get her to stay, willing to fight with her if it meant she didn't leave, but I went too far.

"I drove her away and I don't know how to get her back or what it would even mean if I could. She's supposed to go off to college in the fall, earn a history degree so that she can work somewhere like the Whaling Museum or the damn Smithsonian, places like that. I may not like everything about Nantucket, but leaving would feel like losing a limb." I lift my arm. "I don't have enough working ones left to give up another." I take a breath. "Even for her."

Tate whistles. "I know you liked her, maybe more than liked her, but damn."

I look around the gift shop "It doesn't matter. What could I possibly offer her here?"

"A lot," he says. "From where I'm standing."

"Yeah, well, I'm not standing. And I know what happens when you try and make people stay."

Tate refuses to even acknowledge the first part of what I said. "She's not your mom. And you're not your dad."

"I know."

"Do you? Because from what you've told me, your mom never wanted to be part of this place, and Lili clearly does. She might even want something else too." He reaches out and claps his hands down on my shoulders like he's done a million times before, but this time he gives me a shake. "So stop sitting here and feeling sorry for yourself and figure out a way to fight for your girl."

THIRTY-SEVEN

Lili

I pedal down Main Street, my awareness of every cobblestone and each blooming flower less desperate than it had been at the start of summer. Back then, Nantucket truly felt like the Faraway Land. Now, the sun is warm at my back, as though it's gently guiding me forward, and I don't feel the need to stop and stare at each and every detail like I need to grab hold of it all while I still can.

I pass the Whaling Museum without a second glance, its iconic brick façade quickly fading from view. I don't stop to read the hand-painted signs hanging from shops or slow to admire their colorful awnings. They blur together as I speed up, the wind against my face, until I end up right back where I started all those weeks ago.

It took me all weekend to figure it out. Mom even let me skip lunch at Graham's after church yesterday, especially since he'd been finding excuses to stop by the house every day anyway. I'd seen enough to know that he may be the key to helping her fall just a little bit in love with Nantucket too. He's taking her and Goldie on a picnic today, followed by a stroll down Sconset Bluff Walk. When I left, she was humming to herself while getting ready.

But I did figure it out, and I made the only decision I thought I could. I talked with Goldie and she agreed. Now there's only one person left to convince.

It had felt like the right choice last night, but as I push open the heavy door of McCleave's, my certainty falters.

It's late morning, and the place is bustling with people. Even so, it's easy to spot Tate behind the counter at the gift shop. He's ringing up a few small plush mermaids, tossing each one in the air before catching it in a bag behind his back. He catches two in a row before noticing me and dropping the third.

The wide-eyed shock on his face instantly snuffs out the hesitant smile I'd tried to muster. He hastily finishes with his customer, then pulls out a *Be Right Back* sign from under the counter before vaulting over it to reach me.

"What are you doing here?"

"I'm not staying. I just need to give something to Wren, and then I promise I'm gone." Tate and I were on the verge of becoming friends before everything happened, but it still stings to know we'll never get the chance now.

He makes a show of scanning the area behind me. "Uh, yeah, I don't see him anywhere. Why don't you leave it with me, and I'll let him know you dropped it off?" He reaches for the box I'm holding, but I twist it away.

"I'd like to give it to him myself, if that's all right. Isn't he in the back room?"

Tate freezes for a beat. "I'll go check. Maybe you can help a few of the customers here—you know, for old times' sake?" Then he's off, sprinting through the crowd before I can respond.

I don't understand what he's doing or why he's so determined to keep me from seeing Wren. But it took a lot for me to come back here today, and I'm not leaving without talking to him. I head toward the back room too, moving more carefully through the crowd than Tate did.

Pausing with my hand on the door, I take a deep breath, then open it.

Inside, Tate darts away from one corner while Wren hastily gathers a pile of papers in another. They turn in unison to stare at me. Finally, Wren pushes forward.

"What are you doing here?"

I'd heard those exact words from Tate not five minutes ago, but it's Wren's reaction that makes me want to turn and run. I'd hoped that these days apart would've given him time to calm down, reflect, and maybe understand why I had to quit. But he seems just as upset as the last time we spoke.

And it hurts just as much.

"Good luck," Tate mutters to Wren as he passes by me in the doorway. "You too, *Lili*." The door shuts behind him, leaving Wren and me in a room that suddenly feels far too big.

I search Wren's face for any sign of softness, but all I see is discomfort. The last flicker of hope inside me snuffs out. It was never strong, just a tiny ember refusing to die despite the impossibility of it all.

Forcing a smile I don't remotely feel, I walk past him to our table—*the* table—and set the box down. "This is what I'm doing here." I start pulling out the notebooks, photos, every bit of research I'd collected, and pages filled with the new notes I'd made. "I figured it out, Wren. I know what my dad discovered, what the letter from Edmund Harrington means, and how the map fits in too." I push everything toward him. "All of it."

He stares at me, and then slightly shakes his head. "You did what? How—when?"

"The how came with an assist from Goldie." I start to sift through everything looking for my copy of the letter. "She noticed something about Harrington's letter that we missed."

"Wait, let me get you the originals." Wren spins away, grabbing the album from his desk rather than from a box somewhere, which makes me wonder if he'd been unable to let our project go either.

His eyes meet mine when he hands it to me and I can see the same nervous excitement I feel buzzing through him too. "Show me?"

I do.

I point out the number of lines in the letter and watch his face when I turn to one of the pages in my dad's journal with "forty-three" written on it.

Wren pushes both hands through his hair as his eyes dart from one to the other and back again. I can almost see his mind running through the possible implications just as I had. But he's still missing the final piece of the puzzle.

Carefully, I unfold the map and watch Wren's eyes snap to it, searching. He's significantly more familiar with all the original maps of Nantucket, so what took me hours and countless Google searches to notice takes him only minutes.

"It's the coastal hachure border. That's it, isn't it?" He sounds almost awestruck by the realization. "Those little lines extending out from the island don't represent just the slope or direction of the shoreline, they're too spaced out. They're markers." He hovers his finger over each one, counting though he already knows exactly how many there are. "Forty-three."

I breathe out half a laugh when he turns his wide eyes to me.

"So that's how they communicated? The number of lines in a letter corresponded—"

"—to a location around the island," I finish for him. "Yeah, I think so. That way he could tell her which points to sail through in order to avoid shifting patrols or British surveillance."

He barely blinks as he tries to take in every detail on the map, searching for other markers he may have dismissed earlier. I'm sure there are more, similarly disguised as decorative embellishments, maybe even markers for a smuggler's hole far from any blackberry bushes. But then he stops, and I know why.

"I wanted her to be innocent." His gaze lifts to mine, making me feel like he's holding me the only way he can. "I wanted that for you."

I nod, too quickly, and my chin trembles. "I wanted it too. But Kezia was exactly who they said she was—a smuggler. Her actions, and the actions of people like her, helped destroy Nantucket's economy during the war. She flooded the market with cheap, stolen goods, driving up prices and crushing local businesses. But she didn't care—she was happy making money while everyone else suffered."

"Hey," he says when I'm quiet for too long. "So she was a smuggler. Lawrence McCleave the First lied about capturing a mermaid." Wren offers me a small smile. "Nobody's family is perfect."

I try to smile back, I really do. But then I sniff a little and square my shoulders. "I know, and if it were just that, I'd be okay. But it's not." Slowly, I reach back into the box and pull out an old manila envelope and set that down too.

Wren doesn't ask the obvious question, just looks at me, waiting.

"I found this in my dad's study." I start to unwind the string wrapping around the fasteners. "I never thought to check under the rug, especially once I realized how much time he spent pacing over it. It wasn't until we started packing up the room that I rolled it away and noticed the loose flooring." I tip out the contents. "You were right, he did have pictures of the diary. He also had pictures of the letters and map. I didn't remember it until I saw them, but that first day I met you, Mrs. Mayhew told me he used to help get her Christmas decorations down from her attic. I don't know if that was an excuse to look for something he already suspected was there, or if he stumbled upon the album while actually trying to do something kind for her."

I show him another picture without any writing on the back to indicate where it was taken. The front shows a close-up of an auction listing from 1918 for a lot of early American artifacts from Nantucket that included "a diary of unknown authorship thought to date back to the late eighteenth century, containing entries that may shed light upon the coastal life and trade of the period." It was marked as sold to Mr. Harold W. McCleave of Nantucket for $135.

"That's my great-great-grandfather," Wren says, sounding almost impressed as he moves farther down the table to look at more. "So that's how your dad knew to look for the diary at the museum."

Finally, I lay out the pieces of paper, side by side, even though it's obvious what they are from a single glance, especially once I open my dad's notebook beside them.

The pages were cut out of his notebook so neatly, so close to the spine, that we missed them time and time again, but it's clear now. "Those entries we thought he didn't transcribe? He did, and he figured out everything."

I mentally fought against the accepted narrative surrounding Kezia for so long, not because of some deep-seated need to exonerate my ancestor, but because I wanted to exonerate my dad. And instead, I found all I'd ever need to condemn him for what he took from us.

"All those maybes I said to you last time we were here? They weren't maybes. I think that's why he tried to hide all of this. He made sure I'd find his notebook and see that he was trying all these years to find proof for us, but not all the other pieces that would prove it was all a waste."

My feelings are still very complicated where my dad is concerned. That pendulum has swung from one side to the other this summer, and while it's still swinging, I'm beginning to understand that when it settles, I won't change my mind about this.

"I'm not going to hide from it," I say, pushing it all toward him. "The museum can have all of it, every page of my dad's notebook, if you want it. It's something real now, and if you ever want McCleave's to display any of it and Kezia's story, warts and all, I want you to know you can. All the remaining Gardner family are giving you our blessing."

I hear Wren moving toward me, but he remains silent.

"I know you have your dad and Nerissa to contend with, but maybe it can be a way for McCleave's to start becoming the kind of museum you want it to be."

He's right beside me now, looking over the items I spread out. "And that's what you want?"

What I want is to build it all with him, to stay on this island until no one ever confuses me with a tourist again, especially not him, but there's no point in saying any of that. "I'd like for my dad to be credited for his research. I've thought a lot about that, and I think it's right that people know what he did. He may not have wanted to tell anyone else what he found, but he left too much for me to ignore. Maybe I'll find a way to think that he was trying to protect me from his own failures, but even if I never quite get there, the truth is we wouldn't have found anything without him."

When I look at Wren again, I find him staring at the Shelves, and I can't tell what he's thinking. Maybe he's smiling? I can't really see unless I stretch sideways since he's still not looking at me.

"It's just that I've already been working on a different exhibit, with the harpoons from the wreck of the *Essex* you commented on the first day you came back. I got the idea from something you said about it being like having the weapon that took on Moby Dick."

I stare blank faced at him. "I don't remember saying that, but you're turning it into an exhibit? You're doing it?"

He's definitely smiling now. "I pitched the idea to my dad to tie it into the inspiration for Melville's book, and he went for it. We needed something to replace another exhibit last-minute, and I decided I didn't have anything to lose from trying."

"Wren, that's—" I start toward him without thinking as if I'm going to hug him, only to skid to a stop, realizing that's not okay for me to do. I'm grinning though, I can't control that. "—amazing. I'm really happy for you."

He nods almost shyly. "Yeah, it was time. It's not done yet, but if it goes well, I already have a few more ideas." He half turns to his desk, inclining his head as if he wants me to follow. "This is what

I was thinking of doing next." He gestures for me to go ahead of him, even grabs the back of a nearby chair for me to sit in.

I do, but cautiously, since he's got the oddest expression on his face, almost like he's nervous, which I've never seen him be before.

When I sit and look down at his desk, I frown. "What is . . ." But I don't finish the question. It's incomplete, more so after everything I just told him, but it's all our research into Kezia, including my dad's, only it's organized and laid out like a museum display. There's even a mock-up of what the final exhibit would look like with colored maps and timelines. And there's a picture of Wren and me working that I vaguely remember Tate taking one day, and next to that is a photo of my dad sitting here, at this same desk, reading Kezia's diary.

I bring a hand to my mouth to hide its trembling. "I don't understand."

"I didn't know the ending yet, but I thought maybe the journey into her life was enough to show the world, or at least as many people who come to McCleave's anyway."

I'm still covering my mouth, and I can feel that my eyes are getting dangerously close to spilling over with tears.

"We can make it better now, more complete, if that's what you really want."

I nod, because I do want that, so much I'm afraid of saying it out loud. "Where did you get the picture of my dad?"

Wren's voice is closer now, right behind me. "I was worried he might turn out to be some kind of thief, so I took it in case I needed something to show the police later. I forgot all about it until I started putting this together." He pauses. "I was planning to show you everything once I had a better mock-up, but despite Tate's best efforts, you're seeing it early."

I close my eyes when he moves even closer and says my name. My heart is already a frantic drumbeat threatening to leap out my chest, and I don't trust myself to look at him right now.

"Lili." He repeats my name a second time, but it's not until he softly says, "Tourist Girl," that I chance glancing at him.

"I wasn't who I want to be when you were here last time, and I'm sorry for the way I spoke to you." He clears his throat and adds, "And what I said about you leaving because of everything with me and Eryn—"

"Oh, no." I curl an arm around my midsection and squeeze. "That's okay, we don't have to go into any of that." I stand and step back from the table and raise my hands toward it. "I'm only here for this. And I can go now. We don't have to say anything else about anything."

"—you were right," he continues as if I hadn't interrupted him. "I hadn't dealt with any part of that yet. I needed to before I could tell you what I've been thinking." He pauses and looks down at the work we did together. "I never saw you coming, and I think that's partly why I fought so hard against you in the beginning. I didn't understand how I could be feeling the things I felt for you when I was supposed to already be feeling them for someone else."

My body tenses, and I start to turn away, but his hand catches mine, warm and insistent.

"No, listen," he says, his grip tightening slightly. "I didn't understand because they weren't the same. And that was the problem. I grew up with Eryn, and at first it was easy for us to shift from friends to more. But nothing really changed between us—our feelings never grew past friendship, not the way they should have. I might not have ever realized that if I hadn't met you."

"I don't want to hear this." I tug lightly to free my hand, but he doesn't let go.

"I need you to hear," he insists, his voice low, almost hoarse. "Because I'm trying to tell you I don't regret it. Easy and uncomplicated wasn't enough for either of us, and Eryn knows that now too."

I stop halfheartedly trying to pull away. "She said that?"

He nods. "We talked, and she let me apologize for the way I treated her, but she didn't blame me for realizing the same thing she was realizing herself." He urges me closer. "The love that I have for her isn't the right kind of love. I love her like a friend, but not more than that, and it's the same for her."

His gaze locks on mine, catching every tremor, every quickening breath. He reaches for my face and I cover his hand.

"What exactly are you saying to me?" I ask, my voice barely a whisper.

He smiles as his hand slides over my jaw, his thumb brushing the curve of my cheek with a tenderness that makes my knees weak. "I'm saying that I don't want you to quit, not the museum, and not me. Stay here on Nantucket and help me make McCleave's the kind of place it always should have been, one with the biggest Kezia Gardner exhibit on the island if that's what you want. I know you have more ideas, and some of them might not be awful."

A shaky laugh escapes me

"And I want you, because nothing about you is easy or uncomplicated, and I don't want to think about having to watch you walk away again."

My heart gives a painful thump in my chest, even as it's singing too. "I'm supposed to go to school in Maryland. I want to get my history degree and be able to come back here to Nantucket with something real to offer it."

"I'm not saying don't get your degree," he says quickly, his eyes steady and serious. "In fact, I'm thinking about getting one of my own. I did some research and U of M doesn't offer just in-person degrees. I could get mine without ever having to leave here to get it. You could too."

I just stare at him, my heart pounding harder now. "You're serious."

He doesn't blink. "As a spinal cord injury." Then his hand eases. "Unless you really want to leave Nantucket."

I step back, the sudden loss of his touch leaving a sharp ache behind as my thoughts spiral.

His voice is raw, like he's choking on the words. "I mean, if you do, if that's what you really want, then I won't try to stop you."

I still. "I've never wanted to leave Nantucket," I admit, the truth tasting bittersweet on my tongue. "Not even when I was little."

A slow smile spreads across his face, and I see something close to relief in his eyes.

"But Wren . . . you're saying a lot of things."

His smile falters. "Is it me? Did you change your mind?"

I turn away, glancing up and trying to breathe through the lump in my throat. "You had a girlfriend a week ago."

He doesn't hesitate. "Eryn and I haven't had each other in a long time. We just admitted it to ourselves a week ago. There's a difference."

I nod slowly, my back still to him, but the words come out broken. "But to me, you had a girlfriend a week ago."

He doesn't have a ready answer to that.

I turn to face him, regret hitting me hard when I see the despair in his expression. "I think I need some time to think about everything."

"Okay," he says before his features can smooth into something less dejected. "That's okay. Summer isn't over yet. Your family isn't planning to leave tomorrow, right?"

"No, not tomorrow." Thanks to Graham, Mom hasn't been packing as quickly as she normally does when we're getting ready to leave a newly flipped house.

"Will you still be here on Friday?" he asks, and I can tell how hard he's trying to seem okay in this moment. "You all could come to the private preview for the new mermaid display."

"And your exhibit? Melville and the *Essex*?"

He nods, his mouth lifting on just one side. "It's not going to be highlighted in the program, but yeah, that's the goal."

I don't know if I'll be any closer to figuring out my heart in four days, or everything else he's offering, but I'll have to.

Because Mom may not be in her normal rush to pack, but our ferry tickets for Saturday have already been bought.

THIRTY-EIGHT
Wren

Dad had insisted we both dress for the occasion, and I'd agreed. The difference being my suit didn't come with a fake chest plate and crown like his did.

I didn't comment on his choice of clothing tonight though, and he didn't once suggest I wear so much as a single seashell-encrusted accessory. Not that Tate had left me any. He's playing the part of the real-life Nereus for the evening, and so far, he doesn't seem to mind the extra attention. If he isn't careful, my dad will have him in a tail before long.

"Hey, Nereus?"

Tate looks up from the group of kids he's regaling with stories of wrestling sharks, then wraps up his story before making his way over to me.

"So, what do you think?" He gestures at his chest plate and stretches out his harpoon that was made to look like whale bone with intricate scrimshaw designs carved into it. "Do I look like a prince of the sea or what?"

"You look like something," I agree, muffling a laugh.

Tate ignores my sarcasm. "Do you think your dad will let me have a say in who he hires to play the new Nerissa now that Eryn's officially hanging up her fins?"

"I don't know, maybe." I still feel hollow remembering that Eryn isn't going to be a part of things around here anymore.

I've seen her outside the café a couple of times since that last night by the lighthouse, and while she'd given me a tight-lipped smile and even returned the somewhat awkward hand I'd raised in greeting, we hadn't said anything to each other. I hope it won't always be that way between us, but I understand why it needs to be for now.

After a moment I ask, "Did Eryn say if she's going to come tonight?"

Tate stops admiring his weapon and slowly shakes his head. "She's hanging out with some of her coworkers from the café." He hesitates then adds, "Including that Elliot guy."

I won't lie and say I don't feel anything hearing that, but it's more like expecting pain rather than actually being hurt, like tensing for a shot before realizing the nurse already gave it to you. "She's doing okay then?"

He nods. "She is."

And hearing that doesn't hurt at all.

Tate shifts his weight, clearly sensing a change in my mood. "What about your special guest, she here yet?"

That question does cause a reaction in me, not pain, but something close to it. I haven't seen Lili yet and I don't want to even think about her not showing up.

Tate doesn't need me to say anything. My gaze boring a hole through the front doors is answer enough. "She'll be here. Trust, my friend."

Every time I hear the door open, I try to convince myself that she'll be standing there, smiling at the sight of me, but she's not. Other people arrive, and I know I should be glad that I recognize so many of our neighbors who showed up to support us, but there's only one face I need to see tonight.

And then, suddenly, I do.

I make my way toward Lili, stopping only to say a quick hello to Mrs. Mayhew and Goldie, who's all but yanking the older woman forward to see the mermaid skeleton couple in the center of the museum.

"What a fine job you've done here tonight," Mrs. Mayhew says, leaning in to press her cheek to mine. "Thank you for inviting me."

"Thank you for coming," I reply, unable to keep my gaze from drifting past her shoulder to see Lili. "I'm working on another exhibit that includes some of your late husband's collection. If you want to come by sometime this week, I can give you more details on the progress."

Mrs. Mayhew nods, her eyes following mine. "Oh, yes, I do want to hear all about your *progress*." She squeezes my hand. "Go on now. It seems like you've been waiting long enough already."

"We're late because Lili changed four times," Goldie says.

I glance back at Lili again, noting the way she's gnawing her lip as she scans the room, her uncertainty evident even from across the lobby. But there are too many people between us to see all of her.

"Don't worry," I tell Goldie. "You haven't missed anything. Oh, and there's a T-shirt behind the desk in the gift shop with your name on it. It's the new design with Nereus and Nerissa."

She grins. "Cool. Thanks, Wren." Then she's off, dragging a surprised but smiling Mrs. Mayhew with her.

I catch sight of Lili peering down the Siren's Hall, but before I can follow, her mom and a man I recognize but can't quite place step in front of me.

"Graham Callaway," he says, after I exchange greetings with her mom. "My youngest would have been a couple of years ahead of you in school, Max Callaway?"

I nod, shaking his hand. That's why he looked familiar: His son manages Steamboat Wharf Pizza. "Yeah, I know Max. Great pizza."

"Decent pizza," he corrects. "But you can't beat the price."

I laugh politely. It's still an effort to concentrate on anything other than Lili.

Her mom takes pity on me, linking her arm through Mr. Callaway's. "Let's go get a closer look at those mermaids Goldie's been going on about." She smiles, resting a hand on my shoulder as they pass. "Wren, everything looks incredible."

I nod my thanks, but my eyes never leave Lili's face.

I don't stop for anyone else as I close the remaining distance between us. "Lili."

She spins and my heart stops at my first full sight of her. She's wearing the ocean in her dress and the summer in her smile.

"You look amazing," I say, my voice coming out a little breathless.

Her eyes find mine, and for a heartbeat, everything about her stills—her breath, her expression, even the slight movement of her shoulders. A rush of color rises in her cheeks, and I see her swallow, then almost sway, like the ground beneath her isn't quite as solid as it was a second ago. "Are you wearing a three-piece suit? With a pocket square?" She rests a hand over her stomach like she's trying to steady herself. "You look like Gregory Peck."

I can barely find my words, caught up in the way she's looking at me. "The guy from *Roman Holiday*. You said it was your favorite, so I took some inspiration."

She keeps staring. "It's good. Almost too good."

"I was going for too good." Tate and I hit up every vintage place on the island trying to find something for tonight, finally striking gold at Seconds Shop. It's a little warm with the jacket on, but so worth this reaction. "I guess I should have added the pocket watch?"

"No," she says too quickly. "That might have put me on the floor."

I laugh.

"I love it," she says, meeting my gaze. "Thank you." Then she half turns, looking around. "And the museum looks great. You've changed more than one exhibit."

Two kids run past us wearing gift shop T-shirts that say *I Met the Real Little Mermaid at McCleave's* on the front.

"Not everything is changing," I tell her, "but a few things are. You told me I didn't have anything to lose from really trying to talk to my dad. Turns out you had a point. He's only taken one out of every twenty things I've suggested so far, but that's already more than I would have thought possible a few months ago. And look." I move to the side, giving her a view down the corridor behind me.

Her eyes widen. "Is that your display? With all the people around it?"

I smile at her generous description of a decent handful of people as *all*, but after the crowd around Nerissa and Nereus's exhibit, mine has more than almost any other.

"Can we go look at it?"

I hesitate. "Yeah, but can we talk first? I'm kind of dying here waiting to hear my fate."

"Your fate, huh?" she says, her tone giving away nothing as she ducks her head. "I thought you were the one asking me to completely change all my future plans."

I do everything I can to hide the wave of panic threatening to crash over me. "Not change exactly, more like move them up. And maybe consider how incredible a ramp would look by your front porch."

She laughs, but the sound fades quickly, leaving a subtle tension behind. "Wren . . . I'm not turning eighteen for another month. I couldn't stay here alone on Nantucket even if I wanted to."

The hurt hits, the real kind that doesn't feel like a needle piercing my skin so much as Tate's harpoon plunging straight through my heart.

I nod, but it feels like the gesture's hollow, like my body's going through the motions without me. My brain scrambles to catch up with what she just said. "Okay," I manage, though it sounds more like a question than an answer. My words feel jagged, off. I look at her again, hoping to read something that will make sense of this, but her expression is calm, too calm. "Will you come back? I could wait, I *would* wait."

She reaches for my hand. "I don't want you to wait."

I laugh, the sound dry, almost like a cough. "You honestly think I would want anyone else after you? That someone else could even come close?" My dad barely looked at another woman after my mom, and I never understood that until right now. "Lili, I—"

"No, Wren." She lifts my hand to press it over her heart, where the beat is just as fast as mine. "I don't want to wait either. I talked to my mom and she's agreed to stay till my birthday in a few weeks, maybe even after that if she takes Graham up on his offer to help her with another house she's apparently been eyeing on the island."

My lungs don't want to work. "Wait . . . so you're not leaving?"

She bites her lip again, this time to hold in a smile as she leads me into the back room before answering. "Classes don't start until next month, but I already talked to my academic advisor about switching to online courses, so no, I'm not leaving."

"Me or the island?"

Her smile is almost teasing as she moves to what she thinks is out of my reach. "Whoa, that's not how this is going to work. You're convinced you want me, but you still need to convince me that—"

I move before I can think, pulling her toward me until she's sitting across my lap. Her eyes widen in surprise, but I don't hesitate, lifting her face to kiss her.

The moment our lips meet, it's like diving into the deepest part of the ocean, sudden and overwhelming. I can feel the pull of her, like the tide's drawing me in, and I don't want to fight it. My arms wrap around her, and it feels like I'm holding on to something that could slip away if I let go for even a second. Her lips move with mine, tentative at first, but then she grabs at my lapels and the world outside disappears. There's just the press of her against me, the rhythm of us, like the ebb and flow of the waves, and I never want it to stop.

"I wasn't going to wait a second longer to do that," I whisper, pressing my lips to hers again and tightening my hands along her ribs.

She's still holding my lapels. "I might need a little more convincing."

I know she can feel the rumble in my chest when I laugh, ready to do just that when she leans back and runs her fingers through my hair like it's something she's been dreaming of doing. "So if I'm staying, does that mean you're only going to call me Lili from now on?"

"No, Tourist Girl." I tighten my arms around her, bringing her close again. "But it does mean I'm going to call you mine."

Author's Note

Kezia Gardner is a fictional character, but she was inspired by several historical Nantucket women who shared the name Kezia, particularly Kezia Folger Coffin (1723–1798) and her daughter, Kezia Fanning Coffin (1775–1820). The younger Kezia kept a diary that is now part of the Nantucket Historical Association's collection. The diary, originally composed of fifty booklets, survives only in fragments, with both original pages and copies available for public viewing in the association's Research Library. Most of the entries quoted in this book are excerpts from those original booklets.

Kezia Folger Coffin was a prominent and shrewd businesswoman as well as a British Loyalist. She leveraged her connections with British merchants to achieve great financial success before the Revolutionary War. Remarkably, she gained power of attorney over her husband, Captain John Coffin, allowing her to act independently in legal and business matters—a highly unusual privilege for a woman of her time.

In *Letters from an American Farmer*, Hector St. John de Crèvecoeur wrote of Kezia and her husband: "The richest person now in the island owes all his present prosperity and success to the ingenuity of his wife. . . . She laid the foundation of a system of business that she has ever since prosecuted with equal dexterity and success." In Diana Gaines's somewhat fictionalized account of her life, *Nantucket Woman*, Kezia is even compared to Scarlett O'Hara from Margaret Mitchell's *Gone with the Wind* for her cunning and determination.

However, Kezia's success came at a high cost, both to her and to her neighbors. She was implicated in widespread smuggling operations during the war and engaged in controversial practices, such as buying up and foreclosing on the mortgages of her fellow Nantucketers. In 1780, she was arrested for high treason and, while acquitted of that charge, was convicted of other crimes. She faced numerous lawsuits, including one for attempting to steal a Continental vessel, and ultimately ended up in debtors' prison. She lost her entire fortune and, at age sixty, was evicted from her home. After she refused to leave, her daughter recounted, authorities had to "[take] her up in her chair, carr[y] her out of the house outside and set her in the street."

Though her daughter defended her fiercely in her diary, history largely condemns Kezia Folger Coffin, labeling her as one of the most notorious female smugglers of the Colonial era.

Most of the other historical figures mentioned in this book are also real people, but Edmund Harrington is entirely fictional. The timelines for certain historical events have been altered as well, including the year of the Great Nantucket Bank Robbery, America's first bank heist, which actually occurred in 1795, not prior to the war as stated in this book.

As for me, my parents' best friends used to live on Nantucket, and I have wonderful memories of visiting the island when I was younger. One highlight for any tourist is the very real Whaling Museum. To my knowledge, the museum has never employed anyone named Fanning, but it does house an unparalleled collection of maritime artifacts—and yes, a forty-six-foot sperm whale skeleton. If you can't visit in person, their extensive website offers exhibit information, photos, and videos.

Sadly, there are no mermaid museums on Nantucket. However, McCleave's Museum and Wren's ancestors were inspired by Eliza Ann McCleave (1811–1895), who, according to the Nantucket Historical Association, "gathered together . . . the curios brought by her husband from foreign lands and charged a small admission for exhibiting them."

Off-island, two real mermaid museums influenced the fictional McCleave's Museum: the Mermaid Museum in Berlin, Maryland, and the International Mermaid Museum in Aberdeen, Washington. Several exhibits, including the FeeJee mermaid and the Nerissa skeleton, are based on real "discoveries" that were later debunked as hoaxes or revealed as commissioned art pieces.

The FeeJee mermaid (also spelled Fiji or Fejee) was perhaps the most famous of these nineteenth-century hoaxes. Popularized by P. T. Barnum, the legendary showman behind the Barnum & Bailey Circus, the mermaid was likely constructed by combining the upper body of an orangutan with the tail of a salmon. Meanwhile, the Haraldskaer mermaid skeleton—a creation of Danish artist Mille Rude using human and swordfish bones—was once displayed in the National Museum of Denmark in Copenhagen.

If you're not too squeamish, I encourage you to scroll through my Instagram (@abigailjohnsonya) to see some of the historical images—they're shocking, to say the least.

Some of the other incredible but 100-percent real things in this book include the annual Fourth of July Water Fight (though it's slightly more contained than the free-for-all I portrayed it as) and morning buns! You can try "the love child of a croissant and a cinnamon roll—golden, sugar-crusted spirals dripping with ooey-gooey vanilla icing" for yourself by visiting my website, abigailjohnsonbooks.com and searching for "Eryn's morning bun recipe."

Acknowledgments

I'm incredibly grateful to God for every book I get to write, and for everyone who helps make sure you get to read the best version of it.

That starts with my agent, Kim Lionetti. Thank you for your guidance, encouragement, and unparalleled publishing savvy. I don't have a single finished manuscript collecting dust in a drawer because of you. Here's to seven more.

So much gratitude to my editor, Sarah Homer, for seeing the characters and story I had in my heart and ensuring they made it onto the page. Thank you, thank you, thank you.

I'd also like to thank the many people at HarperCollins and Storytide who invested their time, skill, and artistry into this book, specifically Erin DeSalvatore, Shona McCarthy, Danielle McClelland, Meghan Pettit, and Lindsey Triebel. Special shout-out to illustrator Allie Runnion and designers Julia Feingold and Jenna Stempel-Lobell for this delightfully dreamy cover.

To my book bestie, Cheyanne Young, thank you for all the phone calls about this book in all its various iterations. You are always there to let me vent, help me brainstorm, and encourage me out of a writing slump. So grateful for you.

To my OG critique partners, Sarah Guillory and Kate Goodwin, I wouldn't have published a single book without you two, and the fact that we still cheer each other on after more than a decade of sharing stories together is something I will always cherish.

On the personal side, this book wouldn't exist without the people who shaped my imagination long before I became a writer.

My parents, Gary and Suzanne Johnson, thank you for taking me on that very first trip to Nantucket and for helping to create the memories that led to this book. More than that, thank you for taking me to Middle-earth, to Narnia, and to the Celestial City long before I could read about them myself. What a gift you gave me. What a gift you are.

Thank you to my siblings, Sam Johnson, Mary Groen, and Rachel Lehrer, I love you guys so much. To Ross, Jill, and my new brother-in-law Mike, our family is infinitely better with you in it. To Nate Williams, an honorary Johnson if ever there was one. And to my Uncle Ken, Aunt Jeri, and Uncle Rick, for all your love and support. God only knows what I would do without each one of you.

One of my favorite traditions has been naming characters after my nieces and nephews, and with this book, I have officially included all eleven of you! Thank you to Grady, Rory, Sadie, Gideon, Ainsley, Ivy, Dexter, Os, Gabriel, Goldie, and brand-new baby Tatum for letting me borrow the names of my favorite people to ever exist. Grits forever.